For the Grimlets.

I am honored beyond measure that you

take the time to read my books,

post photos of coffee and half-naked men,

answer the many calls to arms,

and pimp the ever-lovin' heck outta
Charley and the gang.

Thank you, thank you, thank you!

Acknowledgments

Every book creates new challenges and opportunities, and each is a joy to write, but none of them would be what they are without the help of a few friends and colleagues along the way. I am forever grateful to the following radiant beings:

- Alexandra Machinist: for putting up with me!
- Jennifer Enderlin: also, for putting up with me! (No, really.)
- Josie Freedman: for the kind words and enthusiasm
- Eliani Torres: for not putting out a hit on me
- Everyone at St. Martin's Press: for being awesome
- Everyone at Macmillan Audio: for being amazing
- Lorelei King: for bringing my characters to life
- Dana Crawford: for what little sanity I have left
- Lacy Fair: for precious time saved
- Jowanna Kestner: for the giggles and the tears
- Theresa Rogers: for the incredible insight

- Robyn Peterman: for YOU! (and for my boyfriend Kurt)
- DD: for the underwear story :)
- Ashlee and Rhia: for allowing me to pillage your childhoods
- The Grimlets: for help with the you-know-what, especially,
  - Patricia Dechant
  - Jennifer Coffman Love
  - Trayce Layne
  - Wendy McCall Beck
  - Laura Harrison Burleson
- Patricia Whitney: for the sign
- Netter and Kinter: for the light in my heart
- The Mighty, Mighty Jones Boys: for my reason to breathe
- The Readers: for the fact that you love to read as much as I do

THANK YOU SO VERY, VERY MUCH!!!

Eighth Grave
After
Dark

1

Sometimes I crave pickles.
Other times I crave the blood of my enemy.
Weird.
—CHARLEY DAVIDSON

There was a dead tax attorney in my closet, sobbing uncontrollably into the hem of her blouse. She'd been there a few days now. It made getting dressed in the morning awkward.

I would've avoided her altogether if I could, but it was my only closet. And it was microscopic. Tough to ignore chance encounters.

But I had to get ready for a wedding, and sobbing tax attorney or not, I had to get into that closet. I couldn't let my bestie down. Or my uncle, the man with whom my bestie was gracing her presence for as long as they both shall live.

Today was the big day. Their big day. The day they'd been waiting for since they first laid eyes on each other. It took some finagling, but I finally got them to admit their feelings for each other and commit, and I wasn't about to let a tax attorney ruin it. Unless, of course, she was there to audit me. I didn't think so, though. Usually the person crying at an audit was the client, not the tax attorney.

No more stalling. I braced myself and opened the door. She sat curled

in a ball in the corner, crying like there was no tomorrow. Which, for
her, there wasn't. A name tag she was wearing when she'd died read SHEILA
with TAX ATTORNEY stamped underneath that. She must have been at some
kind of convention when she died, but her cause of death was not immediately apparent. She looked disheveled, her chocolate-colored hair
mussed, her tight bun askew on her head, but that could have happened
when she was attacked. If she was attacked. Or it could have been the
result of a few too many mojitos during the after party.

There was just no way of knowing her cause of death without talking
to her, and God knew I'd tried to do that on several occasions. She
wouldn't stop sobbing long enough for me to get a word in edgewise. I
could've told her I could see her because I'd been born the grim reaper.
I could've told her I'd help her find whoever did this. I could've told her
she could cross through me whenever she was ready to see her family,
those who had passed before her.

Most people who died went either north or south immediately following their deaths. But some stayed behind. Many had unfinished business
of some kind, just like the ghosts and spirits in folktales, but some stayed
behind because they'd died traumatically. Their energy grabbed hold of
the earthly realm and didn't let go. They were anchored here, and until
they healed, they would never cross to the other side.

That was where I came in. I helped the departed any way I could. I
found their killers, righted their wrongs, sent messages to their loved ones,
all so they could heal and cross to the other side, which they then did
through me. Through my light. A light that was supposedly so brilliant,
it could be seen by the departed from anywhere on earth.

But Sheila wasn't talking, so there was little I could do at the moment.

As carefully as I could, I pulled a cinnamon bridesmaid's dress through
her quivering shoulders. "Sorry," I said as I patted her dark hair. She released another loud wail of sorrow before I closed the door. Thankfully,
it was a thick door.

"What?" I asked as I turned back to Artemis, a departed Rottweiler who'd been dubbed my guardian by the powers that be. And ever since a dozen testy hellhounds had tried to rip out my jugular, Artemis refused to leave my side.

She sat there, ears perked, head tilted in curiosity as she pawed at the closet door.

"I've tried talking to her." I walked to a full-length mirror and held up the dress. "She only cries louder."

I rubbed to soften the worry line between my brows. As far as bridesmaid's dresses went, this one wasn't the worst. It would've looked even better if I weren't the size of the Chrysler Building. I was currently incubating the girl who would save the world, according to prophecies, but that wasn't what had been worrying me that morning.

Being a matron of honor was just that, an honor, and part of my job was to make sure the bride showed up for her wedding. Cookie had yet to arrive. It was probably that third margarita she'd had last night. Or the ninth. That girl could knock 'em back. In her defense, she was drinking for two. Since I was pregtastic, I'd been restricted to sparkling grape juice. Didn't have quite the same effect, but it was fun watching my sister and BFF belt out show tunes while channeling Christopher Walken.

I dialed Cookie's number to make sure she was headed my way when a voice, deep and sultry, wafted toward me from the door of my bedroom. If that was Cook, she'd had way more to drink than I thought.

"Closing the door on a traumatized dead chick isn't your style," the man said.

Artemis yelped and leapt toward the door, her stubby tail wagging with unmitigated joy.

I swirled to face my husband, the devastatingly handsome supernatural being who'd been forged in the fires of sin, created in hell by the very creature we were in hiding from. As far as we knew, Lucifer, Reyes's father, had sent the Twelve, the hounds of hell, the most vicious and bloodthirsty creatures ever to exist. And he sent them here to destroy us. Our only salvation was literally the land we stood on. The sacred ground that the Twelve couldn't traverse, as we were now living in a convent. An abandoned convent, but a convent—with the requisite sacred ground—nonetheless.

And we'd been here for months in an attempt to avoid being ripped to shreds by the hellhounds that patrolled the border. With help, our job had been to scour ancient texts and prophecies as we searched for a way to kill them. Only Reyes and I were at risk. We seemed to be the only ones the hellhounds wanted for breakfast. Everyone else could come and go as they pleased, which would go a long way toward explaining the lateness of the bride to prepare for her own wedding. We had hours yet, but I figured Cookie would've been at the convent at the butt crack of dawn, waking me up to do her hair. God only knew what would come of that.

Still, my immediate company was nothing to scoff at. His disheveled appearance every time he entered a room of late caused the blood in my veins to surge, the pulse at my throat to quicken.

He bent to pet Artemis. I watched as he gave her a final pat then indicate the Barbie closet with a nod and a gently arched brow. I followed his gaze. The closet had been made for a person with few worldly possessions, aka a nun. And though I was now living in the aforementioned convent, I was not a nun. Not by a long shot. Proof resided in the ever-expanding girth of my midsection.

His signature heat drifted toward me, blisteringly hot, a by-product of his being forged in the fires of hell, and I turned back to him. His hair, thick and unruly and in dire need of a trim, curled over his collar and around his ears. He still wore the button-down from last night. It hung open, revealing the wide expanse of chest he'd crossed his arms over. The cuffs of the shirt had been rolled up to his elbows, showing his sinuous forearms. Beneath them, a rock-hard waist tapered down to lean hips that rested comfortably against the doorjamb. He let me absorb every inch of him, knowing it gave me a thrill. Knowing he'd reap the benefits later.

After taking in his form, my attentions unhurried, languid, I slowly returned to his face. He'd let a small grin soften his mouth. His deep brown eyes sparkled beneath dark lashes that were spiked with the remnants of sleep. As though he'd just woken up. As though he had no idea how sexy that was.

Normally, I would've chalked up his appearance to the bachelor party they'd had for my uncle, but he'd looked like that for weeks now. Exhausted. Disheveled. Sexy as fuck. I could hardly complain, but I was beginning to worry about him. I noticed that he grew hotter when he was trying to heal from an injury, and his heat had been growing hotter by leaps and bounds lately, but he hadn't been injured in months. We'd both been stuck in the convent, on sacred ground, since I was about a month pregnant. That was almost eight months ago, and we hadn't been stabbed, shot, or run down with a runaway vehicle since. I'd have to keep a close eye on him. I did that anyway, so I'd have to keep a closer eye on him.

"Hey! Wait!" I threw the cinnamon dress at him. "You're not supposed to see me before the wedding."

He flashed a set of startlingly white teeth. "I think that only applies to the bride."

"Oh, right." When he indicated the closet again with a questioning gaze, I decided to question him back. "Do you know how many times I've tried talking to her? She won't stop crying long enough to catch her breath, let alone tell me what's wrong. Why did I get this closet?"

His grin spread. "Because it's the only one in the room."

He had a good point. He'd been forced to use a closet in the next room, but still.

"Want me to take care of her?" he asked.

"No, I do not want you to take care of her. Wait, you can do that?"

"Just say the word."

Sadly, I considered it. Her sobbing was taxing, probably because she was a tax attorney, and yet I heard her only when the door was open.

"Check this out," I said, walking to the door. I opened it, and we were met with loud wailing. After a moment, I closed the door again. Crickets. Metaphorically. "This door is incredible," I said, opening it again and closing it several times in a row to demonstrate.

"You need to get out more," he said.

"Right? I'd kill for the delightful décor of Macho Taco."

His face held his expression steady, not wavering in the slightest, but I felt an involuntary pang of regret ripple through him.

I let go of the door and straightened. "No," I said, walking to him.

He pushed off the doorjamb and waited to wrap me in his arms. His heat whispered across my skin and bathed me in warmth as one arm slid around my back while he let his free hand caress Beep, the fugitive I'd been harboring for almost nine months. I felt it was about time to evict her, but the midwife Reyes had hired told me she'd come in her own time. Apparently, Beep lived in a different time zone than I did.

"No," I repeated, blasting him with my best stern face. "We've done okay. We now have a semi-solid plan in place to blow this Popsicle stand once Beep is born that could actually work, if the planets align just so. I've had lots of time to practice my mad skills in grim reaperism slash supernatural being. And I've learned a lot about why I never became a nun: no closet space. This is not your fault."

"At least your father isn't trying to kill us." He stilled, shocked at his own statement, then said, "I'm sorry. I didn't mean—"

"Don't be ridiculous." I dismissed his statement with a wave of my hand. My father had died a few days before we sought refuge at the convent, and I was still searching for his killer. Well, my uncle, a detective for Albuquerque PD was, but I was helping every chance I got. "Reyes, it's not your fault your father is evil. Or that he's the most hated being this side of Mars."

"That's not entirely true," he said. When I silently questioned him, he added, "Not everyone believes in the devil."

"Good point." I was not about to argue with him about his father. He felt guilty that his father would do anything in his power to kill us. To kill Beep, actually. She was the one prophesied to destroy him. I'd tried repeatedly to convince Reyes that this wasn't his fault—to no avail, so I changed the subject instead. "What's with all the dead people on the lawn?"

Departed had been showing up for about a week, standing in what would be considered our front lawn. If we had a lawn. If this were a house and not a converted convent.

A worried expression flashed across Reyes's face so fast, I almost missed it. Almost. "I wish I knew."

He'd been worried a lot lately. I could tell the situation was draining him, and I couldn't help but wonder if he didn't feel like he was in prison again. He'd spent ten years there for a crime he didn't commit. And now once again, for all intents and purposes, he was incarcerated. We both were. We were prisoners of a sort, stuck in this place, and while I was certainly going a bit stir-crazy, my restlessness couldn't compare to his. Still, one foot across that invisible line, the one that marked the sacred, blessed ground from the rest of the area, and that foot would be gone. Along with part of a leg.

We'd fought the Twelve before, and while we didn't exactly lose, we sure didn't win. They came back angrier than ever. Their snarls every time I stepped too close to the border were proof of that. They wanted a piece of me, but it was hard to blame them. I did have a killer ass. Or, well, I used to.

I walked back to the mirror and held up the dress, the one that had to be let out due to the fact that my ass had grown in sync with my belly. Reyes stayed close behind, his hand warm at the small of my back, his heat seeping in and easing the ache there. He was very therapeutic, especially now that the nights were getting cooler.

"They won't talk to me," I said, trying to decide if cinnamon had been my color all along and I just didn't know it. It did match my eyes quite nicely, which were the color of the amber in which the mosquito was preserved in *Jurassic Park,* but it also made me look a little deader than I liked. "The departed on the lawn. I keep thinking they need help to cross, but they just stare straight ahead, their expressions completely blank. Maybe they're zombies." I turned this way and that. "Either way, it's unsettling."

Reyes pressed into my backside and rubbed my shoulders with what I'd come to realize were magic hands. He was clearly the Magic Man Heart had sung about. I'd had no idea anything could feel that good. On bad days—the days there was just no settling Beep—it rivaled an orgasm.

Wait, no, it didn't. Nothing rivaled an orgasm. But it came damned close.

"You're bright," he said, bending until his breath fanned across my cheek.

"I know, but—"

"You're *really* bright."

I laughed and turned into him. "I know, but—"

"No," he said, his eyes sparkling with humor, "you're even brighter than normal. Your light is so bright, it fills every corner of the house."

Of course, only he would know that. I couldn't see my light, which was probably a good thing because how would I put on makeup if all I saw was a bright light? No, wait, he wasn't the only one who would know that. There were others who could see it. The departed, obviously, but also Osh, our resident Daeva, a slave demon who'd escaped from hell centuries ago. And Quentin, a Deaf kid we'd adopted as part of our gang, who mostly hung out with Cookie's daughter, Amber. And Pari, one of my best friends. And Angel, my departed thirteen-year-old sidekick and lead investigator.

I blinked, realizing all the people who would have known that my brightness levels needed adjusting. "Why didn't anyone tell me?"

He lifted a shoulder. "There's not anything you can do about it, right?"

"Right."

"Then why bring it up?"

"It's important, that's why. Maybe there's a reason. Maybe I'm sick." I felt my forehead. My cheeks. My chest. Then I lifted Reyes's hand and pressed it to my chest, glancing up from beneath my lashes as impishly as I possibly could. "Do I feel feverish?"

He darkened instantly. His gaze dropped to Danger and Will Robinson, aka my breasts. His gaze did that often, unruly thing that it was. Danger and Will loved the attention.

"You shouldn't tempt me," he said, his voice growing ragged.

A tingle of desire sparked to life, causing a warmth to pool in my abdomen. "You're the only one I should tempt, seeing as how we're hitched."

He wrapped a hand around my throat ever so softly and led me back against the mirror. It wasn't his actions that jump-started my heart, but the raw lust that consumed him. The dark need in his eyes. The severity of his drawn brows. The sensuality of his parted mouth. My girl parts tightened when he dipped his hand into my shirt. His thumb grazed over a hardened nipple, and a jolt of pleasure shot straight to my core.

"I'm here!" Cookie called from down the hall, her voice breathy, winded from the stairs.

I almost groaned aloud at the interruption. Reyes's grip on my throat tightened. He tilted my face up to his and whispered, "We'll continue this later."

"Promise?" I asked, unwilling to relinquish the impish bit.

He covered my mouth with his, his tongue hot as it dived inside me, as he melted my knees and stole my breath. Then, a microsecond before Cookie walked in, he pushed off me with a wink and strolled to look out the window. Still weak from his kiss, I almost stumbled forward.

"I'm here," said Cookie Kowalski, my assistant who moonlighted as my best friend, as she rushed into the room.

It took me a sec, but I finally tore my gaze off my husband. Cookie's short black hair had been flattened on one side, making her look lopsided. Her mismatched clothes were rumpled and a purple scarf dangled off one shoulder, perilously close to falling to the floor. Though Cook was considered large by society's standards, she wore her size well. She had the beauty and confidence of an eccentric, wardrobe-challenged countess. Normally. Today she looked more like a frazzled scullery maid.

I fought a grin and chastised her for her tardiness. "It's about time, missy," I said, tapping my naked wrist to make my point clear.

She gasped audibly, then looked at her watch. Her shoulders sagged in relief. "Charley, damn it. The wedding isn't for hours."

"I know," I said, stepping closer as she sat some bags on a bench at the end of the bed. "I just like to keep you on your toes."

"Oh, you do that. No worries there. I'm like a ballerina when you're around."

"Sweet." I leaned over to peek inside a bag. "I also want to thank you again for having the wedding here." She did so to accommodate Reyes and me, since we couldn't leave the grounds.

"Are you kidding?" she asked. "This place is perfect. Who gets to have a wedding in a historic convent surrounded by a lush forest adorned with the colors of autumn? Me. That's who." She gave my shoulders a quick one-armed squeeze. "I am beyond thrilled, hon."

"I'm glad."

"And, by having it here," she continued, pulling out a fluff of pink material from one of the bags, "neither you nor Reyes will be ripped apart by hellhounds during the ceremony. I'd love to get through this without getting blood on my wedding gown."

"It's so always about you," I said, and she laughed. Mission complete.

She took a ribbon off the material, then noticed Reyes's tousled state. "I'm not interrupting anything, am I?"

He turned, but only slightly, not wanting to expose the evidence of exactly what she'd interrupted. "Not at all," he said, pointing outside. "We were just talking about all the departed—"

"—who have passed on over the years," I said, stopping him from making a grave mistake. "And, boy, are there lots." I snorted. "Like millions. Maybe even billions."

Cookie stopped what she was doing—namely rummaging through another shopping bag—and turned toward me, her movements slow. Methodical. Calculated. "There—" Her voice cracked. She cleared her throat and started over. "There are dead people on the lawn, aren't there?"

"What?" I dismissed her suspicions with a wave of my hand. Because that always worked. "Pfft, no way. Why would there—? I mean, what would they be doing on—?"

"Charley," she said in warning, her hangover voice low and alarmingly sexy.

I bit down, cursing myself for my utter lack of finesse. This was her wedding day, and her nerves had been stretched thin enough without a last-minute addition of the recently departed to the guest list.

"Only a couple," I said, strolling nonchalantly to Reyes's side and looking out the two-story window. I was such a liar. There were at least a hundred departed standing in front of the convent. Silent. Unmoving. Unblinking. This was going to be the creepiest wedding ever. At least they weren't coming inside, but the wedding was actually outside in a little clearing behind the convent. Thankfully, they hadn't invaded that area. Much.

Reyes leaned down to me and whispered into my ear. "Your nearness isn't helping my condition."

I glanced at his crotch. The fullness caused a flush to rise in my cheeks. But he was right. Now was not the time. "Sorry," I whispered back before turning to Cookie again. "What's that?"

She was busy staring out another window, and I thanked God she couldn't see the departed. "The curtains for the nursery came in," she said absently.

"Oh!" I rushed forward, snatched them out of her hands, and shook out a panel of pink taffeta. "I sure hope it's a girl," I said, trying to change the subject.

"Of course it's a girl," she said, scanning the grounds. "All the prophecies say so. Where are they?"

"The prophecies?"

"The dead people."

"Right." I looked out over the weathered grounds. The grass had yellowed over the last month, the trees burning with the bright oranges, golds, and reds of autumn.

"They're gone now," I said, adding to the long list of sins I was committing in a house of God. "Those people love playing hide-and-seek. Seriously, it's like a thing with them."

I looked up at her, worried she wouldn't believe me, but her gaze had drifted somewhere else, namely to Reyes's reflection in the window. His shirt still hung open, the white material a stark contrast to the dark skin beneath, the muscles leaving shadows along the upside-down T of his chest and the rungs of his abs. "Good Lord," she said to me, her tone silky soft.

I agreed completely. "Good Lord indeed."

We both gawked a solid minute before he realized what we were doing. He dipped his head, unable to suppress a brilliant smile, and cleared his throat before announcing he got the first shower.

"I don't know how you do it, hon," Cook said when he left.

The communal shower was down the hall, a rustic imitation of my shower at home. And the thought of him in it, with steaming hot water cascading over his shoulders, down the curve of his back, sent a tiny shiver through my body. "Do what? Keep my hands off him?"

"No. Well, yes, but also keep your composure around him." She sat against the windowsill. "I'm not supernatural or anything, but even I can feel his power. His . . . allure. Does that make sense?"

"Damn straight it does."

"There's just something so primal about him. So ethereal."

"And?" I ventured. Cookie didn't usually say much without an ulterior motive.

"I worry about him. About him being a dad."

Surprised, I stopped and straightened my shoulders. "What do you mean?" Then, as a possible explanation sank in, I felt my eyes widen. "Do you think he'll be a bad father?" I turned and looked toward the door to make sure he'd left.

"No," she said with a soft chuckle. "I'm afraid he will sever the spine of any boy who breaks our girl's heart."

"Oh," I said, relief flooding me. But she had an incredibly well thought-out point. "Oh. You're right. I didn't think of that."

"You might want to discuss dating guidelines with him now. You know, before she turns five."

"Five?" I screeched. "Why five?"

The smile that spread across her face was one of practiced stoicism, as though she were talking to a mental patient. "And just when did you become interested in boys?"

"Oh, shit."

"Exactly."

2

IRONY: THE OPPOSITE OF WRINKLY.
—T-SHIRT

Two hours later, a wonderful woman named Hildie was doing Cookie's hair—thankfully, because I had no idea what to do with it—Amber was reading nursery rhymes to Beep, and I was eating strawberries atop my lofty position on a very swank divan named David Beckham. David sat by the window so I could look out at all the colors of autumn. He was thoughtful that way. He knew how much I loved fall, and fall in the Jemez Mountains was nothing short of spectacular.

"Humpty Dumpty sat on a wall," Amber said, reading from a picture book she'd bought Beep. She glanced at my belly as though to check if Beep were paying attention.

"Humpty didn't have much of a life, did he?" I commented.

"Humpty Dumpty had a great fall," she continued, ignoring me. It was weird.

"Lack of exercise. No hand–eye coordination."

"All the king's horses and all the king's men couldn't put Humpty to-gether again."

"Okay, stop right there," I said, a strawberry hovering near my mouth. "How are the king's horses going to help put an egg back together? Seriously. They're horses."

Amber was Cookie's thirteen-going-on-thirty-year-old daughter. She had what I'd begun to suspect was a touch of clairvoyance. She'd surprised me on several occasions with her knowledge or her visions of things to come, and she seemed to have a special connection with Beep. If I didn't know better, I'd say Beep was calmer when Amber was around. It was uncanny.

She sat in a chair beside me, her dark hair hanging in long ringlets down her back, her huge blue eyes concentrating on the pages before her. We were all in slips and robes—except Cookie, who was only in a slip underneath a massive hairdresser's cape—even though the wedding wasn't for another couple of hours. But both Amber's and my hair had been done already, our nails appliquéd to perfection, our makeup soft and sparkly. It had a hint of glitter in it. I argued that my face was shiny enough without adding glitter, but Cookie insisted. She wanted princesses in her wedding, and by damn, we were going to be princesses. I refrained from telling her princesses didn't wear glitter. Pole dancers wore glitter.

"It's a fairy tale," Amber said with a giggle, looking toward the door again. Uncle Bob was bringing Quentin up for the wedding. Quentin was her best friend and the current love of her life. I had to admit, the kid had stolen my heart at first glance. I couldn't imagine what he'd do to an impressionable girl. Thankfully, Cookie was too old for him.

"Do you think anyone will show up?" Cookie asked me. Again. While Amber was keeping a constant vigil on the door, Cookie was keeping watch over the drive to the convent.

"Yes," I said, trying not to laugh at her impatience. "Now, stop fidgeting." Poor Hildie. "Do you guys want anything?" I stuffed the last of the strawberries into my mouth and picked up my phone.

"Again?" Cookie asked. "That poor man."

"Are you kidding? Have you seen my ass? This is all his fault."

"Okay, then I'll take a water."

"And I'll take an orange soda," Amber chimed in.

"You got it. Hildie?"

"I'm good," she said, her brows furrowing in concentration.

I texted Reyes. I'd been doing that a lot. Texting demands to my minions. Being fertilized had its upside. Two minutes later, Reyes, wearing a T-shirt and jeans, had raided the kitchen that was down the stairs, past the foyer, and through a great hall—in other words, way too far for me to walk at the moment—and delivered our order.

He handed me a water with a wink. He'd showered, but had yet to shave. Or comb his hair. Or groom himself in any way. Gawd, he was sexy.

"Is that what you're wearing to the wedding?" I asked, teasing him.

In an act that stunned me to my toes, my uncle had asked Reyes to be his best man. They'd grown very close over the past few months—a good thing, since it was basically my uncle Bob who'd put Reyes in prison. But even Reyes had to admit to the insurmountable evidence against him. Earl Walker, the monster who'd raised him, made sure Reyes would be convicted of his murder, and convicted he was. At least until the cops found Earl very much alive.

"This doesn't work?" he asked.

"It works for me, but—"

"Me, too," Amber said, her crush on Reyes adorable. He flashed that brilliant smile of his. It was very unfair of him.

"Me, three," Cookie added.

Reyes walked over to Cookie as Hildie teased her hair. Or tried to tease her hair. She slipped several times, her hands suddenly useless in the presence of the son of what was once the most beautiful angel in heaven.

"I promise I'll look more presentable than this when the time comes, but until then." He took out a small box and handed it to her. "I wanted you to have this before everyone else demands your attention."

"Reyes," she said, her eyes wide. She opened it, absorbed the meaning of what it was he was giving her, then threw her arms around his neck.

A gold chain dangled from her fingers, and she flashed me the pendant, a diamond-studded infinity symbol.

"It's perfect," she said softly, her eyes wet with emotion.

He dipped his head in a bashful smile as she kissed his cheek. Then he turned back to me before I could hide the loving astonishment on my face.

He enchanted.

He simply enchanted.

Stopping in his tracks when he saw my expression, he studied me a long moment before walking over to me and placing a kiss on my cheek. The act was an excuse to whisper in my ear. "You have to stop looking at me like that if we're going to make it through the day without losing our clothes."

I turned to kiss him back. "I have no intention of making it through the day with you fully clothed."

He grinned again. "Do you need anything else?"

"Pitocin?"

One corner of his mouth rose. "What's that?"

"It induces labor. It's about time for Beep to move out. Cut her hair. Get a job. I need a flat belly."

"Have you tried crunches?"

"I just don't get it. I'm supernatural. You're supernatural. Why can't we have one of those quick pregnancies like Bella and Edward? Gwen from *Torchwood*. Scully. Deanna Troi. Or even Cordelia when that demon impregnated her. Twenty-four hours later, bam! Demon child."

"Aren't they all?" Cookie said, garnering herself a glare from her daughter. Ah, to be thirteen again.

"Seriously, what's with this nine-months crap? This is torture." I grabbed my belly and scrunched up my face. "Agony. It's worse than scurvy." I didn't actually know what scurvy was, but it sounded bad.

Reyes chuckled softly, kissed the top of my head, and walked out. Walked out!

"I'm not kidding!" I called after him. "I'm not putting up with this crap much longer."

"He's gone," Cookie said.

"Oh, okay." I cut the act short. "I have to admit, I feel wonderful. Nobody told me it would be like this. I have all this energy. I'm revved up, like, all the time."

"You're nesting."

My brows slid together in doubt.

"You know, getting ready for the baby to arrive."

"So, no actual nests?"

Hildie chuckled as Cookie said, "No actual nests."

"Is this what it was like for you?"

"I enjoyed my pregnancy quite a bit."

"Really?" Amber asked, grinning proudly from ear to ear as though it were because of her instead of in spite of her.

"That's good to know," I said. "What about your labor? How was that?"

"That was fun, too," she said without missing a beat, her smile suddenly as fake as the lashes Hildie had glued onto her eyelids.

"Cookie, I know when someone is lying to me."

"Okay, okay. Fun might be a bit of an exaggeration, but it was, you know, interesting. It was a learning experience. You just have to remember it's not forever. The good part is when you have to push. That's when it feels better. But you can't push too early."

I scanned the area for a pen and paper. "Do I need to take notes? Wait, what happens if I push too early? Katherine the Midwife didn't say anything about pushing too early."

Katherine was the midwife Reyes had hired. I was surprised she hadn't checked in yet. She'd been coming every day, since I was so close to my due date. That woman loved to poke and prod. I only liked being poked and prodded by one person, and his name was not Katherine.

"What'll happen?" Cookie asked, incredulous. "Are you crazy? If you push too early, you'll— You'll—" She stopped and stared into space.

"Did you just have a seizure?"

She blinked back to me. "No, it's just I have no idea what'll happen if you push too early."

She glanced at Hildie. The woman shrugged and kept teasing and tugging Cookie's hair this way and that.

Amber shrugged as well when I glanced at her askance.

"You guys are no help. Now I'm going to be scared to death to push."

"Oh, you'll push," Cookie said.

Hildie snorted and nodded in agreement.

So did Amber, as though she were very aware of what happened during childbirth.

"Someone's here," Amber said, jumping up and running to the window. Artemis, who had been snoring into the pillows on my bed, followed suit, barking at the car pulling into the drive.

"Are guests showing up already?" Cookie asked, panicking. "The food hasn't arrived yet. The decorators aren't finished. The flowers are still in the basement."

I considered getting up for a look, but that's as far as it went.

"Oh," Amber said. "It's just your stepmother."

Just when my day was going so beautifully. At least my sister, Gemma, would be with her, the silver lining to that dark cloud. My stepmother had also been coming to check on me every day. The woman who'd never lifted a finger to help me in her life, who had so little interest in me, she never glanced in my direction unless I was bleeding profusely, was suddenly vying for Mother of the Year. Gemma begged me to be patient with her. Said she was lonely after my dad's death. Said she wanted to make amends.

Maybe she did, but a lifetime of disdain was enough to drive anyone away. I had no interest in anything she had to offer, including an excuse for her behavior. She'd been trying to get me alone to talk to me, but I'd managed to dodge that bullet every time thus far. I just didn't want to listen to anything she had to say.

"And someone else is here. A black SUV."

I finally rolled off David Beckham to take a gander. "Special Agent Carson," I said, a little surprised. I hadn't seen her in months. We'd talked on the phone a few times and emailed quite a bit, but that was it.

"Oh, the FBI woman. She's so cool," Amber said, her voice forlorn. "I want to be in the FBI."

"I thought you wanted to be a hairdresser," Cookie said. "Or a brain surgeon."

"I changed my mind. I want a job where I get to carry a gun."

That was a scary thought. "Why?" I asked.

"Guys dig chicks with guns."

"Excellent reason," I said, giving her a high five.

Cookie shook her head.

"I'll go see what's up. Be back in a jiff."

"Wait!" Cookie said, ducking out of Hildie's grip. "I'll go, too." She unsnapped the cape and handed it to Hildie.

"Cook, no. It's your wedding day, for goodness' sake. And Hildie isn't finished."

"Kit might have a case for us. I need to be there to get the lowdown. Hildie can work on Amber." She raised her brows at Hildie, waiting for confirmation.

Amber had decided she wanted her hair up, and Cookie was game, provided there was enough time to change the style. Apparently, there was time.

"Okay, but as much as I love your undergarments, you're going to need pants."

———

Cookie and I went downstairs in our robes and pajama bottoms, leaving Amber to be pampered and primped by Hildie. Artemis bounded down the stairs right behind us as we padded across the wood floor to the front door.

I opened it and welcomed Kit with open arms. Literally. She eyed me a long moment, then let me give her a hug, patting my back as though she didn't know what else to do with her hands.

"You're very . . . sparkly," she said, her voice sounding a bit like she'd sucked helium from a balloon. Probably because I was crushing her larynx.

I didn't hug halfway. If someone's larynx wasn't being crushed, I was doing it wrong.

"Am I interrupting something?"

I set her at arm's length and took a moment to gaze at her. It made her even more uncomfortable. Score!

But, truth be told, she looked really nice. Her hair had been curled, her suit fit a little tighter than usual, and she was wearing makeup. Stranger things had happened, but not many.

"Not yet. We're having a wedding, but not for a couple of hours."

She gasped. "I'm so sorry. I should have called."

"Don't be ridiculous," I said, ushering her into the foyer along with another agent I'd never seen before.

Every move I made, every step I took, was fashioned with a singular focus in mind. I had to be careful not to look at Cookie. Her hair had been only partially teased, which meant it looked like a hairball with spikes on her head. I'd studied something similar in advanced biology in high school. Knowing a virus like that existed in the world had scared me, had given me nightmares. Or it might have if I'd cared. But I was in high school. All I cared about was boys.

Still, seeing it in person sent a tiny quiver of terror lacing down my spine. Terror that I'd burst out laughing and embarrass her. I had to force myself not to snort every time I looked her way. I had to focus. Concentrate. Channel my inner ninja. They had lots of focus.

"What's up?" I asked Kit as I showed them to our makeshift living room.

I had a feeling the room had formerly been an area for silent reflection for the sisters. I could only hope God wouldn't mind that we'd turned it into a place to entertain guests. On the plus side, we'd partied in it only once. Last night, actually. But I didn't drink, so I was safe from any ramifications we might incur as a result of partying in a house of God. Cookie, on the other hand, was screwed six ways to Sunday. Poor kid.

"I have something I want you to look into," Kit said. "But just so you know, Special Agent Waters was very against my coming here."

I turned to the man trailing behind us. "You must be Special Agent Waters."

"I am," he said, his tone brusque. The energy radiating off him fairly vibrated. He was seething underneath his starched collar. So this would be fun.

All in all, he was very nice looking. Medium height. Slim build. Exotic coloring. His accent would suggest a local upbringing. I got the feeling that in his spare time he liked wearing feather boas and singing karaoke. But that could just be me projecting.

"I'm sorry to hear you won't be happy with my involvement."

"I just don't think there's anything you can do. I don't understand why we're here." He shot Kit a hard gaze.

My protective instincts bucked inside me, but I smiled as graciously as I could. "Well, I hope to disappoint you."

I'd startled him. After a moment, he said, "If you can do what Agent Carson says you can, the last thing I'll be is disappointed."

"Wonderful." I showed them to our limited seating choices, which consisted of a couch, a chair, and a wood bench under a large, bright window. "Then we're in agreement."

The moment we crossed the threshold, I stopped mid-stride, almost causing a three-person pileup behind me. But something had registered in my periphery, and I had to turn to see if my eyes were playing tricks on me.

They weren't.

He was here.

Mr. Wong was hovering in a corner of my living room, just like back at my apartment in Albuquerque. He had never moved from the corner back home in the three years I lived there. Not once. And he was already there when I'd rented the apartment. I just figured he came with it as an amenity, like granite countertops or radiant heating. But now he was here. Hovering. Nose in the corner as always. Toes inches off the floor. Nothing at all had changed except his location.

Artemis noticed him, too. Her stubby tail wagged so fast, it blurred like the wings of a bumblebee. She tugged at his pant leg. Crouched down. Barked. Rolled onto her back with a whine as I stood there, stunned. Cookie covered for me, leading our guests all the way into the makeshift living room. I wanted to cry out Mr. Wong's name, run to him, and throw my arms around him. I'd missed him so. But doing so would probably freak out my unwitting guests.

Agent Waters took the chair and left us womenfolk the couch. Giving up on Mr. Wong, Artemis trotted to the bench and splayed across it to get some sun. I finally forced one foot in front of the other and strolled over to join the gang. As we sat down, we once again did our best to avoid looking at Cookie. It was rather like trying to avoid the hovering ghost in the room. At least for me.

"So, what's up?" I asked Kit after pulling myself together. My mind had instantly jumped to a thousand different reasons Mr. Wong might be there. Departed were showing up by the truckloads, kind of like distant relatives during the holidays. And now Mr. Wong? Why? How did he get here? How had he even found me? Like sands through the hourglass, those were the questions of my life.

Some of them. I actually had quite a few more.

Kit handed me a file. I shook out of my stupor, opened the file, and looked at the picture of a beautiful young girl. She had large, expressive eyes and a sweet smile.

"Missing persons case," Kit said. "Fourteen-year-old female. Last seen with friends at a park in Bernalillo. Her parents noticed she was missing when she didn't come home—"

"—from school one day," I finished for her, scanning the file. "I saw this on the news. Faris Waters." I looked up at Special Agent Waters and saw the resemblance immediately.

"She's been gone for two weeks," he said.

"Is she your daughter?" The anger and helplessness radiating out of him would certainly indicate that.

"My niece."

I bowed my head. "I'm sorry."

"I'm sorry we're wasting your time when you clearly have better things to do."

"Not at all," I said, ignoring his double meaning—as in, I was wasting their time—as I thumbed through the pages, looking for the vital clues. A dark green pickup with tinted windows was seen driving through the area for hours at a time several days before Faris's abduction. It hadn't been seen since. "According to this, she was supposed to meet some friends to go to a party after school, but she never showed up."

"Her parents didn't know anything about the party, but her texts would suggest that was her plan. A classmate was having a birthday party that Friday afternoon."

"I'll need those texts and all her emails," I said without looking up. "I'll also need a list of her closest friends and their contact information."

Kit took out a memo pad and started taking notes. "You got it. I'll get you everything we have by the end of the day."

Agent Waters stood and turned to look out the window. His frustration level showed in the rigid set of his shoulders.

"Agent Waters," Kit said, a hard edge to her voice.

He turned back. "Why are we here? We're wasting time. What can she do that we haven't already done?"

Kit stood. "Jonny, I told you. She solves cases. It's what she does. She's very good at it. These two ladies," she said, pointing to both Cookie and me, "have solved cases that were considered unsolvable. They have closed three cold cases for me over the past year. They found evidence where no one else thought to look. Remember that scumbag in Alaska? That was them."

I was thrilled that she'd included Cookie in her praises. I couldn't do anything without my sidekick.

Agent Waters, or Jonny, raked the fingers of one hand through his hair. I was surprised he had any left when he was finished.

"Now, sit down and pay attention," Kit continued. Her tone was alarming and very curious. These two clearly had a history, especially if the glare he gave her was any evidence.

He rounded the chair and sat back down.

"Have you interviewed all her friends?"

This time the glare was directed toward me. Agent Waters was taking my questions as an indication that he was incompetent. I didn't mean that at all, but he was clearly sensitive about the case.

"Why the guilt?" I asked him. I felt it there, weaker than the other emotions shooting out of him, but it was there nonetheless.

"What?" He acted as though I'd slapped him.

"You feel guilty. Why?"

When he spoke next, he did so through gritted teeth. "Fuck you."

I braced for an attack. If that upset him, what I was about to say was likely to send him over the edge. "Until you explain why you feel guilty, I'm going to have to consider you a suspect."

Both Cookie and Kit gasped aloud. Cookie did that a lot, but Kit was normally so unflappable.

"Charley," Kit said as Cookie placed a hand on my arm. It was an involuntary reflex when Agent Waters stood to tower over me. Not that he was that tall, but I was sitting down. Our positions gave him a distinct advantage. I'd definitely have to go for the crotch if he swung at me. "Jonny—" She caught herself and started again. "Agent Waters was working in the field office in Dallas when this happened. He's been there for two years."

"I'm sorry," I said to her, still doing my best to egg the man on. I hadn't been kidding. Until I knew why *Jonny* felt so guilty about his niece's disappearance, I was going to have to assume he had something to do with it. "But you two have clearly had a relationship in the past. Your assessment can't be trusted at this point in time."

That did it. He came unglued and I prepared for war. Then again, would he really hit a pregnant woman? He lunged forward and I felt certain he would. Reyes exploded into the room incorporeally, his heat like a nuclear blast over my skin. I held up a hand, and though it was meant for Reyes—he had a tendency to sever spines first and ask questions later—Agent Waters stopped instantly. By then, his face was mere inches from mine.

"You are treading in unsafe waters."

Kit rushed between us, pushing the agent back. It was too bad, really. I wanted to see what he was capable of.

"What are you doing?" she asked him.

The agent turned his back on her, and Reyes dissipated only to walk up to the doorway physically and lean against the jamb. He watched Agent Waters, but I nodded my head toward Mr. Wong, trying to clue Reyes in to his presence as nonchalantly as I could. Reyes didn't bite. He wasn't about to let his gaze stray one iota off his target. He had the best attention span.

Agent Waters scraped another hand through his hair, sat back down, then began to rub the palm of one hand with the thumb of the other. "This may be my fault."

Kit had started to sit down again, but she rose to her feet with his confession. "What do you mean?"

He pressed his mouth together before saying, "I think she was trying to figure out who was following her."

"You never said anyone was following her." She snapped up the file and thumbed through it.

"No, I— I didn't want my brother and his wife to know she'd come to me."

Kit sank back onto the couch.

"About a month ago, she emailed me. Asked me how to tail someone. Said that there was a strange man hanging out in their neighborhood, and could I run his plates?"

"Why isn't that in the report?"

"It wouldn't have helped," he said, his ire—and guilt level—spiking again. "She never gave me any more information than that. Just that some creepy guy was hanging out near the park she and her friends hung out at. She's always wanted to join the FBI, and I think she was going to try to investigate this guy on her own."

"What did you tell her?" Cookie asked.

"I told her—" He bowed his head. "I told her that it was illegal for me to run the plates for her. I told her to let her parents know about the man."

"That's not anything to feel guilty about," I said.

He shook his head. "No, but she emailed me again a few days later. She said she figured out who the guy was and asked if I could come to New Mexico and arrest him."

"And?" Kit asked.

"And I told her to give all the information she had to her parents and have them call the police. I told her I didn't have time."

While it sounded pretty legit to me, Kit bolted out of her chair. "You selfish asshole," she said, her jaw locked in anger. "You know how much you mean to her."

Like a dog being scolded, he ducked his head even lower.

"You know how much she admires you," Kit continued. They definitely had a past. "And you know she would do anything to get you to move back here."

"Exactly," he said, raising his head at last.

Kit let that sink in, then scoffed at him. "That's it, isn't it? You thought she was just doing all that to get you to come home."

When he lowered his gaze again, Kit turned away from him in disgust.

"Were you close with your niece?" I asked him.

"Before I moved away, yes. Very."

The interesting part about that statement was not his emotions, but Kit's. The rigid line of her back softened and a sorrow swept over her. Kit straightened her shoulders again, then said, "Now tell her the rest."

For a moment, he didn't understand her meaning; then his gaze narrowed. "Are you kidding me?" When she didn't answer, he asked, "What does that have to do with anything?"

She turned back. "Either you tell her, or I will."

"It doesn't mean anything, Kit. Why even bring it up?"

She stepped closer. "A year ago, I would've said the same thing. Then I met Charley."

His gaze bounced from Kit to me, then back again.

"Tell her."

"Jesus Christ." He stood again as though unable to face me when he gave the next bit of information. "She's been telling everyone for years, since she was about four, she's going to die before she turns fifteen."

I blinked, confused. "And when does she turn fifteen?" I asked.

The next word was spoken so softly, I almost didn't hear it. "Tomorrow."

Cookie placed a hand on her chest in shock.

Kit turned to me. "Like I said, a year ago, I wouldn't have given her premonition a second thought."

"Then you met me."

"Something like that. Do you think it has any merit?"

"Let's just say, I don't believe in coincidences."

"I need to get some air," Agent Waters said. He stood and started for the door, stopping short when he came face-to-face with my husband. My angry husband. As far as he was concerned, Agent Waters had almost attacked me. The agent stopped long enough to let the full effect of Reyes's glare make its point, then stepped past him and strode out the front door, his movements brusque and sharp.

After he closed the door, I turned to Kit. "All right, what gives?"

"What?" she asked.

"I'm sensing a lot of hostility between you two. What's going on?"

She glanced toward the door, then said, "Jonny's my ex."

"You were married?"

"Don't act so surprised."

"No, I'm not. It's just—"

"You think I can't land a man?"

"Kit, that has nothing to do with that. You're just so all-business. I'm a little surprised you took the time."

"Well, I've been married."

"And to a Fed, no less. Aren't there rules against fraternizing with the help?"

She lifted a shoulder. "Kind of. Not really. It depends, but yes, he's a Fed."

I sat taken aback.

"I like to call him my FedEx." A tiny smile broke through her severe expression. "He hates that shit."

"Too bad he didn't take your name."

She groaned. "I know, I know. His name would have been Jonny Carson. I can't imagine why he wouldn't go for that."

"Did you ever go by Waters?"

That rankled her feathers. "No, I'd already been established in the bureau, so I kept my name."

"Maybe that was the problem." I raised my brows, chastising her with them. They were quite unsettling at the right angle. "Maybe you weren't totally committed to the marriage."

Her jaw dropped. "You're going to give me marital advice? You've been married, what? Eight minutes?"

I gasped. "More like eight months."

"And have you taken his name?"

I cringed, glanced over my shoulder at my totally understanding husband, then said, "We were pressed for time."

"Ah, yes." She nodded, taking in the surroundings. "You had to drop everything and get to the 'safe house.'" She added air quotes.

"Exactly."

"Are you going to tell me why you're out here?"

I pulled my lower lip in through my teeth. "You don't want to know."

She leaned closer. "What if I did want to know? Would you tell me?"

An uneasy smile spread across my face. "Probably not. Some things are better left unknown. I'm just so floored you were married," I said, expertly changing the subject. "There's so much about your life I don't know."

"Look who's talking. The woman who solves crimes using almost supernatural methods and yet won't tell me anything about how she does it."

I checked my watchless wrist. "Well, would you look at the time."

"Charley."

"We have a wedding to get ready for, right, Cook?"

Cookie nodded her frazzled head as I shoved Kit past Reyes and toward the front door. I opened it and saw two vans parked in the driveway. One from the caterers. One from the florist. And Jonny was standing on the porch, one hand holding a bottle of water, the other stuffed into a pocket. He straightened when we walked out.

I still couldn't believe it. Kit had been married. I also couldn't miss the spike of emotion that leapt inside her when she saw him again. She was still in love with him. I wondered if I should tell her that he was still in love with her, too.

He turned to us as Kit addressed Cookie. "I'm so sorry. I didn't mean to interrupt your wedding preparations."

Cook waved a dismissive hand. "Oh, please. We've been cooped up here for months, going a little crazier with each passing day."

Before she could run in the opposite direction, I lunged forward and gave Kit another quick hug, but it was an excuse to whisper in her ear. "I'll call you tonight and let you know if she's alive."

Kit nodded, deciding not to question in front of Jonny how I could possibly know that.

When I released her, I added, "I'll do everything I can. I promise."

"I know you will."

Jonny didn't seem quite so confident, but he did have the decency to apologize for his behavior. "I'm sorry I lost my temper."

"Don't give it a second thought. You're upset. I understand upset."

He nodded, probably relieved I wasn't threatening to file a complaint against him.

After waving them off, we hurried back in and closed the door before God and all his creation saw us in our robes.

Reyes walked up to us, and Cookie, suddenly self-conscious, tried to smooth down her hair. It was a bit like trying to tame a hurricane. He wrapped an arm around my waist and I leaned into him, reveled in his heat.

"Did you see him?"

When he finally tore his gaze off the door, he raised a brow in question.

"Mr. Wong. He's here."

The slight lifting of one corner of his mouth would suggest that he already knew.

"How long has he been here?"

"Since this morning. You didn't feel it?"

"Feel what?"

"The shifting of energy." He turned toward Mr. Wong, though we couldn't see him from where we stood, as there was an adobe wall between us. "I just wonder what he's doing here."

"Me, too."

"Me, three," Cookie said, wringing her hands.

I took another look at her, and I couldn't hold back any longer. I burst out giggling.

"What?" she asked, patting her hair. "I'm getting ready. What's the big deal?"

I strode forward and gave her one of my larynx-crushing hugs. "You," I said into her robe. "You are the big deal."

"I think two of the three people standing here would argue with you on that," she said, crushing my larynx back.

The door reopened. A frazzled Gemma tiptoed in and closed it behind her. My blond-haired sister was already sporting her wedding attire, a powder blue cocktail dress with matching ankle boots, only she'd added huge, dark sunglasses that didn't make her look like an insect at all, and she'd gathered her bangs into a pointy ponytail. She'd always loved unicorns growing up, but this was taking it a bit far.

She stopped when she noticed us. "What are you doing?" she said in a hisslike whisper, and I could've sworn she slurred her words. "Cookie, you're getting married in an hour and a half. What are you doing down here? In your robe? With your hair?" Horrified, she pointed at Cookie's head. Then her demeanor changed. "Unless that's how you're wearing it, in which case, it's so pretty. I love it. It looks really good on you."

I laughed out loud and she slammed an index finger over her lips. "Shhhh," she said, hushing me way longer than was necessary.

"Are you hungover?" I asked her softly, appalled. "How many drinks did you have?"

"I don't know. I lost count at three. Or twelve. I'm just not certain."

"What were you doing?" My astonishment knew no bounds. "Why would you drink that much when you knew we had a wedding the next day?"

"I was trying to keep up with Cookie."

"Are you insane?"

She swayed back against the door and shushed me again.

"Cookie's like a competitive connoisseur. The last guy who tried to outdrink her ended up in traction for a month."

Cookie came to her own defense. "Only because a man named Jose Cuervo convinced him he could fly. Not my fault."

But Gemma wasn't listening. "What is up with your hair?"

"Gemma, she's not wearing her hair like that."

"Oh, thank God." She placed a hand over her chest to still her racing heart. "I was worried. Okay, in, in, in." She shooed us forward. "We have a lot of work ahead of us."

I turned toward Reyes and raised a brow. "Some more than others," I teased. He could go naked for all I cared, though I doubted Uncle Bob would appreciate that as much as us girls.

Reyes gave me a quick squeeze, then left us to it.

"Where's Denise?" I asked. Not that I cared where my stepmother was, but I wanted to be prepared for her grand entrance. It always caused an unsettling sensation in my stomach.

"She's out back, ordering the decorators around," Gemma said.

"Sweet. Keeps her out of my hair."

With a chastising sigh, Gemma placed her manicured hands on her hips. "Charley, you have to promise me, for Cookie and Uncle Bob's sake, you will be nice to Mom today."

"What?" I asked, incredulous that she would even say such a thing. That she would trust me so little.

Her expression didn't change. I caved. She was going to be one of those stern mothers all the kids on the playground talked about as though she were something to be feared.

"Okay, whatever. I'll be nice. At least until the wedding's over. But once the rings are on the fingers, it's every evil stepmother for herself."

Gemma rolled her eyes. "You guys need group therapy so bad."

"Oh, hell no," I assured her. "I've had more than enough of that woman over the last eight months."

Denise had been coming out to the convent several times a week. Each time, she had another excuse. She noticed we were out of dish soap or she wanted to make sure I was okay. She was apparently a pediatrics nurse when she'd first met my dad, and that gave her another reason to invade my much-loved privacy. To bombard me with questions about how I felt, my blood pressure, was I taking the vitamins she brought, did I have any swelling? She had never, in my entire existence, paid so much attention to me. I'd learned long ago to be wary of any attention she tossed my way. Everything she did had an ulterior motive. Perhaps without my dad around to give her a sounding board for all things horrid and bizarre about Charley Davidson, she had no one else to turn to. But I was hardly a good alternative.

"She's lonely, Charley." Gemma's expression turned sympathetic.

"Well, let her go be lonely at your house."

"I work. I can't very well have her hanging out at my office all day, scaring my clients away."

"So she has to come here and scare all the dead people away instead? I have clients, too."

"She's hurting right now."

"I know, I can feel it. The sadness. Every time she comes over, all I can think about is Dad, and it breaks my heart all over again. As long as she keeps coming over, I can't heal."

"Charley, maybe she needs to heal, too."

"I'm sure she does. I just don't care."

"You can't mean that."

"You can't be serious. After everything she's put me through, you would still defend her?"

"Maybe she needs your forgiveness. She knows what she did was wrong."

"What she did?" I asked, growing more annoyed by the second. "You say that as though there was only a single transgression. She did everything wrong, Gem."

While Denise took to Gemma like a duck takes to *à l'orange*, she'd never quite bonded with me, if the menacing scowls and the constant digs were any indication. Any mother—step or otherwise—who tries to get her daughter committed to a psych ward because she's a little different from the other kids at the park doesn't deserve that daughter's love. But I'd tried. For years, I'd tried to be more like Gemma so our stepmother would like me. I once studied for two days for a spelling test just so I could get an A on a paper that would sit next to Gemma's on the refrigerator. I was so proud when I'd succeeded that I ran all the way from the bus stop to show it to her, and I fell on the way, but I made it home relatively unscathed. Denise took the paper with the bright red A on it out of my hands, gave it a quick glance, then sent me to my room without dinner for ripping my backpack when I fell.

That night, when I snuck out of my room to get a spoonful of peanut butter, I found the test wadded up in the trash. About three seconds later, I had an epiphany: There would be no winning her over. Denise despised me. Period. It's hard when the only mother a girl has ever known despises her. To learn that at age seven was quite the blow to the ego. I took the test back to my room, smoothed it out the best I could, and pinned it to a corkboard where I kept pictures my dad had taken of my real mom while she was pregnant with me. Before she died giving birth to me. They served as a reminder. Anytime I tried to gain Denise's approval, I looked at that crinkled A and rethought my objectives. The way I saw it, my acceptance of Denise's indifference saved a lot of heartache for me and a lot of disappointment for her.

"And she knows that," Gemma pleaded. "She knows she did everything wrong. What she doesn't know is how to talk to you about it. How to apologize. You make it so difficult."

"I make it difficult?" I asked, astonished.

"Charley," Gemma said, using her clinical voice, soft and nonjudgmental, "until we talk about it, until we sit down and really delve deep into our pasts, none of this is going to be resolved."

What Gemma so often forgot was that no matter how soft and non-judgmental her voice was, I could feel the emotions raging beneath her calm exterior. We'd been having this same conversation for weeks. No, months. And I could feel her frustration. Now that Denise was open to the idea, Gemma wanted us to bond. To be besties and go shopping together.

I'd rather walk into a den of hellhounds.

"You mean if we don't have a long heart-to-heart, issues that have gone unresolved for decades will continue to be unresolved?" I asked, feigning horror at the thought before lifting one shoulder in an apathetic shrug. "Works for me." I turned and climbed the stairs, effectively ending the conversation.

I heard Gemma release a sad sigh.

3

I decided to finish getting dressed in the bathroom while Cookie and Amber put on their final touches in the bedroom. Walking down the narrow hall, I felt the history of the place leach out of the walls. The wood slats creaked beneath my weight, and I could just imagine what it would have been like being a nun here two hundred years ago. Well, not a nun, but a person, interacting with the Native Americans, watching their children play, growing food in the gardens below. What a rewarding life they must have led. And they were brave, the women of the frontier, whether a nun, a native, or a homesteader.

Yet their lives must have been so hard, especially without cell reception. I balked at the challenge of having only one bathroom on the entire floor. Every room had a sink and mirror, but when you had to go, you had to go. Thankfully, Reyes had added central heat and cooling, but I feared him changing the tone of the place, its historical feel, so we hadn't upgraded too much. We kept the rooms upstairs small and sparse, with stoves in each one. Even though they were no longer used, they still worked and could heat the tiny rooms quite nicely. We also kept the downstairs almost all original, patching the walls here and there and fixing the flooring. The former convent would make a great restaurant and B and B for the right owner, but it needed to be registered with the Historical Society to preserve its richness.

Another small renovation we did was add a working bathtub and separate shower in each of the two bathrooms, one upstairs and one down. Though not so fancy as George—that is, the stone shower in Reyes's apartment—the bathrooms had really come along, compared to the originals. While they'd been updated back in the 1940s, plumbing had improved by leaps and bounds since then.

I knocked softly on the bathroom door and, receiving no answer, opened it. A burst of steam hit me in the face, and I could only pray the glitter wouldn't melt off my face. Or melt my face off. Either way. I swiped at the steam and walked in on a half-naked slave demon as he was wrapping a towel at his waist.

"Osh," I said, covering my eyes. "I knocked. What the hell?"

A wicked grin spread across his handsome face. I knew this only because my fingers were accidentally open. It wasn't my fault I could see him in the almost-buff. While he looked nineteen, he was centuries old. Older than Reyes, actually. But somehow that knowledge didn't make me feel less perverted every time I took in his slim, muscular form. Created a slave in hell—or a Daeva, as they were called—he had lived a hard life. I couldn't imagine what he'd gone through. To be a slave was one thing. To be in hell was one thing. But to be a slave in hell? The concept boggled my mind.

Why did they need slaves in hell anyway? What exactly did they do? The only inkling of their duties I had was that some of them were, for lack of a better phrase, pressed into service, forced to fight in the demon army. I first met Osh while he was trying to win souls in a card game. He'd won one from a client, which I wanted him to return. But that's what he did. He supped on human souls. Fortunately, I'd convinced him to sup only on the souls of humans who did not deserve them, like murderers, drug dealers, child molesters, and lobbyists.

But that's where I'd first learned that Osh, or Osh'ekiel as he was called down under, escaped from hell centuries before Reyes did. In fact, he was the only Daeva to escape from hell, and though Reyes didn't trust him at first as much as I did, he'd grown to depend on him for Beep's sake. The demon did seem to have Beep's best interest at heart.

Reyes had once told me that the major difference between Osh in hell and Osh on earth was that his scars were not visible in his human form.

It made my heart ache for him. Normally. Not today, though.

Osh looked me up and down, a wolfish grin softening his youthful face. "I heard you. I was just getting kind of lonely. Figured I could use some company in here."

After giving up the pretense of purity, I lowered my hand and rolled my eyes. "Please. Like you could handle this." I hitched a thumb over my shoulder. "Scoot. I need to finish getting ready."

"I need to shave," he volleyed.

"You can shave in your room."

"My room is the size of a broom closet."

"So is mine. You didn't have to move out here, you know. You could've stayed in your posh house in the city." We'd secretly put him in a broom closet, but what he didn't know wouldn't hurt him.

"And leave you guys to fend off the hounds of hell without me? No way. But, yeah," he said, giving his head a shake, "this place is weird." Water droplets flew off his shoulder-length black hair and onto my face.

I pursed my lips as though that would faze him. "I agree. It's a good thing I was never a nun in the 1800s."

His grin reappeared in full force. "Somehow I don't think, even if you'd been born in the 1800s, you would've become a nun."

He had a point. I shooed him out and turned to the mirror to freshen my makeup, but as the steam cleared out of the room, I saw something unexpected. Names carved into the walls behind me.

Horrified, I looked up as though I could see into the attic. "Rocket!" I shouted, stomping my bare foot.

He appeared instantly. Rocket had died sometime in the 1950s. He was big, over six feet, and cuddly. He always reminded me of a giant bear I'd had as a child.

"What are you doing? I told you, you can't write the names on the walls anywhere but in the attic." Reyes and I had added extra Sheetrock up there so Rocket didn't damage the original structure.

"But, Miss Charlotte, I'm running out of room up there."

"Well, you're just going to have to go over the names that you already have. Think layers. Like you did at the asylum."

"Fine, Miss Charlotte, but I'm going to scratch through the paper. Nurse Hobbs doesn't like it when I do that."

Nurse Hobbs must have been a nurse at the asylum where Rocket had grown up. From what I could gather over the years, which wasn't much, Rocket had been committed to an asylum when he was very young. He'd probably had his gift even when he was alive. He knew the names of every human ever to exist who'd passed away, and he made it his personal goal to document them all. I couldn't imagine what his parents must have thought when he was a kid as he wrote name after name of those who'd passed on anything he could find. Back then, having him institutional-ized would have been the norm.

I grinned at his analogy. Anyone who thought of walls as paper needed to get out more. "We'll get new paper. It's okay."

Rocket had moved in shortly after we did. He'd had something to tell me one day that was apparently of vital importance. It involved a kitten that had wandered onto the property and got stuck in the asylum. It had likely been abandoned by its mother and Blue, his five-year-old sister whom I rarely saw, was very worried about it. So part of Cookie's job for a couple of days was to go search for the kitten at the asylum and bring it to the convent, because by then Rocket had moved in. He said Blue had moved in, too, but I had yet to see her here. Of course, in all the years I'd been going to visit Rocket in the asylum, I'd seen her only three times. She was painfully shy. But I also knew that where Rocket went, Blue was sure to follow.

Unfortunately, so was a sassy little girl named Strawberry. I called her that because she'd drowned when she was nine in Strawberry Shortcake pajamas. She had long blond hair and bright blue eyes and a bluish tint to her pouty mouth, evidence of her cause of death.

She appeared in front of me, hands on hips, glare firmly in place. "Why are you yelling at Rocket? You're scaring Blue."

"Rocket is writing names where he shouldn't. It's against the rules. No breaking rules—right, Rocket?"

He hung his head in utter shame. "No breaking rules. Right, Miss Charlotte."

"Okay, no more names except in the attic. Is that a deal?"

"Deal."

Rocket disappeared, but Strawberry unfortunately did not. I'd gotten to know Strawberry through a mutual acquaintance. She was the departed sister of a cop I knew: Officer Taft. I'd told him that Strawberry moved in with us some time back, so he'd come to the convent a few times to visit her. Not that he could see her, but I was a decent interpreter.

After Strawberry got the glare out of her system, she looked at my face and did a 180. Her huge eyes rounded in awe. "You're sparkling," she said, reaching up.

I kneeled down to let her touch my face, her hand icy against my skin as she patted my cheek.

"You're like a fairy princess."

Utterly flattered, I said, "Thank you."

"You're not as pretty as one or anything. And you're really fat. But you sparkle like one."

I forced my smile to remain steady in the heat of battle. Never retreat. Never surrender. "Thank you again," I said through clenched teeth.

"You're welcome."

"Hey, is Jessica back?" Jessica was my former BFF from high school who'd decided to make my life a living hell by moving in with me when Rocket, Blue, and Strawberry did. But I hadn't seen much of her lately.

"No, she's been staying with her sister a lot."

"Oh. I hope everything is okay."

"It is. I think she's scared of the dogs outside."

"Right. Can't blame her there."

"Okay, well, Blue and I are going to play with Sheets."

"Awesome. Are you going to drape them over you and play ghost? It's really appropriate."

"No, *Sheets,*" she said, her indignation over my ignorance exasperating her. "The kitten."

"Oh, of course. Sounds like a plan." Then, before she could disappear on me, I asked, "Why 'Sheets'? He's black."

"Because he's shiny and black, like David's sheets."

Ah, her brother, David—aka Officer Taft—had shiny black sheets. That was so much more information than I needed today. "Gotcha. Well, have fun."

"Okay." She popped back out, leaving me to my own devices. Probably not a good idea. After all, I had glitter on my face.

Guests started arriving soon after Amber and I finished getting dressed. Amber looked adorable, her hair piled high on her head and sprinkled with tiny bronze butterflies. She was also over the moon that Uncle Bob had showed up. Not because he showed up to marry her mother, but because he'd brought Quentin—*the* Quentin—with him.

Quentin Rutherford was a kid we essentially adopted when he'd been possessed by a demon. He'd been possessed because he could see into the supernatural realm, and at the time, the demon was after me. It had used Quentin as a guide, following my light, the light he could see. Once we'd rid him of said demon, we found out he'd been born deaf. Because he had no family to speak of, we, along with the Sisters of the Immaculate Cross, had adopted Quentin. And it didn't take long for Amber to appreciate that fact. According to the extremely detailed report she gave us, he was dressed to the nines. I was excited to see him myself.

We changed into our dresses while Hildie finished Cookie's hair. I ran to get our bouquets and check on everything while strategically managing to avoid my stepmother. The guests were in the back, where we'd set up several rows of white chairs. But knowing my sister, the whole affair would be absolutely lovely. At least she got to plan one wedding, since mine didn't turn out quite as expected. It became an impromptu thing in a hospital room, and all Gemma's hard work had been for naught. Now she got to start from scratch with a brand-new venue and a fresh set of victims.

When I got back to the room, Amber and I watched as guests got out of their cars. Gemma's former client and current boyfriend, Wyatt, pulled up, as well as Ubie's boss, Captain Eckert, a few detectives I'd seen around and Strawberry's brother, Officer Taft. Garrett Swopes, a colleague, showed next, looking rather delicious in a charcoal coat and tie. Amador, Bianca, and the kids showed up. They'd been coming out on a regular basis to see Reyes, and we'd had several amazing cookouts as a result. In the process, Cookie had grown quite fond of them, inviting them to the wedding. Their seven-year-old daughter, Ashley, would be the flower girl and five-year-old Stephen the ring bearer. I watched as a few other people I didn't recognize got out and walked around back to the makeshift chapel. Several were young girls between the ages of nineteen and twenty-three. Cookie said she had several second cousins. With the stunning array of men who were to attend the wedding, the cousins were sure to have fun.

I relayed to Cookie all the information I could about the guests showing up to set her at ease. She was nervous enough as it was. I'd assumed her knowing that people were showing up would calm her nerves. Instead it made her even more nervous. Go figure.

"Well," she said at last, standing behind me.

I turned and was stunned speechless. Cookie looked incredible. Her short, dark locks had been swept back and made to look like she had an intricate French braid. Just like Amber and me, she, too, wore tiny bronze butterflies in her hair to match our cinnamon dresses. But her dress was a creamy ivory wrap sprinkled with pearls. Her makeup was simple yet dramatic. She was breathtaking.

"Cookie," I said, unable to tear my gaze away from her. "You look magnificent. You look like a movie star from the '40s. You are utterly elegant."

She laughed softly, the act easing some of the tension from her shoulders. "Do you think Robert will like it?"

"Please," I said, astounded she had to ask. "Uncle Bob is going to trip over his own tongue when he gets a load of you."

She crinkled her nose and giggled like a schoolgirl.

"Mom," Amber said as she stared in awe. "You're so beautiful."

"Thank you, sweetheart. You're gorgeous."

Amber dropped her gaze and kicked an invisible layer of dirt bashfully.

"Are we really doing this?" Cookie asked me.

"Hon, if we don't do this, I think that man of yours is going to kidnap you and take you to Mexico. Or Vegas. Or Romania. You two are getting married one way or another."

She dropped her gaze. "I'm sorry we're getting married now of all times."

"What?" I asked, my voice an octave too high. "What are you talking about?"

"I just, I don't want to take away from the birth of your first child. This is such a special time for you."

"Cookie Marie Kowalski, how dare you even think such a thing."

"Are you sure?"

"As sure as I am that my uncle will disown me if I don't make certain you walk up that aisle in the next few minutes."

She laughed and hugged me. Amber joined us in a three-way just as Gemma walked into the room. My sister stood taken aback, a hand placed gently over her mouth for a solid thirty seconds before she shook out of her stupor and waved us forward. Thick droplets glistened between her lashes as she rushed us out of the room and down the stairs. We met Bianca and the kids at the bottom. Ashley's dress was a smaller version of Amber's. Her curls were also piled high on her head with tiny bronze butterflies inhabiting the thick mass. Stephen looked dapper in a black tux and bow tie to match the men's. After Bianca explained their roles again, she went to sit with her husband, Amador, as Gemma escorted us to the back door, where we would step onto the strip of green turf that led to the altar.

Ashley kept twirling in her dress, leaving petals in her wake, while Stephen fidgeted with his tie.

"We'd better do this before we lose them," I said.

Gemma gave us all quick hugs, then went to join Wyatt.

We all took deep breaths as the wedding music started. We sent Stephen down the aisle first, carrying the pillow with the quintessential promise rings. Ashley was next, dropping amber rose petals as she waved and posed for pictures.

I turned to Cookie, forcing myself not to cry. Not yet. There was a time and a place for tears at a wedding, and this was neither. But I couldn't help it. I leaned in and gave her one more colossal hug as a tear escaped despite my best efforts. I gave Amber a quick peck on the cheek, turned, and walked down the aisle.

I had it all planned. I was going to stare straight ahead. I was going to concentrate on my breathing. I was going to focus on not tripping. And it was all going according to plan. I looked at my uncle as he stood waiting for his bride. He looked amazing. Hair and mustache neatly trimmed. Black tux. White shirt. Crisp bow tie. The fact that he looked uncomfortable made me crack a minuscule smile, but I managed to keep my composure as I kept walking, kept breathing, and kept the tears at bay.

Then it happened. My eyes landed on Reyes Alexander Farrow. My uncle's best man, standing in the same black tux, starched white shirt, and black bow tie that my uncle wore. But they seemed worlds apart. Reyes looked like he was born for the finer things in life. His hair had been trimmed since that morning. How any man could look just as sexy in a dirty T-shirt and ragged jeans as he did in a formal tux and bow tie was beyond my immediate comprehension. But the pièce de résistance was simply Reyes himself. His wide shoulders, powerful even beneath the layers of tailored clothing. His face startlingly handsome. His jaw strong, his mouth sculpted to perfection. His thick dark lashes casting minute shadows across his cheeks. And his hair. It was shorter now, but thick dark curls still hung over his forehead. Curled around his ears. He looked like a supermodel. Something exotic and rare. Something not of this world.

One corner of his full mouth tipped up as he watched me watch him. Then the slightest arching of his left brow, and my knees almost gave beneath me. I had never seen anything so beautiful in all my life.

Then I heard a whisper beside me. I looked to my left. Denise sat glaring at me while Gemma's eyes were wide with panic. My heart sped up. My eyes widened to match hers. I was suddenly panicking, too, only

I had no idea why. She nodded toward the front, and I realized I had stopped. The moment my gaze landed on Reyes, I had stopped.

I quickly stared straight ahead, squared my shoulders, and continued down the aisle, wondering if anyone noticed the five-minute pause in the procession. Hopefully not. And if they did, I had a kid fermenting in my belly. I could chalk it up to Beep. But my cheeks burned either way.

I thought Reyes might laugh at me. Or at the very least, find my faux pas amusing, but when I looked over at him again, he was not laughing. He was not even smiling. He had darkened again, his expression almost dangerous as he took me in. He could feel my reaction to him and I, in turn, could feel his reaction to me. How he could have such a reaction with me looking like the Pillsbury Doughboy astonished me. He was kinky. I'd take it.

Once I got to the front, I stepped aside and turned, waiting for the gorgeous bride. The "Wedding March" began to play through the speakers and everyone stood as Cookie and Amber stepped out into the light of the warm fall afternoon. They strolled to the front slowly, taking their time, letting people snap pictures and whisper words of praise.

But my attention had turned to Uncle Bob, and I wished I'd thought to have someone record him, because his reaction to Cookie was worth all the coffee in Albuquerque. No, New Mexico. No! The world!

He sucked in a sharp breath of air at the sight of her, his mouth slightly open, his expression reflecting all the amazement and doubt that was so Uncle Bob. I could tell right then and there he wondered what she saw in him. And I wanted to tell him: *That*. That humbleness. That appreciation of her. That love for both her and Amber. No, not just love. Respect. He respected her. He respected Amber. He was truly grateful for them both. There was no greater gift.

When they reached the front, the minister raised his hands and gestured for everyone to sit. After the guests settled, he asked, "Who gives this woman to be married to this man?"

Amber spoke, her voice quivering only a little. "I, her daughter, Amber Kowalski."

She turned to Cookie, her blue eyes shimmering. She gave her a quick hug, then took Cookie's hand and placed it gently into Uncle Bob's, giving him permission to marry her mother. There was no higher honor. The happiness ricocheting inside me for my cantankerous uncle knew no bounds.

The minister smiled his approval, and I nodded to Quentin, who was sitting in the front row. He stood, took Amber's arm into his, and led her to her seat. The whole exchange was formal and sweet and reverent, and once again I fought with every ounce of strength I had to hold back the floodtide threatening to erupt within me.

The minister went through the vows quickly, garnering an "I will" from both the bride and the groom. And while it wasn't easy for me to take my eyes off the beautiful couple in front of me, I simply could not keep from staring at my husband. I had never seen anything so stunning. His dark skin in stark contrast to the white stiff collar beneath his jaw. His fresh haircut. His cleanly shaven jaw. Although I loved the scruffy Reyes more than pumpkin pie with whipped cream, this one was breathtaking. He was like Tarzan, Clark Kent, and James Bond all rolled into one. I half expected an Aston Martin to be sitting in our drive.

After being given the go-ahead, Uncle Bob wrapped one arm around Cookie's waist and lifted her chin. Only then did I realize she'd been crying. He gave her the gentlest of kisses, the kind that attested to the immense love and respect he had for the woman he'd just married, and the crowd erupted in celebration. It was over. After all the preparation, all the work, all the anxiety, it was over. Fast. Much too fast. We still had the reception, of course, and then I would get to work on the case while Cookie enjoyed her pre-honeymoon honeymoon. It would consist of only one night at Buffalo Thunder, a stunning resort and spa in the Pojoaque valley north of Santa Fe.

Cookie had insisted they hold off on their real honeymoon until after Beep arrived. Odd how Beep had changed all our lives so implicitly. She even added her own little kink in the wedding when the guests started giggling because my dress was moving. I couldn't tell if she was just trying to get comfortable or hosting a kegger. Either way, she was already stealing the show, trying to upstage.

I looked down at her with an *attagirl* grin.

The moment the crowd erupted, Uncle Bob whisked Cookie back down the aisle, which worked for me, as that was where the food sat.

"I have to admit," I said to Gemma as we loaded our plates, "you did good." I chose a kale salad with grilled salmon and an elegant cup filled with macaroni and cheese. I'd definitely be hitting that again, though I needed to leave room for pumpkin mousse, tiramisu, and chocolate truffles. And wedding cake! Couldn't forget the wedding cake!

Gemma had decided on much of the wedding's fanfare. The decorations. The type of food. All the extra stuff that made Cookie's day so special. I owed her. There'd be no living with her now.

"Thanks, sis." She shouldered me playfully.

Wyatt, her beau, asked, "How are you feeling?"

Reyes was close, as in right next to me, so I had to make it good. "Oh, it's awful. I have to pee every thirty seconds. My ankles are swollen. I drool when I least expect it. And I keep getting this weird craving for sardines and green chile on melba toast."

Wyatt had the decency to look aghast, but Reyes just grinned, focusing on the food instead of my suffering. The scoundrel.

"You hate sardines," Gemma said to me.

"Exactly. It's like I'm not me anymore and someone—or something—has taken over my body." I gasped. "It's *Invasion of the Body Snatchers*!"

Gemma giggled. "I think it's called being pregnant."

"Nobody cares about my suffering," I said as Reyes took both our plates to a table.

Gemma and Wyatt followed us. "We care," Gemma said. "Just not a lot."

She was so sweet.

As the afternoon wore on, Reyes and I got to sit back and watch Cookie in action. For once in her life, my very best friend was the absolute center of attention. And she glowed.

"She's really something," Reyes said to me.

I turned to him, his eyes sparkling with appreciation as he watched her and Ubie. "You know, every time you say something like that, I fall a little more in love with you."

His shimmering gaze landed on me in surprise. But he recovered quickly, his expression intensifying as he took me in. It made my insides tighten.

"I wanted to thank you for being Uncle Bob's best man."

He didn't respond. His gaze dropped to my mouth and lingered there as his heat feathered over my skin. He let one finger slide under the hem of my dress and up over a knee. His touch sent a shiver of delight racing up my thigh to settle in my nether regions. He was so darkly sensual, the moment didn't last long. There were too many other women clamoring for his attention, and I sat floored at their brazenness. No idea why. It was like that everywhere we went. Well, when we went places. One actually asked him if he could go out front to check her tires.

Man, Cookie had a fertile set of relatives.

Most people stayed outside to mingle. Fortunately, there weren't many departed in the back. They were mostly on the front lawn. As Reyes helped pull tables together, I chatted with Swopes and Osh, much to the chagrin of Cookie's second cousins, who were vying for their attention at the time, then with my good friend Pari and her beau, Tre. Then I sought out Quentin and Amber after Cookie and Uncle Bob cut the cake. We'd asked Quentin beforehand if he'd wanted an interpreter and he said no, informing us that nobody listened to the words anyway. He just wanted to enjoy the ceremony. What he'd really wanted was to whisper—aka, sign small where no one else could see—back and forth with Amber through the whole thing. They were absolutely adorable together.

The next obstacle I faced that afternoon was of the four-legged variety. Thrilled that Reyes and I were outside, and taking that as her cue to get her freak on, Artemis ran around like a gerbil on meth, turning occasionally to make sure we were still watching. And God help us if we weren't. Every time we turned away, she charged. That was fine for most involved, but she was solid to Reyes, Osh, and me. So while she flew through the guests with the greatest of ease, she'd almost taken me out. Twice. Fearing for my and Beep's safety, Reyes escorted me inside, where more food awaited and guests stood around chatting and eating and generally enjoying the afternoon. But we weren't in there long before he was needed elsewhere.

Turned out, Cookie had a whole plethora of family that I didn't know about. They were all aunts, uncles, and cousins. No siblings and her parents had passed away years ago, but she still had family showing up to represent like true homies. She even had that gaggle of second cousins. Five young women who had decided that Reyes, Osh, and Garrett were the most delicious beings they'd ever seen. Even Quentin and Pari's tall drink of water, Tre, weren't exempt from the Flirtatious Five. I was right there with them, but I did fear for one's life when she made googly eyes at Quentin. Amber's hackles rose to needlelike points, and I was afraid the other girl would not make it home with all her hair. Or all her limbs. Or both eyes. Or a full set of teeth. So many body parts could go missing in such a scenario.

Thankfully, Reyes headed that confrontation off at the pass, and Amber led Quentin to a quiet little table away from most of the guests. But that put Reyes back in the fray. I watched as the five practically assaulted him, each trying to get closer than the next. He took it all in stride, not that I was surprised. He'd been getting that kind of attention his entire life.

And he knew I was watching from inside. I sat at a window as he endured their attention, but the more I watched, the more flirtatious glances he shot my way. The more winks he offered. The more lopsided grins he wore. It was all quite enchanting, but the one that got me, the killer movement that almost sent me into orgasmic bliss, was when he glanced at me from across the sea of guests, gave me a long, languid once-over, then pulled his lower lip in through his teeth. To say the move was sexy would have been like calling a tsunami a ripple in the ocean.

I stood and walked to the door that led outside, about five seconds away from ordering him in, when I heard a female voice.

"Hi, pumpkin head."

I turned to see my aunt Lillian standing behind me, trying to see over my shoulder. Aunt Lil had died some time in the '60s. She was part world traveler and part hippie. Since there were so many people around us, I had no choice but to put my phone to my ear so I could talk to her without looking like a mental patient.

"Aunt Lil," I said, giving her a quick hug before anyone saw us. "When did you get back?"

"Just now, sweet cheeks. What's all the hubbub about?"

"Cookie got married today."

"Cookie?"

I nodded. "She married Uncle Bob."

Aunt Lil cackled with delight at the thought. "'Bout time that boy got hitched. I been worried about him ever since that yogurt incident when he was seven."

I didn't dare ask. "So, how long are you staying?"

"Until you pop, I suppose. I got to see this girl everyone is raving about. Whole place is jumping. Nobody will stop talking about her. Even had to call in the riot police, just in case."

No idea.

"That's so great, Aunt Lil. I'm thrilled you'll be here when Beep arrives."

"Wouldn't miss it, even though I did have to pass up the chance to go skinny dipping with the seventh Tsar of Russia." She wriggled her brows at me. "Now, where is the sexy beau of yours? I need something tall, dark, and scrumptious to look at, if you know what I mean. Men on this side aren't always easy on the eyes."

I laughed softly. "He's right over there, being accosted by Cookie's second cousins."

"Perfect. I'll join them."

I almost doubled over when Aunt Lil disappeared, then reappeared behind Reyes to give his ass a squeeze. He glanced at me, his face accusing as though I had something to do with it. Not to worry. Aunt Lil soon spotted Osh, who was fending off an elderly woman who'd had one too many Chardonnays. The best part, though? Reyes had blushed, and I fell a little further.

4

The day had turned out beautiful in every way possible, but one person was missing through all of it: Angel, my departed thirteen-year-old sidekick. He never missed a party. I considered summoning him, but he already knew about the wedding. Surely he would have come if he'd wanted to. He did a lot of stuff with his own adopted family. Maybe they had something going on today as well.

Still, I doubted it. Angel had been acting strange lately. More so than usual. He popped in at the most inopportune times, acted like he had somewhere else to be when he did stop by, and hadn't hit on me in months. Maybe he was accepting my marriage with Reyes, respecting our union, better than I thought he would. Or maybe the pregnancy freaked him out. Every time he did pop in unexpectedly, he seemed to avoid looking in Beep's direction. I needed to talk to him about it. Get him counseling. Though that could be difficult, considering the situation. If only Gemma could interact with the departed.

After two more hours of mingling, guests started to slowly dissipate.

Not literally, as they were corporeal, but they began giving their final congratulations and saying their good-byes. I wondered why they were leaving before Cookie and Uncle Bob did. The happy couple was supposed to head off to its pre-honeymoon honeymoon bliss while being pelted mercilessly with rice. It was tradition, and it wasn't often I got to throw things at my BFF or my uncle. I had every intention of making every throw count, but they wouldn't leave. Cookie was still in her wedding dress and Ubie in his tux and they were mingling and dancing and eating and drinking as though they had no intention of leaving.

Didn't they just want to be away from it all? I wanted to be alone with my sexy-as-hell husband so bad, I ached. But I didn't want him changing out of that tux before I had my way with him. How many opportunities would I have to rip a tux off him? I could reenact all those James Bond fantasies I'd had since I was, like, two. But I had another appointment to attend soon, so the clothes ripping would have to wait. It was probably a good thing Reyes was being kept so busy. He had checked in off and on, but his attention was always needed here or there. He did give an incredible toast that only once mentioned the fact that Uncle Bob had wrongfully convicted him of murder. So that was nice.

When yet another woman old enough to be his grandmother headed Reyes off and demanded his attention before he could get to me, I giggled at the forced smile on his face. She flirted, batted her lashes, and patted his biceps about twelve times too many for his comfort. He took out his phone and typed as the woman spoke to him, her movements exaggerated. I couldn't be certain, but I had a feeling she was talking to him about how she used to be a pole dancer until her hip gave out.

My phone chimed. I took it out of the delicate clutch that matched my dress and read Reyes's text.

Aren't you going to save me?

I don't know. I'm having a lot of fun right now. Wanna sext?

He crossed an arm over his chest while holding his phone. One corner of his mouth twitched as he leaned back against a tree and typed.

Absolutely.

Sweet. What are you wearing?

His eyes sparkled with mirth.

Animal print boxers and striped socks.

I burst out laughing, gaining the attention of everyone around me. I texted back, only this time I wasn't teasing.

You are so beautiful. How are you even real?

He sobered, staring at the phone a solid minute as the woman described her hip replacement surgery. At least, that's what it looked like from my vantage. He lifted an index finger to put the woman on pause right when she was getting to her recovery and strode toward me. His gaze didn't waver from mine as he walked, his gait like that of a panther on the prowl, the tux adding to the allure, and my body flooded with a molten heat that pooled deep in my abdomen. He took the three steps to the kitchen with one long stride and stopped in front of me.

I looked up and let my gaze trace the outline of his full mouth, the angles of his strong jaw.

After a moment, he wrapped a hand around my neck as though to pull me to him, but Ashley called out.

"Aunt Charley! Uncle Reyes! Mom says we have to go."

After several seconds, he managed to catch her just as she jumped into his arms.

"Can I stay the night? Pleeeeeeease."

Bianca walked up behind her and shook her head at us, adding a threatening glare should we even think about defying her.

I patted Ashley's back, in awe of the death grip she had on Reyes's neck. She put her head on his shoulder and offered me her prettiest pout.

Amador stepped up to take her. "Uncle Reyes has enough women in his life today," he said, peeling Ashley off him with a chuckle. "He doesn't need a fluffy orange tornado following him around." He had been calling our dresses orange all day, mostly because Ashley was not a fan of anything orange.

"Cimmanom," Ashley said, disappointed we weren't having a slumber party.

"Aunt Charley needs to rest," Bianca said, taking her hand when Amador set her down.

"We can rest together," she argued.

I'd spoiled her with our movie nights, not that I regretted a second of it.

"We watch movies while Uncle Reyes makes cockporn."

Everyone in the immediate area stilled while Reyes and I pressed our mouths together, trying not to crack up. This was a serious situation, and cracking up now would just be wrong.

"Popcorn, honey," Amador said. Then he looked at Bianca. "Hon, she really needs to learn how to say that word."

My laughter came out as more of a snort. I coughed to cover it up. Reyes just turned his head, unable to lose the grin.

"I've tried," Bianca said, flustered. "Tell you what, we'll go to McDonald's when we get home. How does that sound?"

That was a pretty big deal. Bianca did not believe in feeding her children fast food.

"Yay!" Stephen said as he ran up, zigzagged, feigned a left turn, took a right before circling the parental units and shooting off in the opposite direction. Reyes caught him just as he sped past. He giggled as he was lifted high into the air, then brought back down into Reyes's arms. "I'm going to be fast like you," he told Reyes.

"I bet your dad's faster," he said.

Amador scoffed playfully. "Don't even start with that crap. I learned my lesson long ago."

Bianca tickled Stephen's bare foot. "If we're going to McDonald's, you'll have to put your shoes on."

Stephen had never been a big fan of shoes. Or socks. Or clothes in general. He'd once escaped from his house in his skivvies. They found him running down the street, telling anyone who would listen that his mother had been abducted by aliens.

"I don't like those shoes," he said, wiggling into the crook of Reyes's neck to get away from his mother while she tried to slip his socks onto him.

"Do you remember what the sign at McDonald's says when you go in? 'No bare feet.'"

He stopped wiggling and looked at her as though she'd lost her mind. "I'm not a bear."

I fought yet another giggle.

"He has a point," Reyes said.

"Yeah, laugh it up, *pendejo*," Amador volleyed. "Your time is coming."

"I can hardly wait," Reyes said to me.

We hugged good-bye, my heart full of hopes and dreams for Beep. Watching Reyes with Ashley and Stephen was one of the highlights of my life. I couldn't wait to see how he'd behave with Beep. If she was half as charming as Amador and Bianca's kids—

Then the truth hit me. I looked down at Beep, then over at Reyes. She would have him wrapped around her little finger in no time. "We could be in trouble."

He laughed and pulled me into his arms. "I have no doubt," he said, walking me to a dark corner of the kitchen.

I giggled when he pressed himself into me. Gasped when he bent to nibble an earlobe. "I'm the size of Nevada. How can you even want me?"

"I happen to love Nevada," he countered, his voice as deep and soft as his kisses.

If it weren't for the lady standing right beside us, the moment would have been perfect.

"You are the oldest soul I've ever come across," she said, astonished as she gazed at me, her eyes unblinking.

"Um, thank you?" I said as Reyes lifted his head at last.

I looked over at the woman. She wore an outdated floral dress and had clearly forgone a bra. She really needed the support a bra could offer her. I'd seen her piddling about, looking in our drawers when she thought no one was paying attention. I was certain she'd gone through the medicine cabinet in the bathroom.

"You're ancient."

That wasn't offensive at all. I straightened. "I'm only—"

"You are older than the stardust in the sky," she said, interrupting. Her eyes were glassed over, and I decided right then and there, no more open bars at weddings. Brought out the crazies.

Reyes stepped out of my arms then, as though something outside had caught his attention, and said, "I have to go check on Artemis."

"Artemis?" I asked, baffled. Since when did he have to check on a departed dog? Seriously, what kind of trouble could she get into?

"You are as old as time itself."

"Look," I said, growing frustrated, "that's just not something a girl wants to hear."

"You are older than—"

"Wow, you know what?" I said as I led her back into the kitchen where Denise was cleaning up. "There's even more champagne in here. Don't let anyone try to convince you we're out. You call 'em on it, okay?"

Cookie walked in then, a horrified expression on her face.

"Lucille, why don't you go find Uncle Tommy? He's been looking for you."

"Oh, my," said the woman, rushing back outside.

"I am so sorry," Cookie said. "Lucille won't bother you again. Uncle Tommy has been gone for decades. She'll never find him."

"Oh, no. How did he die?"

"Oh, he didn't die. He just packed up one night and left to live in the wilds of Alaska. We still get a postcard every few years."

"You have a very eclectic collection of relatives." I looked at Denise as she tried to scrub a stain out of the tablecloth. "But don't we all?"

"No, you're right. Mine is a little more eclectic than others, which is why you're only just meeting most of them."

"They're great. Really, Cook, but you never told me your cousin Lucille was clairvoyant."

"Oh, yeah, she's . . . different. Remember? I told you that one night we were playing Screw Your Neighbor with that couple from the first floor."

"Yes, you told me she's different. You didn't tell me she's clairvoyant."

Cookie cast a doubtful gaze. "Like *clairvoyant* clairvoyant?"

"Yep. Maybe that's where Amber gets it."

Cookie's expression did a 180, shifting from doubt to horror. "Bite your tongue. Amber is nothing like Lucille." I felt a spike of fear shudder through her. "That woman has sample packs of Preparation H from the 1970s."

"That may be, but it must run in your family. There is something very special about your daughter."

"Yes. Special. Just not *that* special."

I cracked up. "You're right. Odds are, Lucille was labeled insane at a very young age. But she's really just—"

"Eccentric," Cookie finished. "I get it. I just didn't know she was gifted."

"I doubt anyone does. But at least you know to nurture Amber's gifts. Not suppress them before they have a chance to bloom and then she becomes the lady that collects samples of hemorrhoid medication."

"I will do anything to avoid that." She indicated Lucille with a nod. The poor woman was asking everyone who was left if they'd seen Tommy.

"Hey," I said, frowning at her, "aren't you supposed to be on your way to your one-night stand? I mean, your pre-honeymoon honeymoon?"

She laughed. "Well, we were, but there is a missing girl out there. She takes precedence."

"What?" A jolt of alarm swept through me, not unlike a body shot might have. "Cook, no. This is your wedding day. You are not, under any circumstances, working. Oh my God, I can't even—"

My phone chimed and I looked down. It was the text I'd been waiting for.

"I have to go—"

"Go?"

"—but you are going on your pre-honeymoon honeymoon, and that is an order."

"Where are you going?"

"I mean it, Cook," I said as I hurried—aka waddled faster than usual—past her. "I don't want to see you when I get back."

"You can't leave the grounds."

I grabbed a sweater, then rushed out the front door, saying just before it closed, "Go!"

I walked quickly past some guests loitering by the cars out front, hoping they wouldn't wave me down for a chat. I also avoided eye contact with the departed who stood between me and my destination, winding through them, hoping I didn't look drunk to the loiterers. Seriously, didn't they have homes? I kept my head down and my stride quick. I had places to be, and I couldn't risk Reyes coming back to find me gone. He would definitely come looking for me.

Fortunately, he wouldn't see me go into the woods from the backyard unless he was specifically watching. I made sure to go straight for the cover of trees and stuck to them until I came around to a path that led to an access road about a hundred yards from the convent. I hurried as fast as my legs could carry the two of us, wobbling through the brush and dry yellow grass, dodging tree branches and departed alike. Even though I knew the Twelve couldn't come onto the sacred ground, I still kept a constant vigil. I'd been attacked more than once. Their teeth were like razors set on thick, powerful jaws. It was not something I wanted to experience again.

I could hear them growling in the distance, the sound a low rumble over the land, reminding me that in all the months we'd been here, they'd never stopped patrolling the borders. The access road came into view at last. The deeper I ventured into the woods, the more nervous I became. A blue sedan sat parked there. I stopped, my ankles aching from traversing the uneven ground. The growls had grown louder, echoing off the trees around me and reverberating in my chest. I fought to control my fear lest I accidentally summon the one man I didn't want to know I was meeting another of his gender. Alone. But it wasn't easy. The hellhounds knew I was taking a direct path to their jaws. I could go only a few more feet before they would latch on to me and pull me off the blessed dirt. I glanced back one more time to make sure Reyes hadn't followed me; then I called out to him.

"I'm here," I said.

A man, tall, in his early sixties, wearing a suit and a military cut, stepped from behind a tree and walked toward me.

"Mr. Alaniz," I said as he greeted me with a once-over.

"Ms. Davidson. I didn't realize this was a formal affair."

"This old thing?" I asked, teasing. "I just threw this on at the last minute." When he winked at me, I added, "Actually, my best friend got married today. I didn't have time to change."

"I understand, but I would advise against walking out here in those shoes again, especially in your condition."

"I know, but I had to sneak away. Thanks again, by the way, for meeting me like this."

"My pleasure," he said, his curiosity about me and our clandestine meetings clawing at him. I could feel it, but it wasn't his place to ask.

Mr. Alaniz was the private investigator I'd hired a couple of weeks after we'd absconded to the convent. Since I couldn't be out there trying to figure out firsthand who murdered my father, I'd hired someone who could. True, Uncle Bob and the entire Albuquerque Police Department were on the case, but I'd never felt so helpless, so useless. Freedom meant a lot more to me than it used to, and I had to conduct my own investigation one way or another. I had to do what I could, and if that meant doing it against Reyes's and Uncle Bob's wishes, so be it.

He looked past me, then said, "I'm not going to ask why we meet in secret like this, but I have to know if you are in danger."

I listened to the heavy breathing of the hounds. If he only knew.

"No," I said, dismissing the thought with a wave. "Absolutely not." And I wasn't. Not in the way that he meant. He wanted to know if I was in any danger from Reyes or anyone else who could stumble upon us.

"And if you get caught? What then?"

What then, indeed. "Let's just say my husband would be upset with me, but, no, I would never be in any danger from him. Never."

He seemed satisfied with my answer but looked past me again for good measure.

"What did you find out?" I asked, trying to hurry this along. Reyes would notice my absence soon. I was a little surprised he hadn't figured out my secret meetings with Mr. Alaniz before now. I was bright, according to everyone around me. So bright, I could be seen from anywhere on the planet. Why, then, didn't he see when I snuck out of the convent? How did he not know where I was every minute of every day?

A growl rumbled not ten feet away from me. I stilled and watched as a glistening of silver appeared, then disappeared in the trees. Fear tightened around my chest as Mr. Alaniz scratched his chin where a smattering of blond stubble grew. He pulled out a notepad.

I'd been to this spot a dozen times. They had never gotten this close. Right after we'd escaped to the convent, Osh had marked the sacred grounds with stakes, then threaded string around the entire area to indicate the border. Either I was closer to the border than I thought, or Osh's calculations were wrong.

I saw another flash of silver as a hellhound's muscles rolled in the shadows of the trees. I could hear its breathing, causing me to retreat involuntarily, but it kept its distance. As long as we had an accord, I didn't feel the need to run screaming back to the convent, but an uneasiness settled in my shoulders and neck, my senses on high alert.

"Your uncle is on the right track," Mr. Alaniz said.

I blinked back to him. "In what way?"

"You were right. After the last time we met, I staked out the place." He gestured toward another small access road above us. "I waited there, and sure enough, a man showed up and parked right about where I am parked now." He indicated his car with a nod, and an excited thrill ran up my spine.

"Were you able to follow him?" I asked. The entire police department had been looking for this guy, but he seemed to be a ghost. Until now.

"I was."

I clapped. It was the first good news we'd had in months. Apparently, some guy had been following me my entire life. My father figured it out and had been tailing the man when he died. We found pictures that my dad had taken of him, but we could never get an ID. So while my father was able to track him, we couldn't get within a mile of the guy. That we knew of, anyway. I began to wonder if he'd vanished until I was out walking Beep and Artemis one day and saw a car parked on the access road. The moment I looked up, the driver started the car and sped off, but I recognized him from the pictures my father had shot of him.

When my dad went missing, we found those pictures along with a whole slew of other photographs in the hotel room where he'd been staying. Photographs of me growing up. Some were as recent as mere days before my father died, and it couldn't have been a coincidence that he died soon after finding this guy. Whoever he was, he could have had something to do with my dad's death. And even if he didn't, I really wanted to know why he had been following me, literally, since the day I was born.

"But there's more to it. While you were right, he does have pictures of you from when you were very young, when I tailed him back to his apartment, I managed to snap some shots through his windows. Just like you said, he had pictures of you, articles, yearbook photos, pretty much your entire life pasted on his walls, but some of them were from just after you were born."

"And?"

"And, he isn't old enough to have been following you that long. He's barely in his thirties. Unless he took up stalking at age five, someone else is involved. Has been involved for a very long time."

He was right, and I had a feeling I knew who—or more precisely, what—was behind this.

Mr. Alaniz handed me a photograph.

I nodded. "That's him. That's the guy from my dad's surveillance photos."

"Then you were right. He does work for the Vatican."

I knew it. A former client, Father Glenn, had clued me into the fact that the Vatican had been keeping a file on me since I was born—but why? And if my dad discovered the truth, would the Church have had him killed? Over a few photos? Either way, I needed proof of this man's existence. And his address.

But first, "How do you know he was working for the Vatican for sure? Do you have any proof?"

"They're paying his bills, for one thing," he replied with a shrug. "He also gets a call from a number in Italy about once a week, a number registered to an office in Vatican City. I don't know much about the Vatican, I have to admit, but I'm sure they have several dozen departments. I couldn't determine which one this number was registered to, however."

"And how did you find out he got a call from them at all?" I asked, liking his results.

"It was weird. The guy just left his phone on a table at a restaurant," he said, lying through his teeth. "By the time I ran it out to him, I'd accidentally scrolled through all his incoming calls. And read his texts."

"One of those freak occurrences?"

"Exactly." He handed me a manila envelope. "And all that information may or may not be in this envelope."

"I'll have to think positive," I said, taking it from him, already coming up with ways to sneak it into the convent. "Did you find a connection between him and my father? Something that might implicate him in my dad's death?"

"No, and I don't think you will."

"Why?"

"He just doesn't seem the type to kill someone and leave his body in a storage shed."

The reminder of how my father was found shuddered through me. "Why do you say that?"

"He's a vegan, for starters. Most vegans are nonviolent. And he never misses Mass."

"Makes sense. He does work for the Vatican."

"I think his only job is to observe and report. For some reason, the Vatican wants to keep a very close eye on you. I just don't get a killer kind of vibe from this guy."

I nodded, trusting his instincts. "I don't suppose you got a name?"

"Howard, if that's his real name."

"Howard?" I asked, a little disappointed. I expected something exotic and Italian like Alberto or Ceasario. But Howard?

"Howard Berkowitz."

"Now you're just teasing me."

He grinned. "Nope. That's what he goes by."

"Okay, I'll look this over. In the meantime, I need you to grab Howard and bring him here."

He chuckled softly. "I'm sorry, Ms. Davidson, but I don't kidnap people."

"I don't mean kidnap. 'Kidnap' is such a strong word. I mean coax. Encourage. Maybe roofie him."

"Well, again, I can't do that. I have a better idea."

"There can't possibly be a better idea," I said, deflating. And here I was, thinking his ethics were on the same level as mine: practically nonexistent.

"How about we tell your uncle, *the APD detective,* so he can at least bring the guy in and question him."

I toed a rock at my feet. "That might work, but I won't be able to be there."

"You don't trust your uncle to get to the truth?"

Not when I could tell if he were lying instantly, but I wasn't about to tell Alaniz that. "No, I do. I guess I'll have to. But we have to get this information to my uncle without him knowing I was involved."

"I think I can handle that."

"Perfect." At least it was a step in the right direction. I scanned the area to make sure they hadn't sent out a search party for me. So far, so good. "Okay, what about that other thing we talked about?"

"Which one?" he asked, his voice full of amusement.

I had him working on several cases for me at once. "The brother thing."

"Ah." He flipped through his notepad.

This was the tricky part. The part Reyes didn't want me looking into. The part where Mr. Alaniz's fears for my safety could actually come to fruition. Reyes would never hurt me, but I couldn't say the same for any unfortunate passerby should my husband find out I'd been delving into his past.

5

When Reyes, aka Rey'aziel, had decided to be born on earth to be with me, he chose a wonderful couple to raise him. Or that's the story I got. But he was kidnapped as an infant. I thought he'd been kidnapped by Earl Walker, the monster who raised him. I didn't find out until just before being banished to the convent that Earl didn't abduct him. A couple in Albuquerque, the Fosters, did. They'd abducted him from a rest stop in North Carolina.

How Earl Walker got ahold of him was a little less clear. Perhaps the Fosters feared they were about to get caught and sold him to Earl, and now they had another son. I'd asked Mr. Alaniz to find out two things: One, was the man the Fosters claimed as their son really their son, or had they abducted him as well? And, two, who was the couple that Reyes had been abducted from, the one he'd originally chosen to be his family?

The latter boiled down to one thing: That couple still lost a child thirty years ago. Their hearts were still broken, their dreams shattered, and I wanted them to know that their son had grown into a wonderful and honorable man.

Because I knew the time frame and the area where Reyes had been abducted—a rest stop in North Carolina about thirty years ago—it wasn't difficult for Alaniz to find his birth parents. But if he knew I'd sought them out, Reyes would be livid. He told me so, made me promise not to look for them, but after becoming pregnant with Beep, after knowing that bond that exists between a parent and a child, I couldn't let them go to their graves wondering whether their son was alive or dead. If he was happy. If he'd suffered.

They didn't need to know that he had indeed suffered. Beyond belief. But I felt they did need to know that he was alive and healthy and happy . . . for now, anyway. Hopefully he wouldn't find out what I'd done, and he would remain happy for a very long time to come. My meddling was a grave violation of his wishes, but I couldn't imagine losing Beep. I couldn't imagine her vanishing without a trace and me not knowing what ever became of her. No parent should ever have to go through that, and if it meant risking my husband's wrath, so be it. At least I would sleep better at night with them knowing what a wonderful man their son had become.

So, I devised a plan once Mr. Alaniz found out who Reyes's birth parents were. I wrote a letter as though it were coming from a neutral private investigator, and he would send it anonymously. I didn't tell them Reyes's name or where he lived or what he'd gone through. I'd told them only the essentials, just enough to bring them closure and allow them to move on with their lives.

Or that was the hope.

"I'm fairly certain, judging from the Fosters' son's coloring and age, he is one of three children that went missing around the time the Fosters adopted him."

"So, he'd supposedly been adopted by the Fosters. Are you sure he wasn't?"

"The adoption agency is out of business, but from what I could find out, they were in business only a few months and facilitated three adoptions."

"Three?"

"Exactly. But I have to admit, he seems . . . okay. Are you sure you want to open that can of worms?"

"Are you kidding? I love worms. And if they abducted him, his birth parents have the right to know. He has the right to know. Wait, do you think he knows?"

"I doubt it. According to his records, he was only a few weeks old."

"Okay, well, we have to decide how to handle this. What about the other thing?"

Writing that letter, the one where I told Reyes's birth parents their son was alive and well, that they could rest easy, knowing he'd grown up an honorable man, was a lot harder than I'd expected. I couldn't find anything about how to tell the grieving parents of a missing child that their son was A-OK in any of Emily Post's books.

Then there was the tiny hiccup in which Reyes had forbidden me from contacting them, so I didn't. I had nothing to do with sending that letter. Mr. Alaniz did. Of course, I failed to mention to Mr. Alaniz Reyes's habit of severing spines before he did it. My love muffin would never in a million years find out anyway. A good thing, because if he did, the power of his anger could destroy this side of the world. Thankfully, I covered my tracks beautifully.

"Well, funny you should mention them."

"Them?" I asked.

He cleared his throat. Studied another envelope in his hands. Glanced over his shoulder.

"Mr. Alaniz?"

"Um, your husband's birth parents."

"Did you send the letter?"

"Yes. Yes, I did." His sudden discomfort had me a little worried.

"And?"

"They're here."

"Who's here?"

"Your husband's birth parents."

It took a long moment for his words to sink in. When they did, a shock similar to being taken from a sauna and thrown into a frozen lake slapped across my body, my nerve endings firing all engines as I gaped at him.

He scratched his head in a nervous gesture. "They . . . my assistant—"

"Please tell me you're kidding."

"—put a return address on the letter you wrote."

"No."

"Yes. And—"

"No."

"Well, yes, she did."

"No." The ground tilted beneath my feet. "Please no."

"Ms. Davidson, they threatened to call the FBI—"

Everything around me blurred, and for the first time in months, I almost passed out. Only no one had hit me or drugged me or run over me with their car. This was au naturel. This was a boiling combination of dread and alarm and stark raving terror.

"—if I didn't explain what was happening. How I knew about their son. I knew you wouldn't want that, so I thought you could explain and—"

The edges of my vision darkened. He was going to kill me.

"—work out some kind of schedule."

Wait! I was pregnant. With his child, even! He couldn't kill me. It was illegal most everywhere.

"You know, maybe you could break it to your husband gently and then introduce them later. Over a bottle of wine."

The last thing I remembered before the ground slipped out from under me was how fluffy the world had become. Then everything went dark.

"Let's get her to my car."

I groaned as an arm went around my shoulders. Then another scooped under my legs followed by a labored groan as I became weightless. My lids fluttered open. Mr. Alaniz was hefting me into his arms and, with the help of two other people, began to carry me off.

I was being abducted!

No, wait, this was worse. I was being taken over the border. Deep, rich growls thundered around me as he carried me closer to my untimely death.

"Wait," I said, trying to blink past the fog. "Wait, Mr. Alaniz, put me down. I'm okay."

He lowered himself to one knee. "Are you sure?"

"Yes, I'm okay."

The minute he lowered me to the ground, I scrambled back. The hellhounds were inches away from me. They could have lunged at me or grabbed a foot and dragged me across, but they didn't. They did, however, growl. Their jaws snapped, their teeth clinking together with each gruesome promise.

I clambered to my feet, then came face-to-face with the woman I assumed was Reyes's birth mother. She was beautiful. With soft blond hair and gentle gray eyes, she'd aged gracefully despite the stress of living with what had happened. They had never had any other children, their sorrow so great. Or that was my guess.

"Mrs. Loehr," I said, trying to calm my racing heart.

"You know what happened to my son?" she asked, her features

suddenly hard, and I could tell she wasn't sure if she could believe that. If she could allow herself to hope after so many years. "You know what happened to Ryan?"

That had been his name at birth: Ryan Alexander Loehr. The fact that he had the exact same middle name and that all three of his first names—his birth name, current name, and celestial name, Rey'aziel—started with an *R* had boggled my mind since I first learned of it.

I looked over my shoulder toward the convent, the roof barely visible from my vantage. While no one had noticed my absence yet, it wouldn't be much longer before they did. I turned back. Mr. Loehr. He had dark hair and brown eyes, which could explain away Reyes's coloring, because he got none of his features from his birth parents. I could only assume he actually did look like Lucifer. He was certainly handsome enough. But I had to stave them off. Even for just a little while.

"Let me start by saying I am married to the man I believe to be your son."

Mrs. Loehr covered her mouth with a small hand, her eyes glistening already.

"If you will go back to Albuquerque, I promise I will get in touch with you. This is something I'm going to have to break to Reyes slowly."

"Reyes?" she said, her voice soft. "His name is Reyes?"

I didn't give his last name. I didn't want them Googling their son and discovering anything before I had a chance to explain.

"Will you please trust me and not call the FBI until I can tell my husband what I've done?"

"You wrote the letter," Mr. Loehr said.

"I did." I placed my hands on my belly. "I wanted you to know that your son was alive and well. That he was beautiful and wonderful and the most amazing person I've ever met."

"I don't understand," Mrs. Loehr said. "Why didn't he contact us? Why haven't you told him you found us?"

I closed my eyes and lowered my head. "He was violently against my contacting you."

My statement hurt her. I could feel a sharp pang pulse through her.

"Not for the reasons you might think."

"Then why?" she asked.

"Because he feels he no longer deserves you."

"What?" Her face showed her astonishment.

I took her hand in mine. "I'm not going to lie to you. He's had a hard life. A very hard life."

She pressed her mouth together to keep from sobbing.

"He doesn't want you to know what he's gone through. He doesn't want you to feel any more guilt than you already must."

She covered her mouth again as Mr. Loehr wrapped an arm over her shoulders.

"Please believe me, he is not going to be happy when he finds out I contacted you."

"Will you be okay?"

"Yes. He won't do anything drastic. He might, I don't know, storm out or something else guys like to do, but that's about it. He dotes on me."

"Can we just—?" Mr. Loehr began, but his voice cracked with the weight of emotion roaring through him. It took my breath away.

"Can we just see a picture of him?" Mrs. Loehr said.

"Of course." I brought up my photos on my cell, scrolled through until I found a shot that wasn't of him half naked, and handed it to them.

They gasped. Both of them.

In the picture I'd chosen, he was wearing a nice button-down. It was casual but nice. Really, really, really nice. Hell, they all were.

Mrs. Loehr touched the screen in disbelief. "He looks like your uncle Sal."

"He looks more like my great-grandfather."

Maybe there really was a family resemblance. Once we got to the point where I could talk to them in public without risking my marriage, I'd insist on full access to the family albums.

"He's beautiful," she said, her voice forlorn.

"That's what I keep telling him," I said, completely serious.

Mrs. Loehr smiled sadly. "When? When can we meet him?"

I bit my bottom lip in thought, then said, "If you will just give me two days, I promise he'll come around."

"Is that our grandchild?" she asked, and the question stunned me to my toes.

I ran my hands over my baby bump again in awe. "Yes," I said, suddenly thrilled Beep would have real grandparents. Denise didn't count. "Yes, she is."

"May I?" She stepped forward, hesitant.

"Of course."

She rubbed a hand over my belly as though I were Buddha. Which made sense. I felt like Buddha.

"What's her name?"

"Um, well, Beep. For now."

They both laughed softly. Even Mr. Alaniz laughed.

"Okay, well, I'd stay longer, but I have to pee."

"Oh, of course," Mrs. Loehr said. She leaned in and gave me a quick hug. Mr. Loehr did the same, and I was overwhelmed by the emotions coursing through the three of us. How was I going to hide this from Reyes until I could talk to him about it? Really talk to him.

Mr. Loehr gave me his business card. "My phone number is on there. We're staying at the Marriott on Louisiana."

"Got it. I will call you the minute I've talked to him."

"Could you tell him—?" Mrs. Loehr started. "Could you tell him we love him? We only want the best for him."

"Absolutely."

I watched as they hiked up the trail that led to the access road above us. They got in Mr. Alaniz's car and drove off as I fought another wave of hysteria.

How on earth was I going to tell Reyes?

I looked toward the Twelve as they paced just beyond the border, their hides glistening like silver fish in a pond. I could only see bits that appeared occasionally, like a mirage of crystal reflections that disappeared as quickly as they'd appeared, their muscles bunching and rolling with sheer power. They growled as I got closer, their snarls vicious and their teeth snapping like starving piranhas, begging for a piece of me. How close could I get? How long was their reach? Could they reach across the border and drag me to them?

I didn't dare get any closer. I couldn't risk Beep, but I was looking for their mark. According to Osh, all creatures from hell had a mark, a symbol of what they were and where their power lay. I thought that perhaps if I could see their marks, if I could draw the shape of them, that would somehow lead us to an answer. It would help us in our investigation. It would help us figure out how to kill them.

But even as close as I got, I couldn't see a mark. I really didn't know what to look for. I saw the silver of their hides, but they were black, so black that they absorbed light rather than refracted it. The silver was literally a reflection off such eternal blackness. But I didn't see a mark. I had yet to see what other supernatural beings saw, though. Maybe if I were more in tune with who I was, with what I was, I would see right through the beasts.

One growled and I saw another flash of silver, this time off a set of razorlike teeth. It lunged at me and I stumbled back, tripping on the low heels of my ankle boots. I caught myself before tumbling onto my backside. Thank goodness, because Beep would not have been impressed with my coordination.

Just as I regained my footing, I heard a male voice from behind me. "One p-push, and you'd be their next m-meal."

Startled, I turned to see Duff standing behind me. He was a departed man in his late twenties who wore a baseball cap, glasses, and a stutter. I'd always found him adorable. The stutter got me every time. But lately he was kind of creeping me out. No idea why, considering almost everything he'd said to me lately seemed to hold a veiled threat.

He smiled when he saw me, but he hadn't been wearing a smile when I first turned around. He'd been transfixed, mesmerized by the beasts snapping and snarling a few feet away, pacing beyond the border, waiting for me to stumble into their grasp. It seemed as though he admired them, but he recovered quickly and forced a warm expression.

"What are you doing, Duff?"

"J-just checking on you."

"Why?" I asked suspiciously. "Did Reyes send you?"

"N-no. No, I just came on my own. I s-saw you leave. I thought m-maybe you were in trouble."

"Why would you think that?"

Duff had been creeping around a lot lately, appearing at times and places where he had no right. He was turning into quite the stalker, and after Vatican Boy, I'd had about enough of stalkers. I kept meaning to talk to Reyes about him, but I also didn't want to ban him from our lives without cause. I feared, however, it was coming to that. He said some strange-ass things. Then again, maybe he just had really bad social skills. I'd met people like him. Cookie's cousin Lucille, for example. Or her second cousins. Or her uncle on her mother's side. Her whole family, in fact, was a Harvard study waiting to happen.

But Duff was getting a bit weird for my taste. I liked weird, don't get me wrong, but he was creepy weird, as though every move he made had an ulterior motive. As though he were testing his boundaries, pushing his limits to see how far he could go with me. He was about to find out.

But nothing could have prepared me for what he said next. "I wonder what would happen if someone just pushed you over the line."

I followed his gaze to the string that marked the boundary; then I turned back to him. "Are you threatening me?"

His eyes widened. "N-no. I would never. I just, I mean, I j-just wonder what they'd do. The hounds."

"Rip me to shreds." Well, that was enough crazy for me for one day. "Excuse me, Duff. I need to get back to the wedding party."

"S-sure," he said before disappearing. I couldn't help but notice the short but intense glance he'd placed on my midsection. Beep, seeming to notice as well, did a somersault. At least it felt like it. I turned to leave and slammed into a departed thirteen-year-old gangbanger.

"Angel," I said, enthusiasm raising my voice an octave. I threw my arms around his neck and kissed his cheek. I hadn't seen him in a while, and his presence had been sorely missed.

He hugged me back carefully, as though he might squish the baby between us.

"Where have you been?" I asked after setting him at arm's length. He wore the same red bandanna over his brow and a dirty T-shirt. The peach fuzz on his face still tickled when I kissed him. And he brandished the same wicked grin as always, the one that made me wonder what he'd been up to.

"Here and there. You're still hot, you know. I'd still do you."

"Wow," I said, forcing my smile wider. "You are too kind, but I'm good."

He lifted a shoulder. "If you ever change your mind, you have my number."

I snorted. "I've missed you. How's your family?"

He lowered his head, still not able to fully accept that his best friend's family had become his. "They're good. My mom and her nieces made tamales all day."

My mouth flooded with saliva. Pavlov totally could have studied me.

"I just wanted to tell you something."

"That sounds serious," I teased.

"You need to stay away from him."

Was this about Reyes? Again? "Sweetheart, I'm married to him, remember? I'm having his child."

He ducked his head to hide his face. "Not him. That guy that was just here. That cracker *pendejo* who pretends to be your friend."

My brows slid together in thought. "Duff?" I asked, surprised. He was the only cracker I'd spoken to in the last few minutes besides . . . My heart skipped a beat. Did he hear me talking with Mr. Alaniz and the Loehrs?

"Whatever his name is. Four-eyed bitch. He looks like a serial killer."

"Angel, it's not nice to judge based on looks. Not all people who wear glasses are serial killers."

"That's not what I mean."

"I know, sweetheart." I put my fingers under his chin and lifted his face to mine. "Are you okay?"

"I just don't trust him with you."

"You don't trust Reyes with me either, if I recall."

He shrugged and ducked his head again. "He's okay."

"I'm sorry. What did you just say?"

"Rey'aziel. He's okay, I guess."

Angel couldn't have shocked me more if he'd slapped me. "Are we talking about the same Rey'aziel? The one you warned me about? The one you've hated since . . . forever?"

He kicked at a rock, missing it since he was incorporeal and all. "He keeps you safe. That's all that matters."

"That's so sweet." I pulled him into an awkward hug since he wasn't really joining in. "You are the sweetest gangbanger I know."

"Okay," he said, wanting the nightmare to end.

"I wish you were alive." I set him away from me again. "I'd totally get you a Charley's Angel T-shirt."

One side of his mouth lifted into an adorable lopsided grin. "Like I would wear it."

"Oh, I'd blackmail you into wearing it." We started for the convent arm in arm. I really did have to pee. "You'd wear it every day and thank me."

"I don't think so, freak."

We trounced through the brush back to the party, and though I had a lot on my mind, Angel helped keep my mind off my impending doom. Reyes's birth parents showing up out of the blue was going to be a tad difficult to explain. Maybe the hellhounds weren't such a bad alternative to life without Reyes Farrow, because that was exactly what I risked by defying his wishes.

Angel gave me a kiss good-bye, saying he had to check on the tamales before trying to slip his tongue into my mouth, at which point I had to swat his ass. Sadly, I think he enjoyed it. I walked around to the front door, noticing most of the cars were gone now, but that the departed had multiplied. There were more now than when I'd left. All staring straight ahead. Waiting for something, which did nothing to put my mind at ease.

I would have to tell Reyes what I'd done. I would have to face the music, a term I never understood because it made whatever confrontation one had to endure seem bearable. I mean, it was music. How bad could it be to face it? The saying should have implied something direr, like, I would have to face the executioner. Much better.

I grabbed the door handle, but before I could open the front door, Denise opened it for me.

"Where were you?" she asked, almost frantic. "We've been worried about you."

Gemma walked up behind her and did the crazy sign, which since she was a psychiatrist seemed very unprofessional.

"You can't just go traipsing through the woods like that and not tell anyone where you've gone."

"But, Mo-o-o-o-om," I said with a schoolgirl whine, "all the cool kids are doing it. And I'm clearly not a virgin, so I'll survive a traipse through the woods should I come across a slasher."

She tsked while dragging me in the front door. "I don't understand half of what you say."

This was like a nightmare. My father gone and my stepmother deciding to pay attention to me after twenty-seven years. Then it hit me. I stilled. It all made sense now. We weren't on sacred ground. Reyes had lied to me. We were in hell!

"You need to go upstairs and rest while we clean up."

I flashed a boastful smile at Gemma and raised my arms in a long, languid stretch. "You're right. I'm awfully tired. And Beep has been especially active today. She's just worn me ragged."

Gemma narrowed her gaze before I giggled and hurried upstairs, hoping the loo was *desocupado*. It was. Thank goodness for small favors. As I washed my hands, I noticed a movement behind me. I turned quickly to find my dad, my wonderful, beautiful father, standing there. I'd caught glimpses of him off and on since we moved to the convent, but he never stayed. He never talked. In fact, every time he showed up, he glanced around nervously, as though he were being watched.

"Dad," I said, walking up to him. Even these few seconds were the longest I'd been able to see him since he passed, and my mind reeled with questions. "Dad, are you okay? What's going on?" I put my hand on his cold face for the first time, and a sob escaped my throat. "Why can't you talk to me?"

"Charlotte," he said, his voice soft. He stared in amazement, as though seeing me for the first time. "My Charlotte. I had no idea what you are. How important you are."

"What? Dad—"

"I'm so proud of you."

As long as I kept contact, he couldn't disappear on me. "Stay and talk to me. Please. I have so many questions."

"*You* have questions?" he asked with a light chuckle. But something caught his attention. He looked toward the bathroom door, breaking my contact, then was gone. I held my hand in the air a few seconds more, savoring the coolness he'd left in his wake, wondering why he disappeared so abruptly.

A knock sounded at the door, followed by a deep, smooth voice. "Charley?"

Even through the door, I could feel my husband's heat. His inferno. Then I looked back to where my dad had just stood. Was it Reyes? Was he afraid of Reyes?

I opened the door, a new worry creeping into my mind to add to the other one already running rampant. Why would my dad be afraid of him?

"Hey," he said, narrowing his lashes on me. "You okay?"

"Me? What? Of course."

He pressed his mouth together, the act causing the most sensual dimples to appear. "Spill."

At least I had an excuse for my nervousness now. I could use that to keep the truth at bay a little while longer. Once Reyes learned what I'd done, he may never talk to me again. The thought made my throat constrict.

"Dutch," he said, almost in warning.

"It's just, I saw my dad."

He glanced inside the bathroom. "Just now?"

"Yeah, but he disappeared again when you walked up."

He frowned at me, his gaze darting to his left, but he didn't say anything. I looked over his shoulder, and he took the opportunity to nuzzle my neck.

"Where did you go?" he asked.

"For a walk."

"An odd time for a walk."

"An odd time to go check on Artemis," I countered.

He stepped back in alarm. "What did you see?"

It took me a moment, but I realized he thought I was checking up on him. If he thought that, then he was hiding something. Crazy how guilt worked. "Trees. Grass. Bushes. The silvery black hides of hellhounds."

A muscle in his jaw flexed with tension "How close to the border did you get?"

"Not very. I was just at the gazebo. But I could see them in the distance."

"If they're that close, maybe you need to stay away from the gazebo."

"Maybe you need to tell me why you were checking on a departed dog who couldn't possibly get into any trouble."

He grinned. "Have you met your dog?"

He was right. I relaxed my shoulders. "Okay, she can get into trouble, but—"

"She's been trying to fight the hounds."

I gasped in surprise. "Artemis? Are you kidding me?"

"I've been trying to keep her away from the border."

I let out an astonished breath. "Thank you. Why would she even do that?"

"She's your guardian and she sees them as a threat to you. She's very perceptive."

I nodded absently.

"So, we're grilling. You hungry?"

"Aren't I always?" He had been a fantastic cook before, but put that man behind a grill, and the heavens opened up to watch him work.

"I'll bring you a plate."

"Perfect." He was still wearing the tux, the sight of him breathtaking. "You can't change, though."

"No?" he asked, the dimples back in full force.

"No. I have this whole James Bond fantasy going on."

"You know, I don't have to return this until Monday."

I curled my fingers into the lapel and pulled him close. "I have a feeling this is going to be a very *Moonraker* kind of evening."

Reyes left me at the door to our bedroom, where Cookie and Amber were changing. I joined them, changing out of my dress into a pair of stretchy pants—they had to be stretchy to accommodate my girth—a sweater, and a soft pair of boots.

"Okay," Cookie said as Amber helped her out of her dress, giggling when her mother's hair got stuck in the zipper, "what's on the agenda?"

I put my hand on my hip. "Your pre-honeymoon honeymoon." When she started to argue, I added, "Amber, Quentin, and I are going to make popcorn and watch *The Rocky Horror Picture Show*."

. Amber nodded exuberantly.

"You're just saying that to get me to leave," she said, freeing her hair at last. "I know you. Quentin and Amber are going to watch *The Rocky Horror Picture Show* while you work the case."

She had me dead to rights. "True, but I can do this while you're banging my uncle."

A loud bark of laughter burst from Amber before she contained it.

"I promise to fill you in the minute you get back. This is your wedding day, Cook."

"Yeah, Mom," Amber said. She winked at me. "I have your six, Aunt Charley."

We high-fived. I loved that kid. But Cookie shook her head as she hung up her dress.

"Robert and I have already agreed. I'm going to help you with the case while he does what he can on his end. He's already gone into town to see if there have been any new developments."

"Cook, this is insane."

She walked to the sink to wash the glitter off her face. "Charley, we aren't going on our real honeymoon until after Beep's arrival anyway. It's okay." I sensed a ripple of apprehension go through Cookie when she mentioned her honeymoon. I'd sensed it almost every time we talked about it. If I didn't know better—and admittedly, I didn't—I would've sworn Cookie didn't want to go on a honeymoon at all.

Still, it was her wedding day, for heaven's sake. No bride should work on her wedding day. I was about 90 percent certain there was a law against it. Then again, who was I to argue?

"Okay, I need everything you can get. Friends. Social media activity. Phone calls lasting more than a couple of minutes."

"She's fifteen," Amber reminded me. "All her phone calls last more than a couple of minutes."

I smiled at her. "Excellent input, grasshopper." I'd make a PI out of Amber yet.

She flashed her pearly whites.

I took a few pages out of the file Kit had left with me. "I'll go check in with Rocket, inquire about Faris Waters's . . . status, and then comb through her texts. If I find anything suspicious, we can cross-reference them with her phone calls. If she was lured somewhere by a predator, I want to know."

Cookie's face brightened as though she'd been champing at the bit to work on a new case. It *had* been a while. We'd done some small side jobs that didn't require our presence, though nothing of this caliber for a long time. But I still couldn't shake the feeling that this had more to do with her honeymoon than with the case.

I reached over and brushed glitter off her cheek, regret consuming me nonetheless. No one's wedding day should be spent looking for a missing child.

"Do you think she's still alive?" Amber asked.

Cookie placed a hand on her shoulder as I glanced up toward the attic.

"One way to find out."

6

My death will probably be caused by being sarcastic at the wrong time.
—TRUE FACT

I left Cookie to get what she could on Faris's social life while Amber went to find Quentin. He was staying the night, since he didn't have to be back at the School for the Deaf in Santa Fe until the next day. While Amber wanted to help with the case, she decided spending quality time with the cutest boy on the planet—her words—would be more fun.

I walked to the end of the hall on the second floor, where another set of stairs led to the attic. Rocket had been staying up there since we moved here. We'd already had to replace the drywall twice. Rocket filled his days scratching the names of those who passed onto the walls. He knew the name of every person who'd died everywhere in the world. There was no way he really wrote them all. I'd read once that there were over 150,000 deaths worldwide every single day. So I wasn't sure why he chose to scratch certain names and not others, but for decades, recording the names of the departed had been what he considered his job. Who was I to argue? Surely there was a method to his madness. I'd

have to pay closer attention someday, to see if the names he inscribed
had any kind of connection to one another.

Just as I was about to ascend the stairs, I felt a rush of cold air at my
neck. It whispered through my hair and caused goose bumps to erupt
across my skin. I turned and saw her, the girl I'd been trying to talk to
for months. Not the sobbing woman in my closet. She'd shown up just
a few days ago. This other girl had already been living in the convent
when we moved in. She was a young, almost childlike, nun, but her habit
was of an older style than what they generally wore now.

I stopped and turned slowly toward her as one would do with a wild
animal one was trying to capture. I didn't want to scare her off. She'd been
trying to show me something; I was sure of it. Every time she appeared,
she would hurry away from me, stopping to glance back every so often, as
though making sure I was following her. But every time I did follow, I'd
lose her in the forest.

"Not this time," I said as she turned away.

She walked quickly down the hall toward the main stairs and disappeared. I descended the stairs and went out the front door, knowing she'd
be waiting for me. And she was, her expression full of fear, her lashes
spiked with recent tears before, just like always, she ran away.

"I'm not losing you," I said to her back. She didn't acknowledge me.

We continued on the same path as always, the one that led in the
opposite direction from where I'd been earlier, the way long since overgrown with vegetation, and as always, she disappeared from there. I
stopped and whirled around in frustration. She couldn't have been more
than eighteen years old. What was she trying to show me?

I continued deeper into the forest. "Where did you go?" I asked the
empty air around me. Maybe I needed to have Angel tail her. Perhaps he
could keep up. She was like Rocket, believing I could run through solid
objects just as she could.

The last time we played hide-and-seek, I'd scoured the forest just to the left of the trail where it dead-ended. This time I went right. I stumbled over the uneven ground then got in some cardio when I passed through a spiderweb, flailing my arms and shuddering a lot. I heard growls in the distance. I stopped and the scent of lavender hit me. Very faint, but there nonetheless. Why would I smell lavender out here? After gaining my bearings, I realized I was getting closer to the border, but I still had a few yards yet. Or I did until I felt a sharp push from behind.

I toppled forward as the land slanted beneath me. Barely able to catch myself on a branch, I held on, but my feet had gone out from under me, the branch broke, and I was sliding down the side of the mountain. The trees around me blurred. They scraped and cut until I was able to grab hold of a root. The sudden stop jerked at my shoulder painfully. I had no idea the mountain was so steep on that side of the house. I fought to get my footing and was startled when someone reached out and grabbed me.

I looked up into the huge frightened eyes of the nun. She pulled and I struggled until I had crawled onto even ground. At first, I wondered if she'd pushed me. If so, then she wouldn't have helped me.

"Thank you," I said, dusting myself off. She didn't answer. "Did you see who pushed me?"

She just stared. I was getting that a lot lately. No matter. I had a very good idea I knew who had done the deed.

After scanning the area, I walked as close to the edge of the drop-off as I dared, keeping a death grip on a tree, because something had caught my attention moments before I went over.

There was one point I could see out over a clearing with a stream running through it. I'd never traveled down there, because it was beyond the border, but neither could Reyes travel that far. Yet there he was, standing pretty as you please by a group of bushes, talking to Angel. My Angel. My sidekick and lead—aka only—investigator.

First off, that was far past the border that Osh had staked out. Reyes should have been mincemeat. Second, what on earth would Reyes and Angel have to discuss?

I eased closer and squinted. The clearing was beautiful. It was one of those places perfect for a picnic. The sun hung low on the horizon, glistening across the field, elongating Reyes's shadow. He looked pensive, angry even, as he spoke to Angel. He no longer wore the tux jacket, and the top buttons of the starched white shirt had been undone, the sleeves rolled up.

He scrubbed his face with his fingers and turned sharply from Angel. He and Angel had never gotten along. Why would they be talking secretively now? Did he know about the Loehrs? Had Angel been spying on me earlier? Fear seized my lungs for a solid ten seconds before reality sank in. I looked awful with a blue face.

I filled my lungs and turned back to the young nun, but she was gone. And being left alone in the woods with someone who was clearly trying to kill me made me a tad uncomfortable, so I hurried back to the convent, doing my best to shake off the dread I felt. Was Duff trying to kill me? He'd said something earlier about pushing me, and I'd definitely been pushed. That couldn't have been a coincidence.

After sneaking back into the house, I rushed upstairs to change again since I was now covered in dirt and grass; then I headed back to the stairs that led to the attic. If the nun showed up again, I was not going to chase her. It was getting dark out, and there was a homicidal pusher roaming the countryside.

I took the steep stairs slowly. I'd been having a pain in my abdomen since my fall, and it was getting sharper with every step I took. I didn't think it was labor. It was too sharp and too concentrated in one area. I'd simply bruised myself on my trip down. Taking in a deep breath, I opened the door to the attic. Rocket was there, scratching a name into the Sheetrock.

He turned and brightened. "Miss Charlotte!" After lifting me into a hug that magnified the pain in my side, he set me down, turned back to his work, and started scratching again.

That was a short conversation. I leaned back against a column and said, "Rocket, I have a name for you."

"I have too many."

"Too many names?"

"Yes. Too too many."

"I'm sorry. Can you check on one for me?"

"I don't think so, Miss Charlotte."

"Why ever not?" I asked, massaging the pain.

"I have too many."

"That was a beautiful wedding." Strawberry stood beside me, holding her bald Barbie doll. "Cookie was so pretty. I wish I could have done her hair."

A sharp stab of horror washed over me at the thought. "Is Blue here, too?" I had yet to see Rocket's little sister. That girl was the best at hide-and-seek I'd ever seen.

"Yes, she's in the round room."

I frowned in thought. "What round room?"

"The tiny one."

"What tiny one?"

"The one downstairs nobody knows about."

This could go on for days. "Okay," I said, acquiescing. "Well, I just hope she's having fun."

"She likes it in there. It's quiet."

"Wonderful." I suddenly wondered if she was talking about the closet we couldn't get open. There was a door to a closet or a room or pantry in the laundry room off the kitchen. A door that was stuck. Or locked. Or both. Even Reyes couldn't open it. It became quite the challenge for a while; then we moved on to other, more interesting things.

What no one understood was that nothing, *nothing,* is more interesting than a locked door nobody could open. I had every intention of getting inside that room. I just didn't know how yet.

"Okay, seriously, Rocket. I need you to check on Faris Martina Waters."

He seemed to sadden. "Not on my list."

"Oh," I said, brightening. "That's good."

"Yet," he added.

That was bad. "So, soon?" I asked, knowing the answer.

"No breaking rules, Miss Charlotte." He continued to claw at the dry-wall.

And though I also knew the answer to my next question, I tried anyway. "Do you know where she is, Rocket?"

"Not where, only if. No breaking rules."

Damn it. "For your information, rules were made to be broken. Just whose rules are these, Rocket? Who gave them to you?"

He looked at me as though I were on the low end of the IQ totem pole. "Nurse Hobbs."

"Okay, and when Nurse Hobbs gave you these rules, what was she talking about?"

"Everything," he said, throwing his arms out wide. "But mostly pud-ding."

I had to ask. "Why pudding?"

"Because of that one time I tried to explain to her that the pudding disappeared yesterday and that Rubin took it, but she gave me the rules: Not when. Not who. Just if."

This conversation was not turning out as I'd imagined. "If?"

"If I took it."

I gaped at him. For, like, ten minutes. Was he kidding? After all this time, the rules weren't even about the departed or how he knew the names of everyone who'd ever passed, but about pudding? After absorbing that little nugget of gold, I said, "Rocket, I don't think those rules apply here."

A loud gasp echoed around me. "Miss Charlotte," he said, chastising me, "the rules apply everywhere. I told you. It wasn't just the pudding, but the corn bread, the honey, the turtle named Blossom—but that was only that one time—and the Thorazine."

I could not believe what I was hearing. All this time, I'd thought Rocket's rules came from some celestial manual or guideline or flowchart, something official—but all along, they were from a nurse at the mental asylum where he'd lived most of his life? Visions of the charge nurse in *One Flew Over the Cuckoo's Nest* came to mind. She was scary.

"Rocket, Nurse Hobbs was not talking about people who have passed away. You can tell me anything about them you want to."

"No breaking rules. You already broke all the rules."

He was scolding me for using my supernatural mojo to heal a little boy—and a few other people—in the hospital a few months back. He felt that using my gift to heal people was breaking the rules, but I saved people all the time. I found murderers and missing children and solved cases incessantly. How was that any different from healing a sick kid?

"Rocket, so I saved that little boy by touching him. So I saved a few sick people. How is that any different from what I do every day? I save people using my supernatural connections every other day. How is one breaking the rules and one not?"

"You probably shouldn't yell at him," Strawberry said, petting her doll's head.

I ignored her. "And I know darned good and well, Nurse Hobbs did not give you any rules regarding me, since I wouldn't be born for decades when you knew her."

"Nurse Hobbs was very smart," he countered as he scratched a *K* into the wall.

I decided to give it one more shot. "Okay, if. You can tell me if. So, if Faris Waters is going to pass away soon, where will it happen?"

"Not where. Only—"

"That's it!" I said, blowing up. "The next time you mention the rules to me, I'm going to take those rules, crumple them in my fists, and set them on fire with my laser vision." I didn't really have laser vision, but it would rock if I did.

Rocket gasped. "Miss Charlotte, you can't do that."

"Oh, I can. Just you wait and see." I rolled onto my tiptoes until we were nose to nose. "Just you wait and see."

He dissipated before me, his eyes saucers.

"You so don't have laser vision," Strawberry said.

"I might. I'm a god, in case you haven't heard."

She didn't buy it for a second. "Unless you're Superman, you don't have laser vision."

Before I could argue further, she followed Rocket's lead and left me standing alone in a dusty attic.

I looked up at the name he'd been carving into the wall and stilled. *Earl James Walker.* The man—the monster—who'd raised Reyes. He was currently living out the rest of his days drinking his meals through a straw in a nursing home. Reyes severed his spine when he'd tortured and tried to kill me a few months back, and now Walker was going to die.

I stood in shock a few seconds, wondering why the man was about to kick, before I realized it was rude to look a gift horse in the mouth.

The first thing I did when I got back to the bedroom was call Kit. She needed to know that her FedEx's niece was still alive. But I felt obligated to tell her that while we had some time, we didn't have much. We needed a break in the case soon.

They didn't have any more information, and all the leads they did have led to a dead end. They were going to question her classmates again, just to make sure they didn't miss anything.

"Charley," Kit said before we hung up, "you have to do your thing. We have to find her."

"I'm working on it. Promise."

I fetched my laptop, the file on Faris Waters, and a hot chocolate, and stretched out onto David Beckham to give my back a break. The pain in my abdomen was almost gone, but it was at that moment precisely that Beep decided to try out for the Olympics, showcasing her floor routine for the judges. I patted what I assumed was her bottom as I scanned the case file on Agent Waters's niece.

I had the distinct feeling I was being watched, but I'd had that feeling a lot lately, so I pretty much ignored it and kept reading the file. I read through all her texts and highlighted the ones that caught my attention. Cookie was working downstairs in my makeshift office. After a while, my hot chocolate got cold. I needed to check up on Cookie's progress anyway, so I went downstairs.

The place was almost good as new. Only a few of the wedding guests remained, and they were all in the kitchen or out back where the grill was. Thankfully, Cookie's cousin Lucille had gone. I headed toward the office but was cut off by Uncle Bob.

"Are you free?" he asked.

"No, but I'm on sale for a dollar ninety-nine."

He sighed, adding fuel to the fire.

"Do you have a minute?"

I patted my pockets. "Not on me, but I can go through the couch cushions."

"Charley." He pretended to be annoyed, but I felt the emotions tumbling inside him. He was happy. Completely content. It was not an emotion I felt from him often, and if Cookie had been there, I would've kissed her on the mouth.

I had to admit, however, I was a little surprised. I'd ruined his pre-honeymoon honeymoon.

"I'm sorry about tonight," I said.

"Don't worry about it. She's like you. Won't give up until she's got her man."

"That's true. She's a good egg. But you already knew that, I'm guessing."

"I did."

"You looked fantastic, by the way," I said. He'd changed out of the tux, but he'd looked amazing in it.

"Thank you." We were venturing onto uncomfortable ground. Compliments weren't part of our MO. Passive-aggressive insults were. Mild threats. A little nagging here and there. "You looked pretty amazing yourself."

My brows shot up. "I'm surprised you noticed, what with that goddess standing next to you."

He almost blushed. "You got that right."

"I hope the captain enjoyed himself."

"I think he did. He's quite . . . taken with you."

Though he didn't mean that in an attraction kind of way, I said, "Yeah, just don't tell the old ball and chain. So, what's up?"

"Well, we still haven't decided exactly where we're going on our honeymoon, and I thought you might know what she's thinking. She won't tell me. She wants me to choose where I want to go, but I want her to choose."

"So, you want me to flip a coin? See who chooses?"

"No, I want you to find out where she really wants to go."

I smiled and leaned into him. "See, that's the funny thing, Uncle Bob. She wants to go anywhere you are. You could book a vacation in Bosnia, and she'd be happy."

"You're no help whatsoever."

"Well, I do have one word of advice: Don't take her to hell. I've heard it's really dry there this time of year."

"You're worse than no help."

"I know. I really do. You haven't heard anything, have you?" He knew what I meant without my having to elaborate.

"No, hon. I'm sorry. We are working the forensics, waiting for lab results."

Unlike on television, real forensic work took weeks or even months. Knowing that didn't help. My impatience knew no bounds. Still, Ubie would have something new to chew on as soon as Mr. Alaniz sent in that anonymous tip about Vatican Boy. I would kill to be there during questioning. Not anybody important. I might knock off someone who groped women in the subway or talked in the theater.

I leaned in to give him a hug and whispered into his ear. "Puerto Rico."

He gave me a quick squeeze before letting me go with a wink and a grin.

Just as I was about to head toward the office again, I decided to take the opportunity to question my investigator about the recent, and rather disturbing, developments. What on earth could Angel have been talking about with Reyes? And why was Angel defending him? Last I heard, he hated the guy with a fiery passion. He'd never trusted him, so why the sudden camaraderie?

I summoned him, determined to find out. He appeared before me, his arms crossed at his chest as though I'd interrupted something important. The kid had been dead for decades. How important could his activities be?

"What are you and my other half up to?"

A hint of surprise flashed across his face, but he recovered quickly. "I don't know what you are talking about."

"Don't try to play the innocent with me. I saw you and Reyes talking in the field."

He lunged forward and pasted his hand over my mouth. "Shhhh," he said, scanning the area. "How did you see us?"

I peeled his hand away. "I looked. You were there. Reyes was upset. What's going on, and why all the secrecy?"

He cursed softly to himself. "I can't tell you."

"Angel," I said, stepping closer and giving him my infamous death stare, the one that frightened man and beast alike, "either you tell me what is going on, or I swear by all that is holy—"

"Please," he said, giving me a light shove of dismissal. "I'm more scared of him than of you, but only on days that end in *Y*."

"Wait, why are you scared of him? Did he threaten you?"

"No. He doesn't have to. Have you seen his angry side? Not something I want to mess with."

"Then clearly you haven't seen mine."

He scoffed. "Your angry side is like when Mrs. Cleaver burns the muffins."

"That is so offensive. I've never made muffins in my life."

"Whatever, *chiquita*. I ain't spilling, so take your threats and—ow!"

I'd taken hold of his arm and sank my nails into his flesh. "What?" I asked, forcing him closer. "What was that?"

"You can torture me. It won't help. I can't tell you, but just know everything he's doing is for you and your baby's safety."

I let go. "For Beep?"

"Yes," he said, rubbing his arm.

"Just give me a hint, then. Angel, if she's in danger—"

"If?" he asked, his voice incredulous. "Have you looked around? Of course, she's in danger. You both are. I'm not sure why that hasn't sunk in."

"It's sunk in. It's completely sunken, but—"

"I ain't talking. You'll have to ask Rey'aziel."

He disappeared before I had a chance to argue further. Damn it. I hated being left out of the loop. I loved loops. People didn't understand that about me.

I heard a loud crash coming from the dining room slash study. While we had assigned a small room past the dining hall to be our office, the dining hall itself had become our study. Reyes, Osh, and Garrett Swopes spent a lot of time in there, scouring over the texts Garrett uncovered, trying to find out how to kill the Twelve. Osh insisted they couldn't be killed. Only sent back to hell. So now they were trying to figure out how to do that as well. While it would be only a temporary fix, we would take what we could get.

I hurried there and came upon a very upset Garrett Swopes and a poor, innocent chair on which he'd taken out his frustration. He'd also knocked over a stack of notes, the same stack he'd been slaving over for weeks. He was funny when he was upset, so I almost didn't intervene. But he saw me anyway and gave me his back, embarrassed.

"What are you doing here?" I asked.

He was still in the nice button-down he'd worn under his jacket.

"I thought you had to leave early to work a skip for Javier."

"I did, but they picked him up this morning."

"Oh, well, that's good." I nodded toward the papers. "No luck?"

He shook his head. "None. There's nothing in here about how to kill the Twelve." He'd hired a doctor of linguistics to translate the texts, and although Dr. von Holstein didn't get through all of them, he'd gone through a good amount. It was all quite fascinating. Much of what this guy named Cleosaurius wrote was about me, aka the Daughter of Light, and Beep, whom he referred to as the Daughter. He did say on one or two notations that she would be a melding of light and darkness, me and Reyes respectively, and he prophesied that Beep, though he never called her that, would be the downfall of Lucifer. That she would destroy him. And while pretty much everything he wrote went against Revelations and the predictions written therein, some of it coincided with the ancient texts. The four horsemen, for example, although Cleo simply called them the bringers of great suffering.

He also prophesied about the Twelve and said what we'd been hearing over and over: Twelve would be sent and twelve would be summoned. So, then, who did the sending and the summoning? Surely Lucifer had sent the Twelve, the hellhounds patrolling our borders night and day. But who summoned the other Twelve? And how did they play into all of this? And how on earth did we kill them?

"I'm sorry, Charles," Garrett said just as Reyes and Osh were walking in. "There's nothing in the texts to indicate how to kill them. At least not in the texts Dr. V translated. There was a lot he had yet to get to. It would have taken him years to translate it all."

"It's okay. I'm going to give Sister Mary Elizabeth a call later. Maybe she found something." Sister Mary Elizabeth could hear the angels speak. Like literally. And though she couldn't interact with them, she did come up with some pretty good intel occasionally.

I sat on a chair and flipped through a few pages. Reyes sat beside me as Osh stood eating a BBQ sandwich. It smelled amazing and my mouth watered involuntarily.

"Food's ready," Reyes said as he studied me. His heat scalded my skin, and even though he was still wearing the white button-down and his hair had been neatly cut, he now wore a day's growth along his jaw. And he looked tired. His eyes had that sleepy look and, while incredibly sexy, Reyes just didn't get sleepy. He had infinite energy. Or that's how I'd always thought of him.

I still couldn't help but wonder what he had going with Angel. He recruited the departed to spy for him. Maybe he was doing something similar with Angel, but why spy on me? It wasn't like I could go anywhere. We were all stuck.

Perhaps that was why the air fairly crackled with tension. Why he was so blisteringly hot. Reyes was unused to feeling helpless, and now he was like a cornered wolf, ready to strike at anything that moved. While he was fantastic today, his energy seemed to be ratcheted tight, like he might explode given the smallest reason.

"Anything you want to tell me?" he asked, jump-starting my heart.

Did he know about the Loehrs? Or my interrogation of Angel? Or how I was pushed? I didn't think he'd seen me. On any of those occasions. And I wasn't about to give him a reason to explode. Not here. Not in front of everyone. I would explain about the Loehrs later, and he could decide what to do then. Besides, he was lying to me, too, in a way. He didn't let me in on what he and Angel were up to. He'd lied about the border, though that could have been Osh. But how was Reyes standing out in a field well beyond where Osh had marked the outskirts of the sacred ground? Was Osh in on it, too? And what was *it*?

"Not especially," I said, offering him my best smile. "Just wanted to make sure the helicopter is all set." We'd come up with a plan a few months ago. As soon as Beep was born, we were going to pile into a helicopter Reyes had chartered that was going to fly us to an island that had once been a leper colony. The entire island was consecrated, thus no hell hounds. We had no idea if it was going to work, but it was the best plan we'd come up with. And we'd come up with many.

"It's set. It's been set for weeks."

"Great." When he kept his gaze trained on me, I looked down at the documents. "What's this?" I asked, finding some notes in Garrett's handwriting.

"Nothing," Garrett said. "I've been trying my hand at translating the texts myself."

I was impressed, but Reyes seemed . . . blasé about it? It was as though he'd expected as much. Or he was still trying to figure out if I was lying.

"Is this about me or Beep?" I asked when I started to read.

"You, I think. Who the hell knows?" He strode back to the table and picked up the notepad. "From what I can tell, it's talking about the beginning and the end of something. I just don't know what."

"Hopefully not the world. Can you read this out loud?" I asked him, getting a new idea.

"A little. I don't know all the vowels, but——"

"Try it," I said, wanting to test a theory.

He picked up one of the documents. We'd had the original texts copied and preserved. They were thousands of years old and locked safely away in storage now, so Garrett was working off copies. After noisily filling his lungs to show his frustration, he stumbled through a couple of lines.

He stopped and glanced down at me as my mind mulled over his interpretation.

"One more time," I said. While I didn't know how to read every language ever spoken on earth, I knew how to speak them. All of them. Every single language, dead or alive, that had ever been spoken, or signed, on earth.

He picked up the sheet again and began.

"King!" I said, gazing up at him. "It's talking about a king."

"No," Reyes said, straightening in his chair. "A queen. If you take into account the first word of the sentence, it is describing a feminine subject. He's just saying the actual word wrong. It's queen." He looked up at Garrett. "Keep going."

Garrett picked up the chair he'd upended and sat down beside us to read the line yet again.

"That's not bad," I said. "I got it that time. The queen, though the first——"

"——will be the last," Reyes finished. Then he looked at me.

"You. It's talking about you, only using the word 'queen' instead of 'god.'"

"It makes sense," Osh said, joining us at the table. "He had to be careful what he wrote or be considered a heretic."

"Or in league with the devil," Reyes added.

Osh nodded. "Like a witch. He would have been condemned and most likely stoned to death."

"What a horrible thought."

"So, if you're the queen in this passage," Osh said. "How are you the first and the last?"

Reyes was staring at me, and I tried to ignore it at first because it wasn't a come-hither stare but more like a *you're a freak* kind of stare. Either that or I was projecting.

"What?" I asked him at last.

"It *is* talking about you," he said as though astonished. "You are the first pure ghost god."

I frowned. We'd had this conversation before. "I thought I was the thirteenth. What the heck?"

He shook his head. "You are the thirteenth god, but the first pure ghost god."

With as much dramatic flair as I could muster, I threw myself—mostly just my head—across the table. "You never give me the entire picture of anything. I'm so confused."

Reyes laughed softly. "Okay, here's what I know: There were seven gods, or what we would call gods, in your dimension. They were the original gods. They created everything there, like the God of this dimension created everything here."

I turned to him, trying to understand. "So, like another galaxy?"

"No," Osh said. "Like another universe. This one is taken."

"There are other universes?" Garrett asked.

"There are as many universes as there are stars in the heavens of this one."

Garrett sat back, as impressed as I was. "Okay, so in mine, there were seven gods. Not just one."

"Yes, for lack of a better term. They are actually very different entities, but we will go with 'god' for now."

"Gotcha. Going with god. And we have seven."

"You *had* seven. Eventually, through time, there were thirteen total entities, including you. But you are the only one left. The last of your kind."

I did the dramatic thing again and Reyes laughed again.

He pushed my hair out of my face. Tucked it behind an ear. "The original seven weren't like your god. They could procreate, but only once."

"Okay, I'll bite. Why only once?"

"Because once they created another god, what I'm calling a ghost god, they melded together and became one. They ceased to exist. Their union created another being—"

"Like Beep!"

"—like Beep, only they converged into one being, a single ghost god, with all the power of the two that merged to produce it. Therefore, the new entity is more powerful than the individual gods that created it. It's like two stars colliding to create a single supernova, one that can live forever and has an endless supply of energy. And now, in a process that took millions of years, or even billions, all of the original gods have converged, either with each other or with another ghost god, until there is only one left. And they were magnificent. They were great celestial beings floating in space with the power of a billion suns."

I sat back, impressed. "Okay, this is a really cool story."

"Thank you."

"But why am I the first as well as the last?"

"If you do that math—"

I gaped at him in horror. I had no idea there would be math involved.

He ignored me. "—you'll realize that seven original gods, and the ghost gods they created, could only have produced a thirteenth if all of them had eventually merged. All seven of the original gods and three of the original ghost gods had merged until only two ghost gods were left. For the first time, two ghost gods, with the power of all those who came before them, merged and you were created from their union."

I squeezed my eyes and tried to envision the process. "I don't think you're very good at math."

"I'm very good at math." He took a pencil and paper and drew me a chart with X's representing the originals and O's representing their off-spring, the ghost gods. He was right. Seven, when boiled down to one, was thirteen total. Seven original and six ghosts.

"So, it's like my mother and my father gave up their lives to create me?"

"Yes, and no," Osh said. "They still live inside you. If this is right, the power surging through every cell in your body could destroy this universe. Could destroy a million universes and everything in them. Thankfully, your species is very kind. I like to think the gods before you are sort of like—" He looked at Reyes for the word.

"Like counselors," Reyes offered.

"Exactly. They're like counselors. They're still there inside you, in the consciousness and memories that define your genetic make up. You're just a separate entity"

"So, to answer your question," Reyes said, "you are the first pure ghost god, the only one created from two ghost gods. And because there are no more, you are also the last."

"That's kind of sad," I said. "But they're all still here?" I placed a hand over my heart.

"Like advisors."

"Think about it, though," Osh said, gazing at me in awe. "All that power, all that energy, the potency of seven original gods, has been harvested and passed down to you."

Reyes looked at Osh and did something I'd never seen him do. He sought Osh's counsel. "This is where I get lost."

Osh nodded to encourage him.

"Why is she here on this plane? If she is the last god of her universe, of her people, the very last of her kind, why is she here?"

"That's something even I can't fathom."

"The first time we had sex," I said, making Reyes a little uncomfortable and Osh perk up, "I saw you see me." I looked at him. "I saw you pick me out of a thousand beings of light. They were all just like me. There has to be more of us."

"They were not all just like you. To give you a metaphor of what your dimension is like, imagine God, the god of this dimension, among his angels. He is not one of them. He created them. He has the power to reduce them all to ash with a single thought, but he still lives among them. And his angels, while more powerful than the mortal life in his realm, are not like him, though they are made of a similar substance. Of a similar light."

"So you saw me among my angels?"

"Metaphorically speaking. And, again, you have to understand, all of this took place over millions of years. Probably billions. The gods of your dimension are more ancient than any other beings I've ever come across."

I had an epiphany. "Then I'm older than you."

"What?" he asked.

"You may be centuries old, but I'm older. I'm millions of years old."

He grinned. "Yes."

"I robbed the cradle," I said, quite pleased with myself. "I wish I remembered all of this."

"From what I understand, you will once you know your celestial name. It's like a safety switch. But you aren't supposed to know your celestial name until your physical body dies."

"But I did die!" I argued. "When the Twelve attacked us. I stuck a blade in my chest and died, baby. I saw the heavens above us. Trust me."

"You died, but you came back," Osh said, struggling to understand himself. "That's the only way it makes sense. You didn't take up your position as the grim reaper like you're slated to do."

"So, the other grim reapers, the ones that reaped, for lack of a better phrase, before me, they were from my world as well?"

"Yes," Reyes said. "But they were like the angels. No god has ever taken on such a menial task."

"Then why leave the gene pool?" Garrett asked. "Why bring in a being—a god, no less—when you already have people for that?"

Reyes nodded, agreeing that the whole thing was utterly illogical. "Like I said before, it's like sending a queen to do the janitor's work."

"Or a god," Osh said, "to clean up someone else's mess."

Garrett sat in thought, then looked at me. "So, whose mess are you here to clean up?"

7

A friend will help you if someone knocks you down.
A best friend will pick up a bat and say, "Stay down. I got this."
—TRUE FACT

Cookie and I compared notes as we ate some of the wonderful fare Reyes and Osh had grilled up. We came up with very little, unfortunately. She was still waiting on information from Kit, and as long as I was stuck at the convent, I just couldn't do much. I felt helpless, and the dread that had taken up residence in the back of my neck concerning the Loehrs weighed on me. I didn't know how to tell Reyes what I'd done.

I begged Cook to go, spend at least the night with her husband in a nice place, but she was adamant about staying. Gemma and Denise were still there, too. They'd been hanging out a lot. It was weird and a little disturbing. Well, Denise was a lot disturbing, but she kept to herself mostly. She picked up our plates and made herself useful. So there was that.

Quentin and Amber went back to watching movies, which reminded me, I needed to call Sister Mary Elizabeth before it got too late. If anyone had the lowdown on what was going on up top, it would be her.

Reyes got up from the table to clean the grill. Gemma found a plush corner in the living room in which to read. Uncle Bob had to get back to the city. Osh was nowhere to be found. That guy kept odd hours. Kit sent over the interviews they'd done with all of Faris's friends, and Cookie couldn't wait to dive in, so I took the opportunity to chat with Garrett, since we were the only ones left at the table. All our conversations were about prophecies and hellhounds. I wanted to know how he was doing. Kind of. Really I wanted to know how his son was doing and his baby mama, Marika.

I gestured him to move closer. He frowned suspiciously, then scooted his chair over. Like half an inch. Jerk.

"So?" I asked, drinking a cup of hot chocolate. Another one. Since I was officially off coffee until Beep was born, hot chocolate had become my friend. We weren't as close as me and mocha latte, but we were getting there. It took time to build a relationship. Trust had always been an issue for me.

"So?" he asked, drinking a beer, his beverage of choice.

"How's Zaire?"

One corner of his mouth went up. "He's good. I get to see him almost every week."

"And what about Marika?"

He lifted a shoulder and leaned back in his chair, straightened out his legs in front of him. "She's doing well. We've been talking."

I scooted closer. "And?"

"She wants to try dating again."

"Dude, that's great."

"I don't know. She used me to purposely get pregnant and didn't tell me."

"Of course she didn't tell you. What would you have done if she had?"

"Run in the other direction. But it's still not okay, Charles."

He was right, of course, but we all make mistakes. I decided to remind him of that. "Do you remember that time I was helping you out with a bust—?"

"You mean that time you butted into my stakeout because you wanted me to lick your coffee cup?"

"Exactly. And what happened?"

"The guy came home. I busted him. End of story."

"No, before that."

"You tried to poison me."

"No, after that." And I didn't try to poison him. I just wanted to know if my cup was poisoned. It tasted . . . poisony. Turned out, I just didn't rinse well. So much for my theory that my landlord at the time was trying to kill me.

He drew out his exhalation to make his point. A long, needless point. "Fine. I get it."

"No, what happened?"

"I went into that diner to get a cup of coffee."

"No. You went into that diner to try to get a date with one of the waitresses."

"I know the story."

"And why was I really in the same neighborhood as you?"

"Because you were staking out that diner."

"I was staking out that waitress. And why was I doing that?"

"Charles—"

I shoved an index finger over his mouth.

He glared.

"Why was I doing that?"

"Because you figured out she was spiking men's coffees with eyedrops."

"Yes. She had this weird vendetta thing going on and was purposely making men sick. I saved your ass. You could have died."

"I wouldn't have died."

"You could have gone into a coma like poor Mrs. Verdean's husband."

"So, where are you going with this?"

"You made a mistake hitting on that woman when your gut told you she was about as stable as a three-legged chair. We all make mistakes."

"What Marika did wasn't a mistake. It was quite intentional."

"I get it. I do. I just hope you give her a second chance is all. Especially now that she broke up with her boyfriend."

"She broke up with him?"

I nodded, knowing that would get his attention.

"I don't know, Charles. Chicks are crazy."

"Duh. That doesn't mean you can't keep trying."

"Maybe it could work. I mean, I've always wanted a family. And Zaire is great. Marika has her moments, too."

"That's the spirit," I said, punching his arm. "So, did you get it?"

"Is that the only reason you're talking to me?"

It wasn't, but I couldn't let him know that I genuinely cared about him. "Of course."

His mouth widened into a grin that made his silvery eyes sparkle. "It's behind that weird box." He nodded toward the potato bin.

"Sweet!" I scrambled up to check out my new toy. "I've always wanted a sledgehammer."

At about half my height, the handle wasn't bad. The head of the sledgehammer was about the size of a Big Gulp. All in all, it seemed pretty non-threatening.

I took the handle and tried to pick it up, ignoring the skiptracer at the table. His snickers would not deter me from my task.

"Fine," I said, dragging it from behind the potato bin and across the floor.

"You aren't going to kill anyone with that, are you?"

"That's certainly not the plan," I said, huffing and puffing as it scraped along the tile with an awful, horror-movielike sound.

"You realize this floor is over a hundred years old."

I felt bad about the floor. I really did, but I couldn't pick the stupid thing up. "It's much heavier than it looks."

"Would you like some help?"

"Nope," I said, winded. I'd traveled about two feet. "I got this."

There was a tiny room off the kitchen with a wooden closet of some kind. Nobody knew what it was, even Sister Mary Elizabeth. It could have been a confessional, for all I knew. Either way, no matter what we did, we could not get the door open. Normally, that wasn't a big deal. But the more I thought about it, the more it ate at me. There could be anything in that closet. There could be a dead body. Or a mountain of gold. Or a staircase to a secret passageway.

After months of trying to pry it open, I couldn't take it anymore. This was my last hope. That door was coming open if I had to tear down the wall around it.

Garrett got up and followed me to the room that we had set up as the laundry room. Though I'd refused his help physically, he decided to help in other ways. He watched and chuckled and assured me I was batshit every so often. So, there was that.

After an eternity, we got to the door, a thick wooden thing set in the middle of a wall in the small room. The wall butted up against the room that Cookie and I had set up as our office, but we'd stepped the rooms off. There was a good five feet of space in between that wall and the office wall. So what was there?

I was about to find out.

As Garrett watched from the doorway, swigging his beer pretty as you please, I pulled with all my might to try to at least get the sledge-hammer off the ground. I wasn't weak. I could lift stuff. Heavy stuff. Well, heavy-ish. This thing was insane.

I set it back down just as Reyes walked up. He wore the same doubt-ridden grin as Garrett.

"Gonna get it open, are you?" Reyes asked, wiping his hands on a towel.

"Yes, I am." I set the hammer down to take a break. "We need to know what's in there. There could be anything. I mean, why is it locked?" I examined the door for the thousandth time. "No, *how* is it locked? There's no lock." I pointed to emphasize the absurdity of it all.

The door was massive. In a convent with regular doors and regular walls, why was this door—the same door that was impenetrable—so thick? So sturdy? Reyes had even tried to see into the closet incorporeally. He couldn't get in!

"I mean, aren't you even curious? What kind of room is impenetrable even to something that is incorporeal?"

I struggled to lift the sledgehammer again, but now I had an even bigger audience.

"She at it again?" Osh asked.

"Hardheaded as the day is long," Reyes said.

My frustration rose to new heights. "Okay, Mr. Smarty Pants, if you aren't going to help, what were you talking to Angel about?"

His gaze narrowed. "What do you mean?"

"In that field today. I saw you."

He straightened. "What were you doing out there?"

"I was following that sweet departed nun. She's been trying to show me something and then someone pushed me and I almost fell to my death and were you there? No."

A blast of heat hit me then, and I couldn't tell if he was angry with me or because someone had pushed me.

"What do you mean, someone pushed you?"

Oh, thank God.

"Who pushed you?"

"Why were you talking to Angel?"

"Is that what happened to you?" He took my arm and indicated a scrape down the back of it, his touch scalding.

"Probably." I shook off his hold and gripped the sledgehammer again. "And I have no idea who it was. I smelled something weird, though." I straightened and thought about it. "Like lavender or something." I bent to my task again.

He stepped to me, curled his fingers under my chin, and lifted my face to his. "Who was it?" The moment he stepped forward, I felt consumed by fire, like I'd been swallowed by a blazing inferno.

"What were you talking to Angel about?" When he didn't answer yet again, I stepped out of his grasp and pointed in the general direction of the living room. "Go stand in the corner with Mr. Wong."

Cookie had joined us then, doing her best to look over Osh's shoulder. "Is she trying it again?"

Reyes turned from me then as though frustrated. "Why is he here?"

"Mr. Wong? I have no idea." But I stopped to wonder as Osh and Reyes eyed each other. "Are you thinking what I'm thinking?"

"Why is such a powerful being in the house?" Osh asked.

"No. Well, yes—that, too—but I was thinking he needed to get out more. Maybe meet a girl. Try the singles scene. He seems awfully lonely."

I pulled on the hammer again, raising it about two inches off the floor, and swung with all my might. It tapped lightly on the door, the sound barely audible above the sound of the spin cycle.

Then someone else joined us. Gemma stood behind Garrett, but I didn't think the high-pitched screech that nigh drew blood from my ears was coming from her. Nope. It came from none other than my stepmother.

"What are you doing?" she yelled, pushing her way into the room.

Ignoring her, Reyes shook off his misgivings about Mr. Wong, the sweetest man alive, or, well, dead, and stepped to me again. "Are you okay?" he asked, taking my arm and caressing it.

His touch liquefied my insides. "I'm fine."

"A sledgehammer?" Denise howled. "What are you doing letting her lift a sledgehammer?"

"I'm calling Katherine," Reyes continued, unfazed by Denise's rant. "I think we need to be sure."

"Katherine the Midwife," I corrected. Since we couldn't take me to a medical team to give birth, we'd brought a medical team here. We even had one of the downstairs rooms outfitted with everything a modern midwife would need.

Denise ripped the handle away from me. "Do you know what that could do to the baby?"

Was she kidding? "The baby is the safest person in this room, Denise."

"Charley, you can't lift something this heavy."

"Yes, I can. Not very far, but—"

A slap echoed along the walls and I realized my face stung. The moment was so shocking, so surreal, everyone stood in complete silence. Even Denise. She seemed the most shocked of all.

Reyes reacted first. His heat exploded around me and I slowed time to watch a hand lift to Denise's throat. He would snap her neck in a heartbeat, before he even knew what he was doing, his anger was so great. I stepped in front of him, put my hands on his wide chest, and pushed with all my might. Then I allowed time to bounce back with my hands still on his chest, my body braced for impact.

It crashed around me, and Reyes, not expecting my influence, took an involuntary step back. I'd hardly fazed him. He started for Denise again, but I put my hands on his face and drew his attention to me.

"Mom!" Gemma yelled, tackling the big guys blocking the doorway to get inside. She didn't know what Reyes was, but she knew he was supernatural and she knew he was as deadly as they came. She got between Reyes and Denise and held up her hands to fend him off.

"I'm sorry," Denise said, trying to calm him.

"Reyes," I said, my voice soft, soothing. "It's okay."

His anger physically hurt, it was so hot.

"You have to calm down." I smiled, trying to lighten the mood. "You're boiling me alive."

He sobered instantly, his eyes shimmering with emotion. A telltale wetness gathered between his thick lashes as he glared at me. Then, ever so slowly, he came to his senses.

I wiped at a tear that slipped past its glistening cage, but he turned from me, embarrassed and furious and, I suspected, afraid of what he would do.

"Are you okay?" I asked Denise.

Both hands were covering her mouth. "Charley, I'm so—!"

"Get her the fuck out of my house." Reyes didn't turn around when he spoke.

"Come on," Gemma said, rushing Denise out of the room.

Garrett helped, ushering them out, and then he and Osh blocked the door in case Reyes changed his mind.

"I'm okay," he said to them, but they didn't move.

Cookie looked on the verge of tears herself.

"We're okay, hon," I promised her.

Even unconvinced, she took that as her cue to leave.

"Reyes," I said, placing a hand on the small of his back. It scorched my skin. "What is going on? You're so hot. Your temper is like a ticking time bomb. You leave and you're gone for hours. And then when you do come back, you stay away from me for the rest of the night. I don't understand." I couldn't even imagine how he'd react when I told him about the Loehrs. The very thought filled me with an all-encompassing dread.

"Tell her," Osh said, leaning against the doorjamb.

"Is it—?" I lowered my head, so afraid of his answer. "Is it me? Is it . . . how I look?"

His temper flared again as he faced me. "I can't believe you just asked me that."

"I'm pregnant, Reyes. I'm the size of a blimp."

The incredulous look on his face stopped me. He was astounded. "You're stunning. You've never been more beautiful. Don't you understand what you are? You're a god and I'm the son of your worst enemy."

I got over the beautiful remark, and asked, "What does that have to do with anything?"

"If you don't tell her, I will." Osh was pushing him. Now was not the time. Or was it?

"What is he talking about?" I asked Reyes as he glared at the Daeva.

"Okay, fine," Osh said. "I'll tell her."

The murderous expression he leveled on Osh made me wince.

He took a step closer to him, his movements dangerously smooth. "It will be the last thing to come out of your mouth."

Osh nodded. "'Bout time you grew some balls."

In the underworld, Osh had been a champion. Their best and fastest fighter. Even faster than Reyes, so my surly husband said. But he was not as big as Reyes. Not in human form. I wondered if that mattered, though.

Reyes took another step toward him. I stopped my husband with a hand on his chest, but only because he allowed me to.

Then I faced Osh. "Tell me."

The grin Osh wore was completely unnecessary. He enjoyed antagonizing Reyes far too much for my comfort. "He hasn't slept since the attack."

"What?" I whirled around. "What attack? When were you attacked?"

"The one eight months ago," Osh explained. "He would be useless in a fight now. If the Twelve somehow get across the border—"

"Eight months?" I asked, astonished beyond belief. "Is he kidding? You haven't slept in eight months?"

We were supernatural, sure, but we had human bodies and human needs. No wonder he looked so tired and disheveled all the time. I'd once gone three weeks without sleep. It about killed me. But eight months?

"Why?" I asked him.

"Oh, but we haven't gotten to the best part," Osh continued.

Reyes's jaw muscle leapt. "Don't do this. I stopped. It didn't work and I stopped."

"What?" I asked, squelching a shudder of fear.

"You stopped after how many attempts? A dozen? More?"

"I stopped, *Daeva*. That's all that matters."

I dug my nails into Reyes's biceps to remind him I was there. "Just tell me," I ordered Osh.

"He thought he might have found a way to kill the hounds." He glanced at me, his eyes twinkling with mirth. "He was wrong."

"To kill them?" I looked from Osh to my husband then back again. "And what way was that?"

This time Garrett spoke, but he did it minus the smirk. "He dragged them onto holy ground, thinking it would kill them."

The shock that jolted through my body was like sticking a fork into a light socket. I turned to Reyes, aghast and appalled and dumbstruck that he would even try such a thing. "You did what?" I whispered.

He didn't answer at first, and when he did, his demeanor was that of a schoolboy being chastised after having been ratted out. "I only tried it a few times. It didn't work, so I stopped."

"Fifteen," Garrett said. "He tried it fifteen times."

The thought of Reyes not only fighting a hellhound, but dragging one onto the consecrated ground—on purpose!—and then fighting it, sent the world spinning beneath me. Before I knew it, the floor disappeared.

"Maybe if he'd had a little sleep, he wouldn't have had his ass handed to him on a silver platter every time," Osh said into the darkness surrounding me. "Those fuckers can fight."

I sank to the ground as though in slow motion. The edges of my vision blurred, then three sets of hands landed on me until Reyes lifted me into his arms. Even though I weighed 1,014 pounds, he carried me with ease to the stairs and up to our room. Where Denise, Gemma, and Cookie were. This was not going to end well.

"She's still here?" I asked Gemma, trying to shake the fog from my head. "Are you kidding me?"

"I had to apologize," Denise said, both hands still covering her mouth. "Is she okay?"

The glare Reyes shot her would have shriveled a winter rose. But no one ever accused Denise of being a winter rose.

"I'm okay, hon," I said, gesturing for him to put me down.

He did so slowly, then steadied me until I had my footing. "I'm not leaving you alone with her, so don't even think about it."

"Reyes, it's okay. She didn't mean to slap the living shit out of me." I said the last bit while leveling my own glare on her.

She had the decency to look embarrassed.

"It's not her I'm worried about. Is that what you were doing in the field with Angel?"

He hesitated, then said, "Yes."

He was lying. I knew it, and he knew I knew it. I raised my chin and turned from him. After a moment, he left.

Then I turned on the woman who'd made my life hell growing up. "What are you still doing here?"

"I wanted to explain."

"Charley," Gemma said, "if you'll just hear her out, I think it would be good for both of you."

"Why? She has never listened to me. Why should I have to listen to her? I should mark her soul for Osh. Oh, wait, she doesn't have one."

"I don't have one?" she said from between gritted teeth.

There she was. I knew the helpful, nurturing routine wouldn't last long.

"You think I'm a big joke," she said, her face the picture of rage.

"Hon, you're not a joke. You're the punch line."

"You didn't even go to your own father's funeral."

Gemma gasped.

"You've been holed up in here for months like you're in witness protection or something."

"The only one I need protection from is you."

"That's it! Sit down! Both of you."

Denise sat on the bench at the end of the bed, while I crossed my arms over my chest again, showing just how defiant I could be.

Gemma reached over, grabbed my ear, and led me to the chair in the corner of our tiny room. "Ow, holy cow, Gem! Katherine the Midwife is not going to be happy with you."

"Her name is just Katherine. You have to stop calling her Katherine the Midwife."

She let go and I rubbed my abused cartilage. "How did you do that?"

"Sit down!"

"No, really. I'm having a kid. I need to know how to completely incapacitate someone by grabbing their ear."

"Sit down."

I sat down. "So, you'll tell me later?"

"You need to listen to what Mom has to say."

"No, I don't."

"She deserves that much, Charley."

"Wait, you were there. Right there through our entire childhood. You saw it. You saw what she put me through. And might I bring up the slap I just received."

It was the second time in my life Denise had slapped me in front of a crowd, and it was just as jolting and humiliating as the first time.

"I saw you both going at each other like children on a playground our whole lives."

"Yeah, but she always started it."

"That's not what I saw."

"What about the time she dragged me off my bike in front of all the neighbor kids because I didn't do the dishes? Or the time a boy threw dirt in my face, right in my face, and she turned away, refused to do anything about it? Or the time she tried to run me down with her car?"

Denise sucked in a sharp breath. "I never tried to run you over with my car."

"Oh, right, I just made that one up. But you admit to the other things."

"Charley, oh my God," Gemma said. "Can we stick with nonfiction here?"

"What? I needed backup just in case you didn't find the other events horrific enough. I know what I'm saying seems childish and ridiculous for me to be holding a grudge for so long, but she was like that every day of my life. In everything that I did. She never complimented me. She never took up for me. She never stopped nagging me about the stupidest things. It was like she made it her personal mission to make sure I knew I was less than she was. Mothers don't tear down, Gemma. They build up. Like she did with you."

"That's not true, Charley," Gemma said in her psychiatrist voice.

"She slapped me in front of all those people. I was five years old."

"Charley, look at that from her perspective. It was a horrible situation. You told a woman whose daughter had been missing for weeks that her daughter was in front of her."

"She was."

"We're mere mortals, Charley. We didn't know that. Mom was mortified. She was horrified and she panicked."

"Like a few minutes ago?" I rubbed my cheek. She had the decency to look ashamed. "Were you panicking then?"

"Yes," she said.

I looked at Gemma and scoffed. "Did you know that same woman sent me a bike after I led the cops to her daughter's body. Your mother wouldn't even let me have it."

Gemma looked stunned. "Of course. You helped bring her closure."

"Even a stranger believed in my abilities, and she—" I looked her up and down. "—made me feel like a freak every chance she got."

"I didn't think you should be rewarded for doing what you did to that poor woman. You had to learn that was wrong. You don't just blurt stuff out like that, even if it's true."

"Well, I learned, all right. Don't you worry about me. Is this over yet?"

"No," Gemma said. "Mom wants to explain."

"I was just trying to teach you."

"No." I stood and paced. "No, you were so indifferent to me. You hated me. That's not teaching. That's punishing."

"I never hated you."

"You were completely indifferent to me. If not hate, then what?"

"I wasn't indifferent."

"You were a monster!" I yelled. "Why are you even here? Why are you even talking to me?"

Her shoulders shook a moment before she cleared her throat and tried to gather herself. No way was she making me the bad guy in all this. Tears may have worked on my dad, but they would not sway me an inch.

"I wasn't indifferent, Charley."

A humorless laugh escaped me.

"I was scared of you."

I sighed, unable to believe she was pulling this shit.

"I was scared to death of you. You were something else, something . . . not human, and I was scared of you."

"Oh, so now you believe in all this?"

"Please listen to her, Charley. It's taken us a long time to get to this point."

"So, you've been counseling her? Five syllables: antipsychotic. They do wonders."

"You owe her at least a little of your time."

"She treated me like shit my whole life. The only thing I owe her is my middle finger and a cold shoulder."

"You're right," Denise said. "You're absolutely right."

"See?" I said to Gemma.

"If you will let me explain," she said, "I will leave tonight and I will never come back if that is still your wish."

"Can't beat that with a stick. Shoot."

Her cheeks were wet and her fingers shook as she stared down at her lap. "When I was little, my mother was in a car accident."

Not her life story. Damn it. I had to pee. This could take forever.

"They had her in ICU. They'd stabilized her, so they let me and my dad in to see her. It was so scary seeing her hooked up to all those machines."

I gazed longingly at the door, wondering if anyone would notice if I just slipped away for a few minutes. Beep was playing hopscotch on my bladder, and this was clearly going to take a while.

"My dad left to get coffee, and Mom woke up while he was gone. She looked at me sleepily and held out her hand right before the machines started going crazy. Her blood pressure dropped. The nurses and doctors came in and they tossed aside one of the blankets that was on her. A blue blanket."

Blue wasn't my favorite color.

"They were working on her, trying to bring her back. I guess she was bleeding internally. She woke up again while they were working on her, but the machines were still going crazy. She looked up at nothing and spoke. Just said things like, 'Oh, oh, okay, I didn't realize.' She had a loving look on her face. When I looked over, I saw what she was talking to. An angel."

I saw an angel once, too, but now probably wasn't the time to bring it up.

"He disappeared. Everyone had forgotten I was even there. They took her back into surgery, performing CPR on the way, but she was already gone. When my father came back, he dropped his coffee. I tried to tell them there was an angel, but all he saw was the blanket. He thought it was a blue towel."

I suddenly knew where this was going. When her father died, I was four. He came to me and asked me to give her a message. Something about blue towels. I was too young to understand. Later, I didn't care.

"They came back and told us she was gone. My dad broke down. I tried to tell him about the angel, but all he saw was a blue towel."

I was going to need a blue towel if I didn't get to the bathroom soon.

"He said sometimes a blue towel is just a blue towel. That became our mantra. Anytime anything unexplained happened, we repeated it. But we didn't talk about the actual event until about two years before I met Leland."

Wonderful. We were jumping ahead in time. I crossed one leg over the other and tried not to squirm. Gemma sat beside her on the bench and put a hand over hers. They were always so close. I'd tried to understand over the years, but some things were just impossible to explain. Like UFOs and bell-bottoms.

"My dad had a massive heart attack, but he survived. Then one day we were having dinner and he looked at me and said, 'Sometimes a blue towel isn't just a blue towel.' Sometimes it's more. But by that point, I'd grown up. I was a bona fide skeptic. And—" She ducked her head as though ashamed. "And I didn't believe him. After everything that had happened, I didn't believe him. I chalked it up to the medication they had him on. But then, right after I met your dad, I was in a car accident."

"So, the point of this story is to not get in the car with you or any of your relatives?"

"Charley," Gemma said, her voice monotone. Nonjudgmental. I loved psychology.

"Your dad rushed to the hospital. He had to bring you girls. They said I nearly died."

Nearly being the salient word.

"I guess because he was a cop, they let him bring you two in to see me." She laughed humorlessly. "I was pretty out of it."

Like now? I wanted to ask.

She looked at me at last. "That's when I saw it."

I had so many comebacks, it was hard to pick just one, so I remained silent.

"I saw your light, Charley. But only for an instant."

"I didn't know about your light," Gemma said. "Not until Denise told me."

"Join the club," I said. "I can't see it either."

Denise stared wide-eyed for a moment before continuing. "I just figured I was seeing things. Then about a year later, I was having dinner with my dad again and I told him what I saw. He tried to tell me how special you were. I scoffed and repeated our mantra. 'Sometimes a blue towel is just a blue towel.'"

"I'm not really sensing an apology here."

Gemma scowled at me. If only she knew about the bladder situation. It was making me cranky. I didn't want to go now, though. It would be my excuse to leave the room when they were getting ready to go home. I could hurry things along then.

"I slowly began to realize my dad had been right. You were special. Different. I didn't know your father was using you to help solve his cases, though. He hid it from me for a long time."

"I can't imagine why."

"It wasn't until the park incident with the missing girl's mother that I realized what he was doing. When I found out, I was livid."

"Because he was paying attention to me?"

"Because I was so against believing what I saw with my own eyes. Despite everything that happened, I had convinced myself that the angel was a figment of my imagination. That my mother did not go to a better place. That supernatural beings like angels and demons did not exist. It went against everything I was trying tooth and nail to hold on to. There was too much hurt and too much suffering in the world for me to believe that an omniscient being would allow it all to happen. I became an atheist. People are just good or bad. There's no devil making us do evil things."

"Well, I have to agree with you on the people front."

"But the devil front?" Gemma asked.

I let a slow smile spread across my face for Denise's benefit. "I'm married to his son."

"Charley, that's not funny."

This time I planted a serious gaze on my sister. "I wasn't trying to be funny, Gem."

She leaned forward and whispered to me. No idea why. "You mean—? Really? As in—?"

"Lucifer's son. Yes."

I was hoping that would send Denise running. Instead, she rambled on. For the love of—

"When you told me what my dad had told you that day in your apartment, the thing about the blue towels, my last desperate grip on atheism slipped through my fingers. I didn't know what to do. How to handle it. But then everything happened so fast with your father."

"After Dad died," Gemma said, "Mom started going to church."

"He's in a better place, right?" she asked, sobbing into a tissue.

"Actually, last I saw him, he was in my bathroom."

They both blinked up at me, their mouths forming perfect Os.

"What? I wasn't naked or anything."

"He's here?" Denise asked.

"No. Not right now." I glanced around just in case. "Not sure what's going on with him. But I really have to pee, so is this a wrap?"

"No," Denise said, her posture suggesting she was going to stand her ground. "I would like to ask for your forgiveness."

"My forgiveness?" I said with a huff.

"Charley," Gemma said, "you promised to listen."

"I did. I am. But that's all I promised."

"No," Denise said, patting Gemma's hand, "it's okay. Charley listened. That's all I can ask. I just want you to know that I am sorry for any suffering I may have caused you."

"There's something you're missing here," I said.

"Okay."

"You've known all along what I was. Or at least that I was special or had a gift or something along those lines. And you denied it and tried to make me feel like shit because of it. Is your knowing supposed to make me feel better? Because trust me when I say that makes you a bigger bitch than I thought you were."

Gemma lowered her head, then spoke softly. "Sometimes we just need to forgive. Not for that person, but for ourselves."

"You're right, Charley. I fought the truth. Fought you. Fought my father and your father and even our Maker. I have no one to blame but myself."

She stood, tucked the tissue in her handbag, then walked to the door. Without facing me, she said, "Thank you for listening. If you can find it in your heart, I want to be a part of your life. A part of Beep's life. I'll do anything you need me to do. I'll help you with the baby. I'll go to the store. I'll change diapers. Anything." Her voice cracked with her last plea. "Please think about it."

She walked out, but Gemma had one last thing to say. "It's taken her months to get through a whole day without crying about Dad. She's come a long way, Charley. She has no family but us. Please consider her offer."

"I'll think about it. After I pee."

8

When I got back from making number one, Katherine the Midwife was there waiting for me, gloves on, in her ready stance. Gawd, she liked sticking her fingers up Virginia.

"Hey, Katherine," I said. "Time for another torture session?"

Reyes was there, too, looking rather ashamed of himself. As he should. Picking fights with hellhounds was not something to be proud of. I would've kicked him out of the room, but I couldn't be too mad. I now had ammunition for when the time came to tell him about the Loehrs.

"Let's have a look at you," she said. "You fell?"

"Yes, in the woods."

"I see that." She lifted my shirt, and a burst of heat washed over me.

Confused, I looked in the full-length mirror and saw what Reyes saw. I hadn't even noticed it before. I had scrapes all along one side of my back and over my rib cage.

Reyes didn't say anything, but I could feel his desire to question me further.

"Okay, no broken ribs. You're breathing okay?" she asked.

I nodded.

She checked Beep's heartbeat, then said, "How about we do this right here? I'll just check to make sure everything is intact."

I knew the drill. She stepped outside the room while I removed my pants and my panties and draped the sheet over me. Then I lay down on the bed and called her back in. Reyes never took his eyes off me. His dark gaze was both reassuring and unsettling. He stared at me from underneath his lashes, his temper held in check by his own feelings of helplessness. I was right there with him.

Katherine the Midwife pushed my legs farther apart and did her thing. The lubricant was freezing and I jumped. "Sorry, hon. Let's see what's going on."

But a barrage of thoughts and images crashed into me as I lay there. The thought of Reyes dragging a hellhound, a fucking hellhound, across the border to try to kill it sank in. That and the fact that someone, or something was trying to kill me in addition to said hellhounds. I wanted to continue to hate Denise forever and ever, but her loneliness—I'd felt it. I'd been feeling it for months. I just lived in a constant state of denial. And the business with the Loehrs. What had I done? What would my actions do to my marriage? Would Reyes forgive me?

It all came bubbling to the surface at the worst possible time. Two fingers. All the way up.

I bit down, covered my eyes, held my breath, but the emotions swirling inside me, the stress of living with a dozen hellhounds just waiting to rip me to shreds—no, waiting to rip Beep to shreds—and being so utterly helpless to do anything about it were getting to me. That combined with everything else, mostly Reyes and his antics and me and my antics, wrenched a sob from my throat.

"It's okay, honey," Katherine the Midwife said. "I'm almost finished. You're dilated, but just barely. You're about a two right now."

She cleaned me up and pulled down the sheet, but it was too late. I covered my face with both hands and fought tooth and nail to hold back the emotions overwhelming me.

"This is a very emotional time, sweetheart," she said, patting my knee.

I felt the bed dip, felt the heat of Reyes near me, felt his fingers push a lock of hair from my face, and cried some more. It was like I'd turned on a faucet and broke the handle. I couldn't turn it back off again.

"I'll leave you two alone, but everything looks good. No damage that I can see."

I heard the door click closed as she left, and then Reyes pulled me into his arms.

"Freaking whore-mones," I said, and he held me tight as deep, cleansing sobs overtook me.

When I woke up, it was dark outside. I lay there listening to the sound of Reyes's breathing, deep and even, and I hoped beyond hope that he was asleep.

"I'm not," he said.

"What time is it?"

"It's only nine. You need to go back to sleep."

"I will if you will."

"Can't."

I rose onto an elbow and tried to make out his features in the dark. Moonlight streamed in from the open curtains and shimmered in his incredible eyes.

"Why can't you sleep?"

"I don't know, Dutch. I just can't. I can't make myself."

"You can't allow yourself. That's what this is about, but eight months? Really? How did I not know?"

"Because you sleep like you're comatose. And you snore."

"You can't watch me every second of the day. What good are you if something happens and you're too exhausted to fight?"

"I know. Trust me. I'm not doing it on purpose. I just can't sleep."

I frowned, worried about him. "Why were you talking with Angel? What's going on with you two?"

"He's doing a little reconnaissance for me."

"What kind of reconnaissance? You aren't putting him in any danger, are you?"

"No." He bent to nuzzle my ear. It sent warm shivers cascading over my shoulders.

"Okay, then tell me exactly what you're doing."

"No." He trailed tiny, hot kisses down my neck.

"Tell me or we are never having sex again."

He smiled behind a particularly sensual kiss where my pulse beat. "I'll put the tux back on."

My lids drifted shut with the thought as a ripple of desire shuddered through me. "Nope. You have to tell me first or that's it. We may as well call the lawyer now because it ain't happening."

"I'll do that thing with my tongue."

My gawd, I loved the thing with his tongue. I had to stay strong. "Nope," I said, my voice as weak as my resolve. "Not even then."

"Katherine the Midwife left the lube. We could try anal."

I stifled a giggle. "We are not trying anal." I rolled away from him and onto my feet. "I need a shower anyway. I just want you to know that whatever happens from here on out is your own fault."

"Really?" he asked, his expression full of interest.

"I tried to warn you. Don't blame me when this becomes a knock-down drag-out war."

"And just what do you plan on doing?"

"You'll see. And, mark my words, you will not be happy." I grabbed my robe from the closet with the sobbing tax attorney and left.

"Just remember," he said as I closed the door. "I was a general in hell. War is my middle name."

Oh yeah. This was going to be fun.

Hot water rushed over my skin, easing the aches from the afternoon's events. I'd already begun to heal.

I called Sister Mary Elizabeth on the way to the shower, hoping it wasn't too late. I'd promised to call earlier and give her an update on Quentin. He had been staying with them, but now split his time between the sisters and Reyes and me. We'd semi-adopted him.

"How's Quentin?" she asked before I could even say hello.

"He's good. He's still watching movies with Amber. Or doing crack. Not sure which. So, have you heard anything?"

"I couldn't find anything out about your nun, but we don't have access to those records. Much of that kind of stuff is archived in the Vatican."

"Wonderful."

"But I did find one very odd occurrence that happened at that convent."

"Hit me," I said, pulling back the shower curtain and turning on the water. It took forever to heat.

"A priest went missing there in the '40s."

"Really?"

"Yep. He was visiting and just vanished."

"Like, into thin air?"

"Not literally, but yeah, no one ever saw him again. There was a huge search. It was in all the papers."

"Okay, well, thanks for looking into it. Anything else on the other front?"

"Besides the fact that heaven is in an uproar? Did I mention that?"

"Yep."

"And did I mention how exhausting their chatter is?"

"Yep."

"And how I'm slowly losing my mind with all the chatter?"

"Hey, it's not my fault you can hear angels talking. Hellhounds."

"No, I haven't heard anything."

"Well, can you ask?"

"I don't ask and you know it. I just listen. It's not a two-way conversation. I can hear them. I can't communicate with them."

"Of course you can. You're a nun. You're pure and good and wholesome. Like Wheaties. They'll listen to you. All you have to do is ask."

"Do you ever listen to anything I say?"

"I'm sorry, were you speaking?"

"You're funny."

"Thank you!" I said, brightening. "So, I keep meaning to ask you something."

"Okay. Is it about abstinence again? I can't keep explaining—"

"No, it's about the night you found out I was pregnant with Beep. And now heaven is in an uproar. Why? I mean, are they mad at me?"

"Oh no. 'Mad' isn't the right word. More like . . . frantic."

"Why? Don't they know about the prophecies?"

"Absolutely, but prophecies are thwarted all the time. I think they were just surprised it was really happening. I mean, you're bringing something onto this plane that, well, maybe doesn't belong? No, that's not the right way to put it."

"So, Beep won't belong here?"

"I didn't mean that. It's more like . . . a birth like hers doesn't happen every day. I'm not sure how to say this without going to confession right after, but from what I can tell, they are saying the daughter of a god will be born here. But that's wrong. There is only one God, so I'm sure I'm misunderstanding them."

"Right. I'm sure."

"I did hear that she will change something that they hadn't expected to be changed. It's kind of freaking them out. It's like when you expect your car to run out of gas before you make it to the station, but you're still surprised when it does."

"Okay," I said, trying to grasp every nuance of her meaning. I gave up. "Bottom line, she isn't in any danger from them, right?"

"From heaven? Absolutely not."

"Oh, good. That's good. Hey, how do you have a cell phone, anyway? I thought cloistered nuns had to give up worldly crap."

"I'm not a cloistered nun, and I have a cell phone because, in my position, it's beneficial. It's all been approved."

"I'll need to see those documents."

"No."

"Have you ever considered the fact that the term 'cloistered nuns' sounds like an appetizer? Or a punk band?"

"Yes."

"Okay, well, let me know if you hear anything. I'd like to lead a normal life someday."

"Ten four."

Showers were God's reward for working hard enough to get dirty. I dried off, wrapped myself up in the plush robe Reyes had bought me, and stepped to a foggy mirror.

Before I could wipe it off, a letter appeared in the steam. I glanced around. No one was in there, but another letter appeared as though someone were tracing letters in the condensation with a finger. I stood back and waited for the full message to appear, then read it aloud.

"Spies."

What did that mean? There were spies here? Did we have a mole in the convent? And if so, who? No, the bigger questions would be, whom was the mole spying for? Whom would he report to?

I reached up and hurriedly wiped off the mirror. Two things came to mind immediately. First of all, that was my dad's handwriting. It was exactly the same, which was odd and a little disheartening that I'd have the same handwriting when I died. I had thought there was hope for me. I thought good handwriting skills were a perk of heaven. That maybe we'd magically know angelic script and have this fluid, flowing handwriting, but no. I was doomed. The second thing was that there were apparently spies among us.

But who? Who would be—?

It hit me like a nuclear blast. I strode down the hall back to my room. Reyes had left, but I knew one person who hadn't.

I opened the closet door to the agonizing sobs of the tax attorney. Reaching inside, I grabbed her arm and dragged her out. As long as I kept ahold of her wrist, she couldn't vanish.

She stumbled to her feet and raised a hand to her face, sobbing uncontrollably.

"Save it," I said, jerking her arm to snap her out of it. "Who are you spying for? Who sent you here?"

For a split second, I actually suspected my husband. It wouldn't be the first time he'd sent someone to watch me. But why would she be putting on a show like that?

No, I suspected it was someone who knew I'd try to help her, and they wanted her to get very close to both me and Reyes.

"Answer me, or I'll—" Crap, I had nothing. What would I do? I was a portal to heaven and threatening to send her there didn't seem like much of an incentive to talk.

But she stopped crying anyway and glowered at me.

"Who are you spying for?" I repeated.

Her glower twisted her pretty mouth into a defiant smirk.

Suddenly, I knew what to do with her. "I'll mark your soul. You will be devoured by a soul-eater and cease to exist."

A split second of fear flashed across her face, but she recovered quickly. "I'm not the only one," she said. "You have no idea what's coming."

"Enlighten me."

"Bite me."

"Hmm, no, I think I'll leave that up to Osh'ekiel."

Her jaw dropped open. "The Daeva? He's here?"

"You're not a very good spy." She tried to jerk out of my grasp, but I held her tight. "Once I mark your soul, there is nowhere you can hide that he won't find you." Then something else hit me. A scent. Lavender. It was coming from the closet and had seeped into her soul. "You pushed me!" I said, appalled, remembering the scent just before I went face-first down a mountainside.

She raised her chin and refused to talk.

Dang it. Where was a waterboard when I needed one? I wondered if an ironing board would work.

But then she had to open her big mouth and make me mad. Not a good idea. "She will never see the light of day on this plane," the tax attorney said, quite enjoying herself. "He'll eat her intestines for breakfast. You have no idea the plans he has for your daughter."

Anger surged through me lightning quick, and before I knew it, I'd marked her. I saw a symbol brand into her soul like a flash of light; then it was gone and all that remained was the burned imprint of the mark.

She gasped, looked at the mark on her chest, stumbled back, but I kept my hold.

Soon, Reyes and Osh burst through the door. Reyes was beside me at once while Osh fairly crooned when he realized what I'd done.

"What have we here?" he asked as the woman cowered away from him.

I turned from him to Reyes. "Your father has sent spies. We have spies! Did you know we have spies?"

Osh's gaze dropped with guilt. But Reyes's gaze never wavered from the woman's.

"Were you planning on telling me?" I asked my husband.

"Not today," he said.

I stood aghast. No idea why. The guy had more secrets than Victoria.

I thought Sheila was scared of Osh, and she was, but when her gaze landed on Reyes, she screamed and fought my hold. Just as she slipped through my fingers, Reyes took hold of her shoulders. "How many more?" he asked as he shook her.

"I don't—" She cried out when his fingers bit into her. "Two. Maybe three."

"What are his plans?"

"I don't know. I—I swear. He doesn't tell us."

He shoved her away from us, the revulsion he felt evident in every move he made. "She's all yours."

She caught herself, straightened, and raised her chin, resigned to her fate.

"Dinnertime," Osh said with a wolfish grin, and what happened next made me pee a little.

We looked on as Osh backed her against the closet door, not as though he were about to eat her alive, but as though he were about to make love to her.

"He's just waiting for the right moment," she said in one last act of defiance, one last attempt to scare us shitless. It was working. On me, at least.

"And what moment would that be, love?" Osh asked as he caressed her neck and lifted her face to his, his touch as gentle as a summer breeze.

She curled her hands into fists at her sides, waiting for the inevitable. "That moment when no one is looking."

He leaned into her, pressed his hips into her, ran his lips along her neck. "We're always looking, love."

The grin that spread across her pretty face was both sad and terrifying. Her gaze landed on me and her grin widened. "Not always."

Before I could ask what she meant, Osh bent over her and covered her mouth with his, the sensuality of the act surprising. And arousing. A shimmer of light escaped from between their mouths, and Osh pulled back from her, just enough for me to see her soul passing out of her and into him. His eyes were closed, his hands holding her head as she stared wide-eyed at the ceiling. She seemed to weaken almost instantly, her fists relaxing, her arms falling limp. Then her body grew more and more transparent. She began to dissipate. Pieces of her drifted into the air like ashes until she disappeared completely.

Osh braced an arm against the door and rested his head on it, his shoulders rising and falling with each heavy breath he took.

"How did you know?" Reyes asked me.

"My dad, I think. He told me there were spies and it just made sense. Mostly because she didn't make any."

"Any?" Osh asked, still panting.

"Sense. She didn't make any sense. She was way too put together, too smart to be so upset she couldn't even talk to me. And why in here? Where Reyes and I slept?"

"And talked," Reyes added.

I sat on the bench, Reyes still holding my hand as I said, "That was kind of amazing."

"Thanks for the meal," Osh said, crossing his arms over his still-heaving chest. His shoulder-length dark hair hid most of his face, but from what I could see, he was quite satisfied.

"I probably shouldn't have done that. Isn't that, you know, God's job?"

"You *are* a god."

"Not here. Not in this realm."

"Since she was sent from hell, I doubt he minded."

"From hell?" I asked, surprised.

Reyes looked down at me, his presence so powerful, I wanted to melt into him. "Who else would spy for my father?"

"You mean, she had been sent to hell and Lucifer sent her back? To spy on us? Is that even legal?"

"It would seem so," Osh said. He laid his head back against the door, still recovering.

"Can you take someone's soul who is still alive?" I asked him.

"Only pieces of it unless it's been marked. Otherwise, I have to wait until those who have lost their souls to me die." He bowed his head and looked at me from underneath his lashes, the wolfish grin back and darkening his features. "Then they're all mine."

"But, as per our agreement, you can eat only the souls of those undeserving of them." I knew that good people had lost their souls to him. I'd saved one from him a few months back and made him promise to be more selective.

He lifted a shoulder in agreement. A reluctant agreement, but an agreement nonetheless.

"Hey," I said, "I could mark my stepmother for you."

Reyes sat down. "You can't mark your stepmother."

"Just a little mark. Barely visible."

Osh laughed softly and stuck his hands in his pockets.

I grabbed a bottled water off my nightstand and nestled back beside the son of evil. "So, why do Daeva eat souls?"

Reyes spoke from beside me, his gaze hard on Osh's. "It's what they were created to do. Work. Fight. Entertain. Live off the suffering of others."

"And what were you created to do?" he asked.

"Send people like you to their deaths."

"Wait," I said, holding up a time-out sign. "When did this turn south? We were all friends a minute ago. Weren't we all friends?"

"It's all good," Osh said, sobering. "Rey'aziel tends to forget where he's from sometimes. And that we were created by the same being."

"But not in the same fires," Reyes said. "Not of the same substance."

Osh shrugged an eyebrow, unfazed.

"Maybe you're a spy as well," Reyes said.

"Maybe," Osh replied. "And maybe you know more than you are letting on."

"Maybe."

So, now we were playing the maybe game. What was going on? They'd been getting along famously, then this. I decided to change the subject.

"So, explain to me this whole marking thing," I said to Osh. "Are there others on earth who eat souls?"

"Yes," he said without elaborating.

"Are they all Daeva?"

"No. I'm the only Daeva ever to both escape and make it through the void."

He was right. Reyes's tattoo was a map to the gates of hell. It was how he could traverse the oblivion, the void between this plane and his. He was literally a portal to hell while I was a portal to heaven. And we hooked up. Stranger things had happened; I was certain of it. He told me once that most all of those who tried to get onto our plane from hell never made it through the void. They were stuck there, slowly going insane. I wondered what would happen to one of those creatures if it finally, after centuries of living in the void, actually made it onto this plane. What would it be like?

A shudder rushed through me with the thought.

"You know," I said, realizing something else, "all twelve hellhounds made it through the void and onto this plane. Someone had to have helped them."

Reyes nodded. "I would guess that whoever summoned them had a hand in that."

"But it took your father eons to create you, you who had the map imprinted on his body. He created a portal. Without the map that you and only you have, even he can't cross onto this plane easily. Is that right?"

He lowered his head in thought. "Yes, it is."

"Then how would he help them get here?"

"She's right," Osh said. "Whoever summoned them must have already been on this plane."

Reyes stood and started pacing as Osh bent his head in thought. They were trying so hard to figure out the puzzle. They had been for months. I still couldn't imagine why Osh was helping us. He hated Satan. I got that. But there seemed more to it than just hatred. He had an ulterior motive. I could feel it.

And why tell me what I could and could not do? I could destroy him with even the minute amount of information he'd already given me about my past, about my powers. I decided to learn more while I could.

"Why can I mark people?" I asked out of the blue. "I mean, why me?"

"Comes with the gig," Osh said, his head still bowed in thought. "Only the reaper can mark the souls of humans. Well, God can, of course, but why would he need to? And I think Michael can. And the Angel of Death, naturally."

"The Angel of Death? For real?"

"For real."

"Wow, so what else comes with the gig?" I asked, fishing. "I mean, what other marks could there possibly be?" He'd let it slip once that I had five marks, five avenues of judgment as the reaper. Since I can see into people's souls, I can see what they did with their lives and how they treated others, I had the ability to judge, jury, and execute. I wanted to know every avenue I had at my disposal.

"You have five marks, and what you say is law. Only God can supersede your decision on any soul." He looked up at me then, his brows knitting in suspicion. "Why?"

"I just want to know what I can do."

"You will know," Reyes said, "when you pass and you ascend to become the grim reaper. If you take the job."

"Why wouldn't I?"

"Because you are a god. You have an entire universe to run." He looked away from me. "Why would you stick around here?"

"Good point," I said, teasing him yet marveling at how matter-of-fact they made it all sound. How everyday.

"What other marks?" I asked Osh.

Osh eyed Reyes a moment before continuing. "You can brand a soul for heaven or for hell. You can brand a soul for termination, which is essentially what you do when you mark one for me. It's kind of like free game. You can mark one as a wanderer, a soul with no home who must wander the wilds of the supernatural realm, forever considering their mistakes. And you can give the mark of designation."

"Designation?"

"You can assign that soul a special purpose on earth, and no other supernatural being can argue with your decision."

"Like when the president appoints a chief of staff?"

"Pretty much. That soul can no longer be touched."

I was still confused on a couple of points. "So, if I marked a soul for termination and you weren't here to eat it, what would happen to it?"

"It would burn away over the course of a few days. It would be very painful. So, in a way, I'm performing a public service."

"Of course you are. And when I found you, what were you doing then?"

"Hey, everyone has to eat, and I can only bargain for souls. They must be given willingly."

"But you trick them into giving up their souls."

He spread his hands wide, acquiescing. "That was the old me. This is the new."

"You no longer trick them?"

"Oh, I trick them. Really, it's just too easy. But I only trick the bad ones, remember?" he added quickly when I scowled at him. "Child molesters and such. As per your request," he mocked.

"And people who talk at the theater. Don't forget people who talk at the theater."

One corner of his mouth tipped up. "I wouldn't dare."

Reyes walked to the window and looked out over the lawn. Even as dark as it was out, we could still see the departed.

"I once ate this woman—," Osh started.

"Dude, I don't think I should be hearing this."

"I ate her soul," he corrected.

"Next time, open with that."

"And she tasted horrible, like an ashtray with kerosene in it."

I fought my gag reflex. "No way."

"Crazy thing was, she didn't even smoke while she was alive."

"Then why? Surely she wasn't born bound for hell?"

"She was a very feared drug lord. Ruthless. Barbaric. She killed anyone who got in her way. A lot of people died in her crossfire. Even children. We are all tainted by the decisions we make."

"And the taste of our souls reflects that?"

"It does."

"Huh. I wonder what mine would taste like."

"Cherry pie." He grinned from ear to ear. "Very tart cherry pie."

"How would you know that?"

He ignored the threatening scowl Reyes had cast him and winked.

"You've tasted me? Oh my God, I feel violated."

"Please, it was just a nibble."

"I totally should have paid more attention in Bible school."

"I don't think they teach about the Daeva. We aren't important enough to merit a mention."

I narrowed my eyes on him. "Somehow, I don't think that's true. Are there more?" I asked Reyes.

"Exponentially more."

His shoulders took up the entire expanse of the window, so I nudged against him. He wrapped an arm around me and stepped to the side. He was right. Our shindig had grown exponentially.

"Do you think there are spies among them?"

"I do." He looked down at me. "But they could be anywhere. Anyone."

I nodded. "Is that what you and Angel were talking about in the clearing today?"

When he didn't answer yet again, I tsked. "Just remember, you brought on the wrath of the reaper all on your little lonesome. By the way," I added, looking at Osh. "I was just kidding about the people who talk at the theater."

"Damn it," he said, feigning disappointment.

Now if I could only figure out a way to convince my husband to get some rest. Too bad there wasn't a mark for that.

I stood and walked to the door to check on Cookie, but before closing it, I offered Reyes one last chance to come clean. "This is your one last chance to come clean," I told him, deciding not to mince words.

He sat on the bed, leaned back, and folded his arms behind his head.

"I mean it. If you don't tell me what you and Angel were talking about, why you were meeting, I can't take responsibility for my actions."

He grinned.

I tapped my toes in impatience.

He grinned wider.

"Okay, war it is. I have to warn you—"

Before I got much further into my intimidation process, a pillow slammed into my face. I stood there, eyes closed, mortified while the ball and chain laughed softly.

It was so on.

9

I went down to check on Cookie. Uncle Bob was still in the city. Working. On his wedding day. I felt so guilty, though I didn't know why. I had nothing to do with his working. Just Cookie's.

"Hey, you," I said, watching Reyes in the kitchen from the corner of my eye. He was making us both a hot chocolate. God bless him. Chocolate had become my best friend in the absence of coffee, which I'd given up for Beep. Come to think of it, I'd given up a lot for her. I'd have to make sure she knew that. Remind her. Daily. "It's almost ten o'clock, Cook. You have to go to bed."

There was a small couch in the office, on which Amber and Quentin sat. Well, Amber sat. Quentin slept, his blond hair hiding his face, one arm hanging over the side, the other thrown over his head. He had a massive shoe on Amber's lap, but she didn't seem to mind. She sat reading, completely content.

"I've been going through everything," Cookie said, apparently ignoring my prime directive. That happened a lot.

Reyes brought my hot chocolate in. "Anyone else?" he asked, offering his own mug. A true gentleman.

"I'll take some, Uncle Reyes," Amber said, her smile flirtatious.

He chuckled and handed her his mug. "What about you?" he asked Cookie.

She was so engrossed in her work, it took her a moment to blink up at him. When she did, she stopped, blindsided by the picture before her. He stood in a pair of lounge pants, black and red plaid, with a dark gray, form-fitted T-shirt. I felt a flush of heat radiate out of her—a feat, considering Reyes's heat knew no bounds.

When she didn't answer, he flashed her his famous lopsided grin and said, "Hot chocolate, it is."

He winked at me before venturing back to the kitchen, and for a split second, I thought I saw odd lines across the back of his shirt, but I dismissed the thought when Cookie came back to earth.

"Did he say something?" she asked.

"He forgot the best part!" Amber said, scuttling out from under Quentin's enormous shoe and following after her uncle Reyes. "You forgot marshmallows!"

"He's getting you a cup of hot cocoa," I told Cook.

"Oh, right." She shook the fog out of her brain. "That man makes it impossible to concentrate."

"He does, at that. So, can I ask you something?"

"Of course." She turned in her chair to face me.

"It's about your pre-honeymoon honeymoon."

"Charley, really, it's no big deal."

"I think it is, but not in the way that you are letting on."

She shifted in her chair. "What do you mean?"

"It's like you were relieved that you didn't get to go."

"What? There is a missing girl. There was nothing for me to be relieved about."

"Which is exactly why I'm concerned."

"Well, don't be."

"Hey," I said, using reverse psychology, "at least when all this is over, you two will get the honeymoon of your dreams."

That ripple of concern shuddered through her again. "Absolutely."

"Cook," I said when she turned back to her computer, "what's going on?"

Her shoulders lifted as she filled her lungs before facing me again. After a quick glance down the hall, she said, "Robert is not my second marriage. He's my third."

A jolt of shock rocketed through me. "Oh my God, I can't believe you didn't tell me that!"

She slammed an index finger over her mouth to shush me.

"I tell you everything," I whispered loudly. "I even told you about that time Timothy Tidmore tried to use Virginia as a garage for his Hot Wheels."

"I know." She hung her head in shame. "I know. But my first marriage lasted all of two days."

"No way." I wiggled closer, suddenly very intrigued. "What happened?"

"Well, I was in Vegas with my aunt and uncle. It was my eighteenth birthday and they were there for a trade show. Anyway, my cousins and I had a lot of free time and, well, I met a guy by the pool and we had a really great day and we . . . um . . . got married."

I blinked, unable to reconcile the vision of a carefree wild child and Cookie.

"That night." When I didn't interrupt—I didn't dare—she continued. "So, we're in his parents' hotel room later that night, on what we were calling our honeymoon, and his . . . pants . . . kind of—" The longer she spoke, the softer her voice became.

"His what did what?"

"His pants caught on fire."

"Of course they did. He was eighteen."

"No, I mean, literally."

"Oh, like, *on fire* on fire?"

"Yeah. He'd spilled wine on his pants while we were having a candle-light dinner, at his parents' expense, naturally, and when I jumped up to help him, I knocked over the candle and . . . well, you get the idea."

"Oh, man. That had to hurt."

"I'm sure it did, but he was never the same after that. He was actually quite a jerk. Thankfully, his parents had the marriage annulled as soon as he told them what we'd done."

"Okay, so your first honeymoon didn't go so well. But surely you had better luck with Amber's father."

"My second honeymoon was worse."

"No," I said, intrigued again.

She nodded. "We lived together a whole year. Everything was wonderful until the day we got married. Everything changed."

"Cook, what happened?"

"Well, it started out okay. We had the wedding. It was a huge event. All the crazies from my side showed up, and his family numbered in the thousands. It was nice, but not really me, you know?"

"I do."

"I was so nervous that I drank a little wine before the wedding."

"Uh-oh."

"Oh, the ceremony went off without a hitch. I slurred my vows a bit, but other than that, perfection."

"Okay," I said, growing wary nonetheless.

"So, we had the reception and I drank some more."

That was never good.

"And we did the whole rice thing and left in a limousine for the hotel. We were going to stay the night, then fly out the next morning to Cancún."

"Awesome. Loving it so far."

"Well, I'd had a bit too much to drink, we both had, and Noah decided to moon the people on the freeway."

"Wait, who's Noah?"

"Amber's father," she said, suddenly annoyed.

"Oh, right, I knew that. Okay, so he's mooning everyone."

"Yes, but I started to get sick."

"Understandable."

"And I just reached for the closest door handle."

"No."

"Yes. I opened the door while he was mooning everyone. He fell out of the limo on I-25."

I sat stunned.

"South," she added.

I still sat stunned.

"Near the Gibson exit."

"Cookie," I said at last, "what happened?"

"He suffered multiple fractures, a ruptured spleen, and a mild concussion."

I slammed my hands over my mouth.

"I know. Things just changed after that. Even after ten years of marriage, we never found what we had again."

"I'm sorry, hon."

"I just don't have the best luck with honeymoons."

"No, that's not true. Those were total coincidences."

She smiled sadly. "You don't believe in coincidences."

I squeezed her hand. "I do now."

"This is so much better," Amber chimed as she skipped back to her seat.

"I can't believe you're that girl," I said softly as Amber tried to get back under Quentin's shoe and balance her hot chocolate at the same time.

"What girl?"

"The one who meets a guy and marries him twelve hours later."

"Nine."

I stifled a grin.

"And a half."

I leaned forward and gave her my best hug. "But now you have Uncle Bob. Nothing is going to change his mind about how unbelievably perfect you are."

She giggled. "You might be surprised."

"Never."

"What are you guys whispering about?" Amber asked, her hair in her face as she shimmied up the back of the couch under the weight of an anvil.

Cookie leaned back and wiped at her eyes. "We're talking about the boarding school we're going to send you to if you don't start earning your keep."

Amber blew her bangs out of her face. "You have to come up with some new material, Mom. That hasn't worked on me since I was three."

"She catches on quick," I said. "So, any luck with the information Kit sent over?"

The frustrated sigh that escaped her lungs told me everything I needed to know. "Nothing. Everything they have is right. Faris was supposed to go to the park after school, and then she and her friends were going to walk to a party."

"A party her mother didn't know about," I added.

"I don't get it, though," Amber said, scanning a handful of pages, and I realized she had been going over the case with Cookie. "Why are the cops so worried about that party or the park?"

"Because according to all her friends, that's where she was going."

"Which friends?" she asked as though we'd lost it. "Certainly not the one she was texting that day."

I straightened and walked over to her. "What are you talking about?"

She pointed to a copy of Faris's texts that were in the file. "Right here. Did Kit talk to this guy? Nate something or other? Because according to these texts, they were ditching the party and meeting at a skater hangout."

Cookie thanked Reyes as he handed her a piping hot cup, then stayed to listen in.

"Amber, where does it say that?" I asked.

She pointed again as I dialed Kit's number. I still didn't see it. She was pointing to a text that said,

COP at tunnel.

Feeling like an idiot, I said, "I don't get it, hon."

Before she could explain, Kit picked up. I put her on speakerphone.

"Okay," I said, forgoing the pleasantries, "you're on speaker. Who is this Nate kid that Faris was texting?"

"We don't know," she said, sounding exhausted but not sleepy. I hadn't woken her. "She has a friend named Nathan, but he says it wasn't him in the texts. Still, there were only a few texts from Nate, and they seemed pretty innocent."

"Nuh-uh," Amber said. "There were only a few from him *as* Nate. He also texted her as Caleb, Isaiah, and Sean. It's their favorite show."

"Yeah, we couldn't find any one of her friends with those names. What do you mean their favorite show?"

"*NCIS,*" she said as though we were daft. "It's right here." She thumbed through the pages and pages of texts. "Back when he was Nate the first time."

"The first time?" I asked, trying to see what she saw.

She rummaged through the pages until she got to a set of older messages. I'd remembered them talking about *NCIS,* but how on earth did Amber get the name thing out of it?

"Right here. He tells her if her parents catch on to let him know and he will switch to the next episode."

This was getting ridiculous. I was still young, for goodness' sake. I wasn't *that* out of touch. Was I? The text read,

If PAW, will start next episode.

Clearly I was. "You're going to have to explain."

"Don't worry," she said, sympathizing with me. "Okay, this says if your parents are watching, *P-A-W,* then I'll start the next episode. I'll go to the next letter. Thankfully, when the phone company sent a copy of her texts, they sent them in order instead of by user. That's how we figured it out, because right after that, like ten seconds after, Caleb wrote this."

She pointed at a text that read,

Starting next episode now.

"Caleb," I said, realizing at last what they were doing. I'd have to go back completely and find all the transitions and texts from this same guy. "But what about a skater hangout?"

"Right here," she said, pointing for the third time to the same text,

COP at tunnel.

"Isn't that just warning her away from a tunnel? That there's a cop there?"

"No, it says *C-O-P.* 'Change of plans.' And to meet him at the Tunnel. Aka, a skater hangout. Not that I've ever been there," Amber assured her mother.

My jaw dropped open. "How did we miss this?"

Cookie shook her head, flummoxed.

"We missed it, too," Kit said. "We just thought they were planning a little underage drinking and were trying to dodge the cops."

"Which is probably exactly what he was hoping we would think," I said. "This wasn't a crime of opportunity, Kit. If Amber's right, he planned this. Got to know her through texts. Spent weeks planning the abduction."

"And he sent her pictures," Amber said. "But that's not him." She held up one of the shots he'd sent. "I can't believe she fell for that."

"Why?" I asked. "Who is it?"

"It's the Target kid. The one who got famous when a girl snapped his picture and tweeted it to her friend? It went viral?" she said, trying to clue us in. "It was, like, everywhere? And this one," she said, holding up another, "is a kid who got famous on YouTube for doing 'Paparazzi.'" When we stared at her, she added, "Lady Gaga?"

"Oh, the song," I said, finally getting it.

"Seriously, though, they don't even look alike." She compared the pictures. "What was she thinking?"

I took the seat at my desk, the one opposite Cookie. "They'd been texting for weeks. She thought she knew him."

"She thought she could trust him," Cookie said; then she looked at Amber with a new determination. "That's it. Where's your phone? You're grounded from it for seven years."

"Mom," she said with a roll of her eyes.

Kit spoke up then, sounding more energized than before. "Charley, this is it. I think you guys are on to something."

"Not me," I said, waving a hand, then pointing at Amber. "Amber Kowalski."

"And Quentin Rutherford," she added, gazing at him adoringly. It took true love to overlook drool. "He was the one who caught the *NCIS* thing. He loves that show."

"We'll check out these numbers, see what we can get. I'm sure they're burner phones, but we might get a hit on one of them."

"He went to a lot of trouble to get to Faris," I said. "He had to have known her from somewhere. Became obsessed with her. Maybe a coffee shop she and her friends frequented or even their school."

"I'll call Agent Waters, now. We're on this."

I hung up and gave Amber a high five. "You may have just saved a life, Amber."

She smiled bashfully. "I hope so."

After scouring the texts one last time, making notes based on Amber's keen eye, we scanned them all and sent them back to Kit with our observations before wandering off to bed. I led Reyes to the communal bathroom and insisted he take a long, hot shower for two reasons. One, I wanted him to relax enough to fall asleep. Eight months without a wink? Unfathomable. How was I not married to a zombie? Two, I wanted to get a jump-start on this war.

Because the rooms were so tiny, we'd had to stash Reyes's clothes in the room next to our bedroom. I'd dubbed it his dressing room. He was a prince, after all. Sure, he was a prince of the underworld, but the title still counted. I hurried inside and carried out my dastardly plan, ransacking his dresser until I found every stitch of underwear he owned. I stuffed them into a plastic grocery bag—ever a champion of recycling— tiptoed back into our bedroom, and hid them in Beep's bassinet. Then, giggling like a mental patient, I grabbed the book I'd been reading and scrambled into bed.

My insides tingled when I heard him walk down the hall. Open the door to his dressing room. Pull out a drawer. Then another. I wiggled farther into the covers when I heard his footsteps get closer.

By the time he appeared at the door, a playful grin on his face, I lay reading in bed, completely innocent of anything he might accuse me of.

He folded his arms over his chest and leaned against the doorframe. "You wouldn't happen to know where my underwear ran off to, would you?"

I closed the book and thought. And thought. Then I crinkled my nose and thought some more. "Nope," I said at last. "Weird that you don't, though, since it *is* your underwear. This could get really awkward."

He dropped the towel and my gaze darted to his glorious nether regions.

"Not for me."

Damn him and his rock-hard body. I tore my gaze away and went back to reading as he pulled on a pair of loose pajama pants, the kind that tied in front, and a powder blue T-shirt, all the while watching me like a panther readying to pounce.

"Going commando?" I asked as he crawled onto the bed. The mattress sank under his weight.

Ignoring me, he read the title of the book I kept firmly between our gazes. "*Lover Awakened*." He nestled his head on my shoulder. "Weren't you reading this book last month?"

"No."

He raised a brow.

"Yes. I can't stop. I've read it twenty-seven times in a row."

He chuckled. "Do you need to be awakened?"

" 'Parently."

"You know, you don't need a manual for that. I can walk you through it step-by-step." He ran a finger down the curve of my neck, his heat licking across my skin, soaking into my nightgown.

"That's okay," I said, fighting a grin. "This author covers the basics. Her hero seems very well informed. I think I'm getting the general idea."

"But can he do this?" He slid a hand under the covers and over my knee. Separating my legs, he wrapped one of his around one of mine, locking mine apart as he pushed the other knee, distancing them farther. He kissed my shoulder and slid his fingertips over the delicate folds between my legs, parting them, easing inside. His touch was like liquid fire. It rippled over me, settled deep inside, melted me until the warmth pooling in my abdomen ignited. I curled one fist into the sheets and opened even wider, greedy for more.

"Well, I can't say," I said breathlessly. "I've never met him. But he seems very capable."

"What about this?" He peeled back my nightgown with his free hand and took Danger's hardened nipple into his mouth. Sucking softly, he did the tongue thing. The fucking tongue thing that set me on fire. He had me squirming in seconds, begging for release as he tasted and teased.

I reached down and took hold of his rock-hard erection through the pants. He sucked in a soft breath and even through the material I could feel the blood rushing beneath my fingers. I started to turn into him, but he pulled me up from the mattress. Locking me to him from behind, he walked me to the full-length mirror, pushed my gown over my shoulders, and let it drop to the floor.

When I tried to look down, he wrapped a hand around my throat from behind and forced me to look into the mirror, as though wanting me to see what he saw. But what I saw was a very large, very round woman.

He must have sensed my misgivings. He tsked softly and placed my hands on the wall on either side of the mirror. Then he pulled a chair over with one foot and lifted one of my legs over the back of it. My toes barely touched the seat and by that point, I was shaking visibly.

He wrapped a hand around my throat again and whispered into my ear. "Now I'm going to do things to you," he said, his voice deep and smooth and accented with a brogue, and I realized he was speaking in Manx Gaelic. "Very bad things," he added, his brogue almost as sexy as he. It set my soul ablaze. "And you're going to watch." He cupped Will. Kneaded her. "And you're going to learn." He grazed his teeth over my lobe, his warm breath fanning over my cheek. "And you're going to understand exactly what it is that you do to me."

What I did to him? Was he insane? I was just thankful for the wall; otherwise, I doubted I could have stood as his erection slid between my legs, so hard it pulsed there. I started to reach under and take hold of it, but he quickly set my hand back on the wall.

"Not yet," he warned, giving my wrist a firm squeeze.

Then he did the strangest thing. He pulled back my hair, sweeping it into one hand so he could caress my face with the other. He watched me in the mirror, and while I got the feeling he wanted me to see what he saw, all I could look at was him. His eyes shimmering beneath his long lashes. His mouth full and parted ever so slightly. His jaw strong.

He dropped my hair and moved to my shoulders. Ran his fingertips over them until he came from behind and cupped Danger and Will. Massaged as he nibbled on my neck. Skimmed his fingertips over their peaks, causing a spasm of pleasure to shoot to my core.

But everywhere he touched, he left a scalding heat, and I realized he was doing it on purpose. He could control his heat, at least to some degree.

I needed to see. I needed to watch him from the other side. From the supernatural side. And while I had yet to master the leap from one plane to the other, I released the breath from my lungs, relaxed my body, and concentrated until I saw the flames that forever engulfed him. I'd seen them a couple of times before, but never like this. While normally he had blue flames licking along his skin as though he himself were an accelerant, this time he glowed with a bright orange fire. And everywhere he touched, every part of me he stroked, he left a trail of flames in his wake.

I watched mesmerized as the prince of the underworld set me ablaze. Literally.

His hands brushed over my belly, infusing his warmth deep inside me, and my legs started to give beneath my weight. I lay my head back against his shoulder as he found the cusp between my thighs again. Holding me to him with one arm, he breached the folds, brushing softly, stroking until the tinder he'd ignited in my abdomen blazed to life. I clawed at his arm, wanting more, but once again he placed my hand back on the wall.

Then he was gone.

I opened my eyes and he was on his knees in front of me. My nails dug into the plaster when he opened me further and branded me with a fiery kiss. I gasped. Pleasure pulsed through me as his tongue caused stinging tendrils to swirl inside me like a dust devil struggling to become a tornado. I sought that peak, but I didn't have to look hard. He grazed his teeth along the sensitive apex, then feathered his tongue in sweet, short sweeps, stoking the embers, coaxing me closer and closer until a riptide of raw lust engulfed me. The orgasm rocketed through me, sending out pulsating swells of unimaginable pleasure to every nerve in my body. I plunged my fingers into his hair and held him to me as the tidal wave rose to exquisite peaks, then ebbed slowly, the sharp contractions tapering off.

With the release of all that energy, I almost fell against the mirror, but Reyes was behind me at once, his quest only just beginning when he pushed his pants over his hips and entered me from behind in one long thrust. A twinge of delight leapt inside me as the orgasm that had yet to ebb entirely reignited.

He captured my gaze in the mirror, daring me to watch, his eyes sparkling with unspent passion.

And how could I not? He was magnificent. His muscles strained against the T-shirt he wore as he buried himself again and again.

He pulled me back against him, locking me there as he whispered into my ear. "Come with me again," he said in the same Gaelic brogue, the fires around him fueled by the friction our bodies created. "See what you do to me, *my ghraih*." My love.

I focused on him as his powerful strokes fanned the flames around him. His brows furrowed, his expression one of almost agony as his own climax neared. He braced one hand on the wall, clenched his jaw. His breathing grew labored as a biting pleasure brushed over my skin, nipping and scratching in rapturous delight. He thrust harder, an exquisite hunger swelling inside me, as though he could siphon the pleasure from the very marrow of my bones.

I felt it the moment he erupted inside me. He groaned as his orgasm crested, as it surged from him and into me, and then I saw it. I saw him. He exploded into a sea of flames. They consumed him and engulfed me in a torrent so savage, so volatile, I wondered if I would survive.

The air left the room, and my lungs seized. My eyes rolled back as wave after wave of scalding fire crashed into me. The desire was overwhelming and earth shattering and wonderful.

I tumbled to earth slowly and blinked back to this plane. Disentangling myself, I turned to him and focused on his impossibly handsome face.

He still had a hand braced on the wall, struggling to catch his breath as one final spasm shuddered through him. Then he stepped closer until he had me pressed into the cool mirror. He placed his forehead on the hand braced against the wall and wrapped an arm around me.

"You saw?" he asked, and I felt the tiniest ripple of insecurity radiate out of him.

"I saw. It was amazing."

He wasn't so sure. Doubt settled deep in his core. I stroked his back to assure him that everything I saw, everything he showed me was incredible, but I realized his shirt was wet. Very wet. Too wet.

I lifted my hand and gasped. It was covered in blood.

Pushing him off me, I stepped away to see what had happened, but he quickly turned until he was facing me again.

"Reyes, you're bleeding," I said, trying to turn his body.

He steeled himself, his jaw working, his gaze hard as he stared down at me. He hadn't expected me to notice anything amiss.

"That's why you're wearing a shirt." It suddenly made sense. That little niggling in the back of my mind as he'd made love to me half dressed. That just didn't happen often. "Take it off."

"I'm fine," he said, jerking the pajama pants into place and tying them.

I did the same. I picked up my nightgown and slipped it over my head. "Wonderful. Then show me."

"Dutch," he said as though in warning, turning to face me when I tried to come around again.

But I saw the long streaks of blood in the mirror. Slashes that started at one shoulder, cut across his back, and ended under his rib cage. Claw slashes that only a bear or a hellhound could inflict.

I erupted in anger. "Take off your shirt or I'll take it off for you."

He knew I could. He knew I could completely incapacitate him with one word. But instead of the explosion I'd expected, he stilled. His lids narrowed, but not out of anger. An emotion more like pride spilled out of him. One corner of his sensual mouth tilted up, but he shook his head nonetheless. "No. You've seen enough over the past few months. I won't have you exposed to the depths of my stupidity."

The anger inside me dissipated immediately. "Mr. Farrow," I said, twirling my finger, instructing him to turn around, "the depths of your stupidity are the least of my concerns."

With a resigned sigh, he lifted the shirt over his head, his muscles bunching as he did so, and turned to face the mirror. And that was when I decided to take up gardening as I planted my face in the floor behind him.

"It's hormones," I said when Osh brought me a glass of water.

He had apparently been headed to the bathroom for a shower when he heard a thunderous crack and the ground shook beneath his feet—his words. Surely my fall wasn't that thunderous.

"I just got light-headed."

He winked at me, his signature top hat back in place, since the wedding festivities were over. Reyes held a cold rag to my temple, his expression severe. I'd scared him. I'd scared me too, but not for my own sake.

"I fell on Beep." I poked my belly, hoping she'd respond. "Do you think she's okay?"

"Better than you, *loca.*" Angel had dropped in, too, because I needed to be insulted as well as disoriented and humiliated.

"Angel Garza," I said, pointing at him threateningly. "I can do things now. Scary things."

He raised his hands, the boyish grin he wore perforating my heart.

"Duct tape?" I asked Osh.

He raised it, then tore off a strip to tape up Reyes's back. He'd been wearing duct tape under the dark gray T-shirt he had on earlier. I knew I'd seen odd lines across his back. But, thinking he'd healed for the most part, he peeled it off when he took a shower. He was wrong. His back bore two long slashes across it with four gashes each. One set extended from his shoulder to just under his rib cage. The other across the small of his back. The hellhounds' claws were like razor blades and the cuts were bone deep. Which would explain my sudden but blessedly short departure from reality.

"I think if I were you," Angel said to Reyes, "I'd stop trying to cuddle with hellhounds."

Reyes shot him a glare that didn't even faze him. Normally, Angel was scared to death of my husband. Clearly, they'd grown close enough in the last few months to give Angel's mouth free rein.

"If this happened yesterday," I said as Reyes bit down, steeling himself against the pain of Osh's administrations, "why are you not healing faster?"

Osh answered for him. "Because he's not sleeping. He hasn't been in stasis for months."

"Reyes," I said, drawing his gaze, "you have to sleep. Why aren't you sleeping? Eight months? How is that even possible?"

Osh applied one final piece of duct tape, then slapped it into place, causing a muted groan to escape his patient. "Good as new," he said. Then he grew serious. "But if this gets nasty, he'll be no use to us in this condition." He winked at me before grabbing his supplies and leaving.

"I'll be around," Angel said. "Just shout if you need me."

"Why?" I asked before he could disappear.

"Why?"

"Why are you here? What are you two up to?"

I didn't miss the warning glare that Reyes flashed him. He chewed on his lower lip, and said, "I'm just looking out for you."

Before I could push the subject, he vanished.

I crossed my arms over my chest and focused on my husband. "Why are you not sleeping?" I asked him, deciding to address his health instead of my curiosity about what Reyes had been up to with Angel.

He eased onto the bed, his large frame taking up most of its surface. "I can't let my guard down."

"Reyes," I said, straddling his hips, not an easy feat in my current state, "Osh was right. If you don't sleep, you won't be able to bring your A-game should things go south out here. It's like we're in a pot of hot water and someone is slowly turning up the heat. We can't stay out here forever. The hounds will figure out a way in. I can feel it."

His mouth widened into an appreciative grin when I crawled onto him, as though completely dismissing everything I'd just said. He rested his hands on my hips. "I'm learning about them," he said at last.

I leaned over him, tucked a lock of hair over his ear, ran my fingers along the outline of his lips. "About who?"

"The hounds. I'm learning how to fight them."

I bolted upright. "Is that why you continued to antagonize them even after you realized the holy ground wouldn't kill them?"

He lifted a playful brow. "Antagonize them?"

"You know what I mean."

"Something like that."

"But you're stopping, right? You said you're stopping."

"I'm stopping."

I lay down beside him. "What happened when you pulled them onto holy ground? I mean, did they writhe in agony?" I bounced up. "Did they smoke like the ground was burning the flesh off their bodies?"

He tucked an arm behind his head in thought. "That's just it," he said, his voice curious. "It didn't seem to faze them at all."

"I don't understand. The consecrated soil didn't hurt them?"

He shook his head. "Not even a little."

I lay awake, listening to Reyes's even breathing, but I now knew he was faking it. Had been faking it for eight months. My right foot was more asleep than he was. His revelation about the hellhounds kept my mind racing in overdrive. If the ground didn't hurt them, then why weren't they crossing it to rip out our throats? Maybe it did hurt them, just not visibly. They were freaking hard to see. Perhaps they were more focused on tearing my husband apart.

Or maybe they were simply waiting, patrolling the border to keep tabs on us. But why? What could they be waiting on?

My phone rang, but due to the limited number of electrical outlets in the room, Piper, my phone, was way across the other side. True, the room was tiny, but I'd still have to get out of bed to answer her summons.

I tried to roll out of Reyes's arms. He tightened his hold. I tried to lift an arm off me, but he clasped his fingers, essentially locking me in.

"Reyes," I said, stifling a giggle, "I know you're awake. You can give up the game."

"Never," he said into his pillow.

I laughed and leaned all my weight forward until he finally let go. By the time I got to Piper, my voice mail had picked up. It was Uncle Bob, so I put on my robe, tiptoed out of the room, and called him right back.

"Are you still at work?" I asked him, looking at the clock before I closed the door to a pretend sleeping Reyes. It was 1:32 A.M.

"We found him," he said, his voice hurried. "You won't believe this. He works for the Vatican."

"No," I said, adding a flare of astonishment to my voice.

"Freaking hell, Charley, did you already know that? Are you the one who called in with the tip?"

"No." Though I sounded super convincing, Ubie didn't buy it.

"Charley—"

"I suspected. It's a long story. So, what's going on?"

"We can't hold him, hon. He says he had nothing to do with the murder. Says your dad was following him, not the other way around. But we do have enough to charge him with stalking if you will press charges. Just say the word, pumpkin."

"Does he know anything about Dad's murder?"

Uncle Bob let out a long breath. "He says no. Says your dad threatened him if he didn't stop following you, then that's the last he saw of him."

"He's lying."

"How do you know?"

"Because, he wasn't just following me. Look at the pictures in his apartment."

"What pictures? There aren't any."

Damn it. He got rid of the evidence. Must have sent it all back to his boss at the Vatican. "He had pictures of Dad on his wall."

"You've been stuck at that convent for eight months. How do you know that?"

"I've been working with someone on it."

"Even after I asked you not to?"

"Kind of. He had pictures of Dad."

"Well, we got nothing now. And because he checks out, I can't hold him."

An idea hit me hard. As well as the corner of a hutch as I tried to traverse the house in the dark. I walked into the living room to hang with Mr. Wong.

"Put him on the phone," I said.

"Charley, I can't do that."

"Tell him who you're talking to and tell him Father Glenn sends his love." I'd suspected he knew Father Glenn, a man I'd helped with a nest of demons a few months ago, for a while now. He was the one who told me about the file the Vatican had on me. I wondered if they were connected somehow.

"Okay. Hold on."

After a few minutes, a timid male voice came on the phone. "Hello?"

"Hey, Blondie," I said, "been stalking anyone I know lately?"

"I don't know what you're talking about."

"Have you told the Vatican yet?"

"Told them what?"

"That your cover has been blown."

"Again, I don't know what—"

"How about we skip all this and get to the heart of the matter?" I didn't give him time to respond. I was hoping to disorient him so he'd slip up. "You tell my uncle, and you know damned well he's my uncle, who was following my dad. You had pictures of him and another man. Hand those over, and I won't tell anyone at the Vatican what a royal fuckup you are, *capisce*?"

He didn't say anything, which meant he was considering my offer.

"In turn, you can keep doing your Vatican crap, whatever the hell that's all about, and just do a few side jobs for me every once in a while, starting with a nun that died at this convent. I want her name and what happened to her. I also want to know what kind of trouble the priest that vanished was in."

"Which convent?"

"Dude, seriously, if you start playing games with me now, I will stop your heart in your chest. Funny thing is, you know I can do it. You've been stalking me for years. How do you think that makes me feel?"

Silence.

"Angry, Howard. It makes me feel angry."

"If they find out—"

"You'll lose your job?" I scoffed. "You're about to lose it anyway. You've been busted by your mark. A mark who is going to rain hellfire down on your boss's city. How do you think that will end?"

"I'm just an observer. I don't do research."

"Bullshit. Try again."

He sat thinking over his options, but the fact was, he didn't have any. Not if he didn't want to lose his cushy job.

"O—"

Before he could even finish the *okay* part, I said, "Get that picture you have of my dad and that other man to my uncle tonight and find out about the nun and the priest. You have two hours."

When I was met with only silence again, I said, "Howard, give the phone back to my uncle now. You're burning moonlight."

"What did he say?" Uncle Bob asked as he walked away from Howard. I could hear his footsteps in the background. "Is he going to cooperate?"

"He didn't have anything to do with Dad's death, but I think he might have a photo of someone who did. Dad seemed to be confronting a guy, and they both looked angry. He's going to give you that photo, but you have to let him go. Like immediately." I was so excited to be getting somewhere on my dad's case, I didn't want to waste another moment.

"You got it, pumpkin. What are you going to say if Reyes finds out you've been working on this case? He is afraid doing so will put you in danger."

"He won't find out. Don't worry about me."

"I like him. He's . . . a good man."

"Thanks, Ubie. I like him, too."

"Oh!" I almost forgot. "I'm sure he already knows it, but make sure Howard has my phone number. I'm expecting a call."

"Do I need to stay on him?" he asked.

"I don't think so. Once you get that photo and anything else he has on Dad, you need to come have sex with your wife."

"Charley," he said, and I could almost feel his cheeks heat up.

"I'm telling you, she's out here with three—no, four if you count Quentin, which why wouldn't you?—of the sexiest men on the planet. Just sayin'."

"I'll be there in an hour."

"It takes an hour to get here and you still have to get that photo."

"That's what sirens and flashing lights are for."

10

I decided to work on the door to the locked closet again while I waited for Vatican Boy's phone call. He'd better come through, or I was totally marking him. Not with anything bad. I'd give him a designation like head toilet bowl cleaner at the Pit, Albuquerque's sports complex. Man, that would suck. Though I was pretty sure the designation thing didn't exactly work that way, it was a thought.

I walked to the laundry room, this time with a flashlight, and studied the door from top to bottom. How was it even locked? There was no doorknob, no latch. And what would be the purpose of it locking from the inside? Then the occupant couldn't get out.

I gasped. That was it. Maybe someone was locked inside and they'd suffocated or starved to death. Maybe it was the priest. Maybe that was how he'd vanished.

This was getting exciting. I lowered myself onto all fours and shone the light under the door, hoping to catch a glimpse inside. Nothing. It was sealed tight.

Beep decided to practice the splits while I was down there. I crawled to the washing machine for leverage. Getting up was not so easy as it had once been. But since I was already in the vicinity, I decided to do a load of laundry.

Denise's voice scared the crap out of me. I startled when she said, "I was going to do that. I'm washing all the baby stuff and getting it ready."

"Wow, you don't give up, do you?"

"I have no intention of losing you."

Gemma was right. I felt Denise's loneliness cut through to my marrow. But whose freaking fault was that?

"Is Gemma with you?"

"No, I drove. Your friend Lando Calrissian gave me a room. It has a cot."

"Lando?"

"Long black hair, looks like he's still in high school?"

"Osh. His name is Osh. Lando is—"

"I know who Lando is."

"Oh. Well—"

"Are you taking your vitamins?"

"Yup."

She nodded. "Have you had cramping? Any spotting?"

"Nope." When she only nodded again, I said, "Okay, then. I'm going to go . . . do stuff. Other stuff. Somewhere else."

I couldn't miss the relief she felt when I didn't throw her out. I was not forgiving her. I refused. But she could do my laundry if she wanted. And, maybe, help with Beep when she arrived. All babies need a grandmother.

"You should get some rest," she said.

"I'm waiting on a phone call about a case. But the minute I get it—"

"A case? You're still working cases?"

"'Parently."

She started to chastise me. I could see it on her face. She wore scorn like a trophy wife wore Louis Vuitton. Instead, she lifted a shirt out of a laundry basket that said DEAR DIARY, HAD TO CUT A BITCH TODAY and didn't say a word. No terms of aghastment. No scathing remark. It was weird, and I was more convinced than ever that she was possessed.

I decided to wait for the call in the theater room, which was really a few chairs and a television. I ended up curled into a recliner and watching an episode of *Andy Griffith* when my husband walked in. I eyed him. Yep, I could do him again.

He walked into the theater wearing the lounge pants and nothing else. Even his feet were sexy. But now I understood the scruffiness of his appearance. The sleep-deprived features.

"You're not coming back up?" he asked.

"I'm waiting for a call."

He nodded, picked up a magazine with Oprah on the cover, and sat in the chair beside me. "You know," he said right as Opie was going to knock some birds out of a tree. Such a bad boy. "You can tell me anything."

I snorted. "No, I can't."

He stopped and gave me his full attention. "Why would you say that?"

He was magnificent, and I didn't want to disappoint him. But now was as good a time as any. The thought of what I was about to do to him—to us—saddened me. I was about to turn his world upside down, but he needed to know what I'd done.

My nerves jumped to attention. My heart raced. He would hate me come morning. But where could he go? We'd be stuck in the same house for God knew how long, hating each other. Or, well, him hating me. I could never hate him. Not even if he ate the last Oreo, though that would be pushing it. "What if I told you—?"

My phone rang. I paused midsentence, swallowed back my fear, and picked up my phone. I had been given a momentary stay of execution, and I damned well was going to take it.

"It's Howard," the voice on the other end said.

"I figured as much. What did you find out?"

"There was a novice there, about to take her vows when she accused a priest of molesting her."

"Let me guess, the priest who went missing."

"Yes. But nothing ever came of her charges, and there's nothing about anyone dying there. Not a young nun anyway. The novice was excommunicated."

"Of course, she was." I stood and paced the room. "Coming forward to accuse a priest of misconduct back then usually meant excommunication." That would explain why her death had not been recorded. But how did she die? Did the priest kill her and then disappear? "What was her name?"

"Bea Heedles."

"Sister Bea?"

"I think she went by Sister Beatrice. So, is that all?" he asked.

"Did you get the picture to my uncle?"

The moment I asked, I heard a car pull up. That would be Ubie. Reyes stood to open the door.

"Yes. I did as you asked." I could hear the resentment in his voice.

"Okay, then answer me this: Why?"

"Why what?"

"Why does the Vatican—I mean, seriously, *the Vatican*—have a file on me?"

"I'm just the observer," he said, trying to pull that innocent-as-the-driven crap again.

"Howard, if this relationship is going to work, we have to be honest with each other. So I, honestly, will let your heart keep beating if you stop bullshitting me."

He took a long moment to get back to me. When he did, his voice was a tad more reverent than before. I'd take it.

"All I know is that you are of interest to them. They— They have prophecies, and apparently when you were born, all the predictions started to come true."

"How did they find out about me in the first place?"

"We have people, too," he said. "People like you. People with gifts. They, they saw you, I guess."

I knew that they paid very close attention to what Sister Mary Elizabeth had to say. They'd wanted her in Italy when she was a novice, but she wanted to stay in New Mexico, near the girl causing all the uproar in heaven. Were there more like her?

"What about you? Do you have gifts?"

"No," he said.

Uncle Bob came in, gave me a peck on the cheek, then went upstairs to find his wife. Cookie was about to get a nice surprise. Reyes walked up behind me and draped his arms over the back of the recliner so he could rub my Beep bump. His hands felt wonderful. His heat soothing.

"What about other . . . people like me?" I asked. "Do you know about them?"

"There are no other people like you."

"No, I mean, what about other people they observe. How many are there?"

"Look, I was hired to observe you and report back. That's it."

"That doesn't answer my question."

"I know that your husband is special, too."

He had that right. He was busy nibbling on my earlobe, causing ripples of pleasure to race over my skin.

"Do you know what he is?"

"I know that he's from hell."

I stilled. That was more than I thought he'd know. "Is the Vatican aware?"

He'd grown more hesitant as the conversation wore on. I sensed a spark of fear in his voice, but he soldiered on. "Everything about you goes into my reports."

"Will they take any action?" What would they do, really? What could they do? But I needed to know if this was going to be an issue.

"I have no idea. I don't have that kind of clearance."

I believed him. I also believed that this guy was going to come in handy.

"Howard," I said, letting a smile spread across my face. "I think we're going to have a long and beautiful relationship."

"But I thought—"

"How many years have you been stalking me?"

After another long pause, he said, "Observing. Seven."

Holy cow, how did I not know these things? I was so oblivious sometimes. "Then the way I see it, you owe me seven years of indentured servitude."

"Crap," he said.

"You'll be like a double agent. It'll be fun!"

"I'm going to hell."

"Not anytime soon, you're not. I need you, buddy. It's you and me against the world. Oh, hey, so do you know how to kill a hellhound?"

Determined to stay up with Reyes—if he couldn't sleep, I couldn't sleep—I fell asleep in the theater room about five minutes after we snuggled together and he started rubbing my Beep bump again. I remember being lifted—and thankful that I was only dreaming that I was being airlifted—and carried to our room. I woke up a few hours later to an empty bed.

The sun was just breaching the horizon when I put on my robe and padded down the hall to find the community toilet. I peed and was in the process of brushing my teeth when I looked out the postage stamp window. I had a view from the back of the house. All the wedding goers had left and only an occasional flower or silken streamer remained as evidence of Cookie's special day.

I started back for the mirror, as my tongue was on fire—freaking cinnamon toothpaste—when I noticed a movement along the tree line. It was Reyes and he was sneaking out. To go fight another hellhound? Hadn't he proved that dragging them onto sacred ground wouldn't kill them? Maybe he was meeting that traitor Angel again.

I rinsed and spit, waving a hand in front of my face as I rushed into the darkened bedroom to throw on some clothes and hurried down the stairs. Denise was up, making breakfast. I ran, kind of, past her, then stopped and turned.

"You made bacon?" I asked, my mouth watering.

"It's veggie bacon."

"Isn't that an oxymoron?"

"Do you want to try it?"

I eyed it distrustfully. "I'm not sure."

"Sit down, I'll fix you a plate."

"No time. I have to catch my husband in the act." In the act of what, I had no idea, but I was damned well about to find out.

She pursed her lips as I grabbed a piece and ran, kind of, out the door. "Okay, I'll keep it warm," she said.

"Thanks!" I said, not too loud, though. I had to be like a grasshopper on the wind. No! I had to *be* the wind.

Initializing stealth mode: now.

I skirted the tree line to get to where I'd been the day before. I had a pretty good view from there. I really just wanted to make sure my psychotic, sleep-deprived husband wasn't wrestling hellhounds. That would have been such a great metaphor if it weren't real. I'd have to remember it. Use it metaphorically later.

I climbed through the trees, all the while keeping a sharp eye on the drop-off. It still boggled my mind that Reyes didn't notice me right off. If I was so bright, how could he miss me? But there he was, walking through the clearing that was supposedly beyond the border. Freaking Osh. He'd been in on whatever was going on from the first.

Reyes stopped in the middle of the clearing and Angel appeared. He'd summoned him! My investigator. I felt violated. Betrayed. Trampled on like a used napkin at the Frontier, my favorite restaurant.

The Frontier.

I started to drool again as I watched them. Easing over a fallen log and negotiating the uneven ground, I kept my head down and my breathing steady. No idea why. I totally felt like a sniper in the marines. Only I was pregnant. Other than that, and the fact that I couldn't snipe if they'd paid me to, I embodied all that a sniper should be. Stealth. Grace. The patience of a panther on the prowl. Gawd, I had to pee.

A face in my periphery caught my attention. It was the nun. She snuck up beside me and, following my lead, kept a close vigil on the men below. I finally got a good look at her, albeit from my periphery. I didn't want to scare her off.

She had a tiny, upturned nose, a soft face that still had the puffiness of youth, and a small, pretty mouth. The veil she wore covered her hair, but even through the grayness of her coloring, I could tell her eyebrows were light brown and her eyes hazel. We both kept our gazes locked on our targets as Reyes and Angel talked.

An idea hit me, and I finally turned to her. "Can you maybe pop down there and listen in?"

Without taking her eyes off me, she shook her head.

That was disappointing. "Can you read lips?"

No again, only this time she fought the twitching of a grin. Okay. Two could play that game.

"Then can you run up to them, jerk their pants down, then run away?"

She giggled softly. Then she was standing about ten feet from me. I decided to give up on my sniper career and see where Sister Beatrice took me today.

"Okay, but seriously, you have to wait for me this time. I mean it."

She kept disappearing and reappearing farther down the overgrown path. If it ever was a path. We went deeper and deeper into the woods, but I had yet to come across the string that marked the border. Even so, the growls in the distance grew louder with each step I took.

"Beatrice!" I said, calling out to her. I'd lost her again and I needed to catch my breath. But before that could happen, she appeared beside me. My heart tried to leap out of my chest. I pressed a hand to hold it in and took a few deep breaths. "All right, Sister. What are you trying to show me?"

She pointed down. I followed her line of sight to the ground beneath me and realized I was standing on slats. Wooden slats. I knelt down and brushed the dirt and leaves away. I couldn't be certain without a flashlight, but it could have been a well.

"What's down there, sweetheart?"

Her gaze dropped to her saddle shoes, her hands wringing nervously.

"Is it you?" I asked. Did the priest kill her and dump her body in a well?

Without looking at me, she shook her head.

It hit me then. I sat back on one leg. "Is it him?" I asked her. "Is it the priest?"

She closed her eyes as shame consumed her. I had to admit, I didn't expect that. Did she kill him? Or maybe he attacked her and she'd defended herself. It could have been any number of situations.

"Can you tell me what happened?"

She stepped forward and held out her hand. I took it, but wasn't sure what she wanted until she nodded and closed her eyes. She was allowing me access to her memories.

They catapulted me back to a moonless night slick with freezing rain.

I saw her journey through her eyes as she ran. Fear thundered through her. As she climbed as high and as fast as she could, her shoes slipped in the mud. But someone caught her wrist. Someone else was with her. Another young novice like herself. One whom she loved with all her heart and soul. It was hard to see her clearly through the rain, but the nun had features similar to Beatrice's. And she was just as scared.

Beatrice's fear paralyzed me. Her heart beat so hard, it hurt. He was going to kill her. He was going to kill them both. One of them, and he didn't know which, had written to the bishop, accused him of forcing himself upon her. He'd been drunk, he said. He didn't remember doing it, he said, let alone which girl it was. But he was not about to lose his entire career, his livelihood, over a whore. And since he didn't know which one he'd accosted, he was going to kill them both. They saw it in his eyes when he asked them for help with a pen outside. They'd gone with him, feeling safe since there were two of them. They'd been wrong.

He swung a hammer, hitting Beatrice's friend on the temple, and they ran into the night. Holding hands, they found a spot and hid from him. But he was not about to give up the search easily. He kept at it for what seemed like hours. Eventually, he found them.

The girl she was with motioned for her to run and then lunged at the priest. Beatrice couldn't, though. She couldn't run. She couldn't leave her friend. Instead, she attacked the man from behind. He was choking her friend. She beat his head with her fists and scratched at his eyes, but he elbowed her in the face. The force knocked her back against a tree and she lost consciousness for a precious few seconds. When she came to, her friend lay motionless, his fingers so tight around her throat, she'd turned blue.

He shook the girl, squeezing the last remnants of life out of her as hard as he could, then let her go and came after Beatrice. She no longer cared. She gaped at her friend, unable to process the fact that she was gone.

The priest walked toward her slowly, suddenly interested in her again. He would have his way with her before he killed her. Or after. Either way, he would win.

No, she thought. She brought out the knife she'd taken from the kitchen. The one she'd been carrying around since that night. To use on him. To protect herself. But she decided to use it on a part of him instead. The baby he'd left inside her body. He stopped and watched as she took the knife into both hands and plunged it into her abdomen.

He watched for a while, surprised, then shrugged. She'd done the work for him. When she fell to her knees, a searing pain paralyzing her, he walked back to the girl and dragged her higher up the mountain. Beatrice watched as he pulled back a wooden cover of some kind and dropped her friend into a well. He turned to come back for her, but the rain had softened the ground. He slid, caught himself, then slid again and toppled over the side and into the well.

She heard him groaning at first; then he came to and started yelling for her to get help. Instead, she crawled to the well, her hands and stomach covered in blood, and pushed the wooden cover with all her might until it canopied the entrance. His screams faded as the barrier slid into place, but they were still audible. So she worked for an hour, dragging dirt and grass and tree branches to cover the wood. To insulate the sound.

Finally, his screams were barely a whisper on the wind. With grief consuming her, she walked farther into the woods until the sun came up and drenched her in its light. Dreaming that it was God. Dreaming that he would forgive her, that he would touch her face as gently as the sun and welcome her home. She took her last breath thinking only of one person. Her twin sister. The girl lying at the bottom of a well with a murderer.

Her heart contracted for the last time, and then she was no longer cold.

I jerked away from her, fought to catch my breath, struggled to keep at bay the wetness threatening to spill over my lashes. I lost. Fat, hot tears streaked down my face as I looked at her.

"Beatrice, I'm so sorry."

She shook her head. Pointed to herself, and finger-spelled, "Mo."

"Mo? That's Beatrice in the well?"

She nodded.

"Are you Deaf?"

She shook her head, curled one small hand into a fist and held it over her mouth.

"You're mute. And your sister?"

Her signing was archaic and not really American Sign Language. It was a jumble of signs she'd probably done at home with her family, gestures, and ASL. I did understand that her sister could talk, but that night, she didn't want the priest to know which girl he'd raped. So she'd refused to talk, refused to give away which sister was the threat. She'd given up her life for her twin, who had been mute most of her life. The priest knew that, and had believed that disability would keep her from speaking up for herself. He'd been wrong.

"Mo, I'm so sorry."

She was crying, too. All the emotions I felt came straight from her. Her heart had been ripped out that night. Her life and her happiness stolen. But the worst part was the loss of her beloved sister.

She signed to me again, and it took three times for me to figure out what she was asking. I felt stupid and inept for making her repeat herself so much. But I finally figured out she was asking me if God hated her because she let a man lie with her. Because she got her sister killed and then killed herself. Because she took away the life he'd given her.

"Can he forgive me?" she asked. "If I do something good?"

"Oh, sweetheart," I said, standing up, after some effort, and hugging her. "He doesn't hate you. I promise with all my heart. You did do something good. You tried to save your sister." I set her at arm's length. "You can cross through me if—"

I heard something before I could finish. A crack. A sharp crack. Like wood. And I thought to myself, wouldn't it be crazy if—?

Yep. The cover broke beneath my weight. My eyes wide, I gazed at Mo. She gazed back. Then I dropped.

11

The wood didn't exactly break cleanly. It scraped across my back and arms as I fell, but I managed to grab hold of a slat on the way down. I hung there, my legs dangling. A jagged point had torn into my face by my ear and up across my forehead. I didn't realize it until my vision blurred due to the blood gushing from my head.

Mo tried to pull me up, but there was simply no way. I weighed too much. It was Beep's fault. Apparently, she weighed around eighty-seven pounds. My ribs burned and I had a difficult time breathing, but I took in a lungful of air and was just about to scream for my husband when the plank I held on to for dear life broke.

I dropped longer than I thought I would have, falling into a deep pit of darkness. In that instant, I prayed there would be water at the bottom. My prayers were not answered. I hit hard. My legs crumpled beneath me. My hips exploded with pain as my femurs drove into the sockets by the force of the sudden stop. The drop knocked the air from my lungs, and I raised my arms over my head, trying to catch my breath. Both

those tasks caused jolts of excruciating pain in my side. I'd cracked a rib.
Possibly more.

The ground was uneven beneath me, and in the back of my mind I
knew I was sitting atop the bones of at least two people. I fell back against
the side of the well. Most wells in the area weren't dug so wide. They were
just wide enough for small children or animals to fall in. This was a bona
fide well with lots of elbow room. I was lucky. I could have been stuck in
a pipeline. Beep could have died.

Mo appeared beside me. My question was, why didn't Reyes? He loved
to pop in when I was in mortal peril. What the heck?

There was just enough space for Mo to stand beside me. Had she been
alive, it would have been terribly cramped. As it was, she could stand half
inside the wall of the well.

I glanced around and could see two things. The round top of the well,
which reminded me of a horror movie I'd seen, and Mo. I could've seen
Mo no matter how much light I had. Or didn't have. But the light seemed
to stop about halfway down the well.

Tree roots zigzagged across the opening above me. That would explain
some of the burning I felt on my back and arms. And I honestly didn't
know if I was sitting on more roots or bones. Either way, this was not a
place I wanted to stay long.

"Reyes," I said weakly. Screaming for help was no longer an option.

"I'll go get help," Mo signed, but before she could go, Reyes appeared
at last, his incorporeal form shrouded in a massive undulating robe. It
filled any leftover space.

Mo fell back against the side of the well, her eyes wide.

"It's okay, hon," I said through gritted teeth. "He's with me."

His incorporeal form disappeared, and I heard someone running and
then sliding to a halt above us. Dirt trickled down from overhead.

"What the hell, Dutch?" Reyes asked.

I was in too much pain to offer a smart-assed comeback. And though there was no water in the well, I was wet. Very wet. I closed my eyes, mortified. My water had broken. This could not be good.

I heard Reyes whisper above me, the sound echoing around me, the walls like an amphitheater. "Osh'ekiel," he said.

Osh would be there soon. He'd probably bring Garrett as well if he was still at the house.

I was safe. I knew I was safe. With that thought, I decided to drift off for a while. Regain my strength. Gather my thoughts.

Reyes yelled at me, but I couldn't stop my fall into oblivion. It certainly felt better there.

I heard arguing overhead. Every once in a while, a voice would drift down to me. Osh. Garrett. Uncle Bob. Poor Ubie. Reyes and Cookie argued with him. He wanted to risk it and have me medevaced to Albuquerque. He didn't understand the consequences of such an action. It might take the hellhounds a while to find me, but find me they would.

I didn't care at that moment, though. If it would save Beep, then we needed to risk it. I tried to tell Reyes that, but no one was listening to me.

"Charley!" Cookie called out to me. She was hysterical, racked with sobs. I felt bad that I was causing such uproar.

"I'm okay," I said, and looked over at Mo.

"What can I do?" she asked. Either that or she said I needed to dye my hair. Maybe it was time. I was getting older now. Had a family and a kid. Almost. I needed to be more adultlike. Dye my hair. Get my nails done. Go to water aerobics.

"What the fuck?" Osh asked me.

He grinned down at me from up high. It actually wasn't so deep as the fall that lasted forever would have me believe, but it was deep enough to make getting me out of there a problem.

There it was again. A pain across my stomach and abdomen that crept around to my back. Crap on a cracker. I was in labor.

"So, guys," I said, looking up at heads in a circle. It would have been comical if— Who was I kidding? It was comical. "My water broke. I'm in labor, so if we could just hurry this along. Also, I think I broke a rib. Or two. And possibly my hips. And my ankle hurts."

"The way I see it," Osh said, "you got yourself into this mess. You can get yourself out of it."

Cookie whacked the back of his head.

"Just kidding."

"Who's the girl?" Quentin asked, his signs difficult to read from my vantage.

I tried to sign back, to no avail. "Amber, can you tell Quentin this is Mo? She's mute but uses mostly home signs. I need a Deaf interpreter."

She relayed my message and I could hear Artemis whimpering in the background. I was surprised she wasn't down here with me. After a moment, Quentin nodded.

"Okay," I said, looking at Mo, "are there any neighbors close by with a rope of some kind?"

"Yes," she said, pointing repeatedly. I'd been at the convent all this time but had no way of visiting our neighbors. Even if I could have ventured out, we were trying to keep to ourselves, to allay any questions our new neighbors might have about why we were living there, so I had no idea what lay beyond our holy border. "Quentin, can you let her lead you to them? We need rope and boiling water."

"Why boiling water?" he asked.

"I don't know. They just always boil water when someone's having a baby."

"Not the boiling water," Reyes said to Quentin. "But we do need rope or ties or, better yet, mountain climbing gear, but that's aiming high."

He nodded and Mo disappeared to lead them to the closest neighbors. Hopefully they'd have at least one item on our list.

"Can you lift me out of here?" I asked Reyes, only half teasing.

He didn't smile. "How are you?"

"I'm okay. I need some ibuprofen. Or some morphine."

He nodded. "I've called Katherine."

"Katherine the Midwife. You have to say her full name."

"She's on the way," he continued without even cracking a smile. I was losing my touch. "But it'll take her almost an hour to get here."

"Okay. I'll wait," I said, just as another spasm ripped through me. It made breathing impossible with the rib situation. I grabbed hold of a tree root—hopefully—nearby and squeezed.

"Lower me down," I heard someone say. "I was a pediatrics nurse, and I even helped deliver a few babies in my day. I need to check her."

No way. They were going to put me in an enclosed area with Denise?

"This won't hold," Reyes said.

"It won't hold you, but it'll hold me. We're risking the baby's life."

"If it doesn't and you fall onto her—"

"I won't. I'm the smallest one here besides Amber, and I'm pretty sure she wouldn't know what to look for."

I drifted away again, wondering how far under the dirt the bones were. Someone needed to know that they were here.

I looked up to tell them, but found myself staring at a butt. A butt I'd recognize anywhere. It was Denise's, and she was being lowered with sheets that had been tied together. She was so going to fall on me. I closed my eyes as dirt tumbled down on me, and it felt good and I fell into oblivion again until an excruciating pain jerked me out of it.

"I hate labor!" I yelled, but it came out as a whisper.

"Here," I heard Denise say before feeling the rim of a water bottle at my mouth. She'd brought Katherine the Midwife's case with her. "I called Gemma. She's on the way, sweetheart. You just hang in there."

I pushed it away. "Were you possessed? Is that why you're being nice to me?"

She laughed softly. Like laughed. At something I said. Oh yeah. She was possessed. Bedeviled. Entangled in Satan's snare.

She lifted a bottle to my mouth again. "Just a tiny sip," she said. "Once you go into hard labor, you can't eat or drink anything. I need to see how far along you are, but it's too cramped."

"I was fine until you showed up."

"Can you get onto your knees?"

Now she was just expecting miracles. "My femurs have been shoved into my hip sockets."

"If that were true, you would be screaming in agony. You may have pulled some tendons, though, so be very, very careful."

She was standing over me and slowly slid to her knees. Moving one of my legs, she parted it at the knee, and while it hurt, it wasn't excruciating. She tried the other one, with the same results. "If I pull your arms, can you grab hold of my shoulders and get into a crouching position? It'll help with delivery if it comes to that."

"Delivery?" I asked, my voice an octave higher than normal. "No way."

"Hon, we may not have a choice. We need to be prepared."

"Like the Boy Scouts."

"Exactly."

"Okay, I can try."

"First we're going to have to get your pants off."

"Oh, hell no," I said, suddenly self-conscious. "We have an audience."

"And we," she said, smiling at me, "have a sheet. Several, in fact."

With Denise's help, I got onto my knees and we managed to get my pants off me.

"Can't the guys just lift me out of here with the sheets?"

"No, it's too big of a risk. If you fall again—"

"You could have fallen on me. Why was that not a risk?"

"Charley, every risk has to be weighed. It was riskier for you and for the baby for me not to come down here and check you. But it's riskier for you both if the sheets don't hold and you fall again. What is that?"

She pointed to my left. I'd been sitting on a skull. "So that's what that was. Killed my tailbone."

"Is that—?"

"A skull. Yes, we have to tell people. There are two bodies down here." Even in the low light, Denise's face paled visibly. It was awesome.

"You okay?" I asked.

"Yes, We need to get a sheet under you, then I'm going to check you."

It took some creative thinking, but we managed to get the sheet mostly underneath me.

She'd brought gloves from Katherine the Midwife's stash and put them on. "Can you straighten up just a bit?"

I grabbed a protruding root and straightened as much as I could. A blistering hot pain shot through me. Every part of my body hurt, but she was able to get a hand between my parted legs. "Okay, you are at about a seven with ninety percent effacement."

"Should I push? I don't want to push too early. I've heard stories."

Reyes's heat felt good. I could feel it from where I sat.

"How long was she out?" she asked Cookie.

"About an hour."

"An hour?" I asked, surprised. "It felt like minutes." I fell onto my palms again, my head resting in her lap as a spasm of pain clawed at me and squeezed my midsection like I was a bottle of ketchup. I gritted my teeth and sucked air in and out through them. My hands curled around handfuls of the sheet until the pain began to subside.

"Charley," Cookie said from overhead. "I can't believe this is happening."

"Me neither."

"Do you remember that time we went to the movie and that woman went into labor but she wouldn't leave because she didn't want to miss the ending and then, bam, it was too late?"

"Oh yeah. That was crazy. That ending sucked."

"Right?"

"Do you want to tell me what you were doing out here?" Reyes asked.

"I was following you."

"Why?"

"You snuck out of the house and—" Anther spasm ripped through me and all I could wonder was why in the world had women been doing this for thousands of years? This was barbaric. This was torture. Never again. Never again as long as I lived would I have another baby, so Beep had better be pretty awesome.

"And what?" he asked me. I realized, of course, they were trying to take my mind off the pain. Off the situation.

"And you met with Angel again."

"Don't bring me into this," Angel said.

"Angel!" I said, happy to see him. Or hear him, since my face was planted in Denise's crotch. "Why were you meeting with Reyes?"

"I can't tell you. He's meaner than you are."

I lifted just to glare up at him. "Clearly you don't know me very well."

"I would go down there to be with you, but I draw the line at child-birth."

"Chickenshit."

"And proud of it."

"I would have told you," Reyes said. "You're holding my underwear hostage. I would've had no choice."

"Does that mean you aren't wearing any?"

"Your blood pressure is too high," Denise said. She'd checked me with one of those wrist models that fascinated me. She looked up. "We need that rope."

"Got it!" Amber called out. "He didn't want to lend it to us. He didn't believe we had a pregnant woman stuck in a hole. So he came to help."

"Hey, there," a man called down to me. A Native American, judging by his accent. "I'm thinking we might need to get some professionals out here."

"So, yeah, I'm not wearing pants," I said to him. "Sorry."

"I'm okay with it if your husband is."

Another spasm, this one harder than any of its predecessors, tried to tear me in half. I cried out between locked teeth and tried to breathe in a pattern. It didn't work.

"We need the rope," Denise called.

"I'm getting it ready," Reyes said.

"Got the board," Osh said as he ran up.

He put a wide board across the opening. "What's that for?" I asked. "It will just break like the ones before."

"Not this one," he said. "It's from your kitchen table."

"Oh, okay, that might work." I doubled over and clenched my fists so hard, my fingernails pierced the flesh on my palms. "There's so much pressure," I told Denise. "I feel like I have to push."

"Okay, sweetheart." She eased me back and reached between my legs to check again. "You're ready. If you have to push, push."

"But they can pull us out now."

She shook her head. "It's too late. We are going to have to do this here."

I glared at her. "I don't want my baby born in a well," I gritted out.

"I know," she said as I pushed with all my might. I couldn't not.

She instructed me on how to do it. Push to the count of ten, then rest. Push to the count of ten, then rest. It occurred to me that she hadn't done this in a very long time. They might have changed things since her day. Maybe babies were born differently now. Maybe ten was no longer the magic number. But I couldn't argue with her. I could barely speak through the labor.

She rubbed my back until it was over and I could take a breath; then she listened for Beep's heartbeat again.

"I need the rope!" she screamed; then she shoved me back against the wall, wedged her palms against my lower abdomen, and pushed up.

I cried out in pain and tried to get her off me.

She said something I didn't comprehend; then she did it. Again. For the third time in my life, she slapped me.

My temper flared and the ground shook beneath us, causing dirt to fall on our heads. It didn't faze her.

"Look at me," she said, her face inches from mine. "Beep is in trouble. If you push, she could suffocate."

Alarm sobered me instantly.

"I lost her heartbeat for a few seconds. The cord could be wrapped around her throat. You may have to have a C-section."

"We can't leave the grounds," I said, my agony ripping a sob from the deepest core of my being. "She'll be in danger."

"Charley, she already is. I don't understand."

"There are—" I stopped as another sob shook through me, my horror was so great. "There are beings who want her dead. Huge supernatural beings with large razor-sharp teeth and claws the size of Pittsburgh. They'll kill her the minute we step off this ground."

She gaped at me as though I were a child telling a tall tale. In her eyes, I could see the instinctive desire to chastise me for being ridiculous—then understanding dawned. "Charley, are you serious?"

"Trust me, I wish I weren't."

For a long while, she sat stunned, at an utter loss for what to do. My muscles seized again. She coached me through it again, pushed my abdomen to keep the umbilical cord from strangling my daughter. As painful as that felt, I could only be grateful. Then it hit her as I tried to catch my breath and get comfortable, both of which were impossible.

She nodded and straightened. "Lean back," she said, all business.

I sat on my heels, my knees spread as far as they could be in the cramped quarters.

She squatted down and perched elbows between my knees. "I'm going to reach in and loop the cord over her head. I'll have to push her back a little to do it. This is going to hurt, Charley."

"I've been hurt before," I said, determined to do anything it took.

Then Reyes was there, his incorporeal form scalding, the sensation welcome until he reached around me from behind and held me to the prickly wall of the well, forcing me back so Denise could do what was needed. She reached inside me and ripped me in two from the inside out.

I screamed, long and loud and guttural, as Reyes pinned my shoulders against the well wall. I clawed at his arms, but he was the only thing keeping me from doubling over as my stepmother pushed Beep back up and then searched for the cord. The sheet beneath us was covered in blood, as were my legs. And my shirt. And pretty much everything around me.

Another spasm hit just as she said, "I think I got it. I think she's in the clear." She listened for the heartbeat again with the stethoscope as Reyes kept his hold tight, this time monitoring the entire time I pushed. I grabbed a handful of his hair and gave it my all.

She sighed in relief. "I think she's okay. We can do this, Charley."

I heard the Native American man argue with Osh and Garrett. He was going to call an ambulance, but they insisted one was already on the way. They'd lied, but they had to hold him off.

"You're tearing, but I can't do anything about it down here."

"It's okay," I said, my entire body slick with sweat. "It's coming again."

"You can do this, sweetheart," she said.

I nodded and pushed when the spasm hit. I felt myself splitting as Beep's head passed through.

"Okay, stop pushing!" she said, taking one of the sheets and working on Beep. Then she took a sucky thing out of the bag. Though I couldn't see what she was doing, I heard a soft wail of annoyance waft up to me, and I let my head loll back against Reyes's shoulder. But Beep was still halfway in me, though, and I really needed to push. I fought the urge with all my strength.

"Okay, I'm going to pull her out one shoulder at a time. Don't push."

"What?" But with one final jolt of pain, Beep was out. And pissed as hell.

I covered my mouth with my hands. "Reyes," I said, unable to take my eyes off her.

"She's perfect," he said into my ear. Thank God he continued to hold me. I doubted I had the strength to hold myself upright anymore.

Denise worked to get our daughter cleaned up. I could relax and focus on the broken rib and the nigh-fractured hips and the blood still running out of my head.

I smiled at Reyes. "What a day, huh?"

He shook his head.

"So, do you still need the rope?" Osh asked.

"Yes, but not for a few minutes," Denise said. She cut the cord, clipped it with a clothespin from the looks of it, and wrapped our bundle in a clean-ish sheet. Then she handed her to me.

All I could see was a little round face still covered in spots of muck, but she was the most beautiful thing I'd ever seen in my life. Dark lashes. Full mouth. Stubborn chin. She was Reyes incarnate, and my heart swelled with pride. "She's so perfect," I said.

"Yes, she is, but we need to get you both out of here as soon as possible."

"Katherine the Midwife is here," Amber said. "Can I hold her?" she asked me.

"You'll have to ask Katherine, hon."

She laughed. "I meant Beep."

"You absolutely can, just as soon as we get out of here."

"One more thing," Denise said.

"What?"

"We have to get the rest out of you."

"What rest?"

I shouldn't have asked.

They lifted Denise out first while she carried Beep. Then the guys lowered Reyes to get me. He lifted me into his arms and they hoisted us both up at the same time using some kind of pulley system Garrett had jerry-rigged. I lost consciousness about halfway up, exhausted and broken, but as long as Beep was okay, I was okay. I knew she'd be well taken care of. She had a large family.

I awoke hours later in bed beside Reyes with a tiny bundle between us. One lamp fended off the darkness in the small room, and I could see Katherine the Midwife snoring in a chair close by. Though I didn't much care what time it was, I did wonder how long I'd been out. How many hours of Beep's existence I'd missed.

They'd dressed her in the first outfit Cookie had bought her. When I first saw it, I'd remarked that it looked too small. Babies couldn't possibly be that tiny. Now that she was wearing it, however, it looked too big. Beep didn't seem real. She was like a doll with thick lashes, a perfect nose, and a widow's peak. She was surreal and angelic and mesmerizing.

I rolled onto my side and loosened the blanket. Her tiny fingers splayed in reaction to my touch, and I marveled at her fingernails—exact replicas of Reyes's—as I counted them. An even ten. Just what the doctor ordered. I felt as though my eyes were glued to her. I couldn't stop gazing at this little person we'd been waiting so long to see. I fought back tears as I looked at her, ignoring the fact that I felt like I'd been run over by a train. I'd been run over by trains before. The tenderness between my legs, however, was novel. And nature wasn't calling. She was screaming, ranting and raving like a lunatic.

Unable to ignore my bladder any longer, I kissed Beep's head, then her cheek, then her hand, before rolling out of bed. I glanced at my husband, wondering if he was really asleep at last. He lay on his side with his head propped on one arm, the dips between his biceps forming deep, alluring shadows. His long lashes fanned across his cheeks, just like Beep's, and I stilled to watch them just a few seconds more, until I heard Denise.

"She's perfect," she said softly.

I turned to see her sitting in another chair they'd brought in. "She is, isn't she? She's so tiny. It's like she's not real. She's like a pink flower floating on a big blue sea."

"They're always smaller than you think they will be."

She and my dad had never had more children, and I always wondered why. Not enough to ask, but . . . "How long have I been out?"

"Since yesterday morning. About eighteen hours."

"Eighteen hours?" I asked, scanning the room for the clock. "She had to face the world without me for eighteen whole hours?"

"They said you were in stasis or something. That you had to rest to heal."

"Yeah, well, I don't think it worked this time." I tried to stretch. It was just too painful.

"Do you want to hold her?" she asked, stepping forward. "We finally wrangled her away from your husband long enough to let Katherine check her out. A pediatrician is coming tomorrow, though, just to make sure."

"Oh, good. Let me go pee, then she's all mine."

I grabbed my phone, then walked to the bathroom, my pace that of a snail in its late nineties. The soreness I felt was beyond anything I'd experienced before. My hips hurt the worst, then Virginia. Poor Virginia. She'd never be the same again. Then my ribs, et cetera. It hurt to brush my teeth and wash my face, too. I had a nasty bruise on the side of my head with a lovely gash in the middle and a black eye.

I checked messages while sitting on the toilet. Multitasking had always been a specialty of mine. And I peed forever, so I had a lot of time. I had a text from Mr. Alaniz, my PI, asking me if there was any progress on the home front. Meaning, had I told Reyes yet? I was going to have to tell him. The Loehrs had given me until tomorrow. Maybe now that we had Beep, he would understand what I did. Either way, I dreaded that conversation.

By the time I got back, Reyes was up with Beep. Shirtless, he held her in his arms as he turned to me, and my breath caught in my chest. Here was a man so powerful, he could make the earth quake beneath us, holding something as fragile as fine china. It was charming and endearing and sexy and exquisite.

I walked to stand beside him. He grinned down at me, pride evident in his every move.

"Did you get some sleep?" I asked, placing a hand on his arm.

"Sure," he said, lying through his teeth. His sleepy eyes and unshaven face awed me for a moment.

"I'll leave you two alone," Denise said, barely audible above Katherine the Midwife's snoring. Then she turned back to me. "You have some pretty great friends."

Reyes had just set Beep in my arms when I walked over to Denise. "You saved her life," I said, my gratitude limitless. "I don't know what would've happened if you hadn't been there today."

"Yesterday."

"Yesterday," I corrected.

She bowed her head. "I'm just glad I could help." She turned and left.

"And you," I said to the ball of perfection in my arms, "I have to show you something. Coming?" I asked Reyes as Beep and I left the room.

He followed us downstairs and outside, where we sat on two lawn chairs to gaze at the stars. I told her all about the constellations, pointing out each one and reciting its name, at which point, Reyes corrected me.

Naturally, I ignored him. "And see that star?" I asked her even though she had yet to wake up. "I'm claiming that one for you. It's all yours. Its name henceforth shall be known to all the lands as Beep."

"I'm pretty sure that one's already named."

I turned to Reyes as he lay beside us. Still shirtless despite the crisp night that didn't seem to faze him.

"And I'm pretty sure it's a planet, not a star," he continued, a playful grin lifting one corner of his mouth.

"Really?" I looked at Beep. "Did you hear that? Daddy is dissing your star. And he's wearing duct tape. Duct tape is so last June."

"Venus," he said.

"Beep," I volleyed with a stern brow.

He laughed softly. "Beep it is. I found something about her very interesting."

"Just one thing?"

His grin widened. "This is interesting in a different way."

"Really?" I asked, intrigued.

"Seven pounds, thirteen ounces."

I gasped and gazed at her wide-eyed, making everything I said and did into a Broadway production. Not sure why. "Did you weigh seven whole pounds and thirteen ounces? No wonder Virginia is under the weather." Then realization dawned, his point sinking in at last. I glanced at Reyes. "Seven original gods, thirteen altogether."

He lifted a shoulder. "Just found that interesting."

"I do too. Like, bizarrely interesting."

"You seriously need to hydrate and eat something. What do you want?"

"Dude, you can make eggs into a gourmet three-course dinner. Surprise me."

"Oh, I didn't say I was going to cook. I was just offering to hold our daughter while you cooked. I'm kind of hungry, too."

I laughed.

"Eggs it is. I have some red chile potatoes made up, too."

"My mouth is watering just thinking about it." Then I bolted upright. "Coffee," I whispered, the word like a delicate snowflake on my mouth. "I can have coffee now."

It was like the heavens had opened up and God smiled down on me.

"Aren't you going to breast-feed?"

And they closed again. "Yes."

He shook his head and went to scrounge us up some grub. I sat back in despair until I really examined the situation. Maybe it would be best for Beep if she built up a tolerance to caffeine now. Start her off young.

Reyes made breakfast, cooking eggs to go on the potatoes and chile, and brought me a huge plate. I handed Beep off to him.

Watching Reyes hold her, as though she were made of glass, afraid to wrap his arms too tight, was priceless. It amazed me to see how one tiny creature had the power to turn a man made of pure, natural prowess into a bumbling mess. Not that I was much better, but we'd get there. We had all the time in the world.

12

*It was a sad and disappointing day when I discovered
my Universal Remote Control did not, in fact,
control the universe. (Not even remotely.)*
—MEME

We went inside after we ate, not wanting Beep to get pneumonia. The house began to stir a couple of hours later. Kit and Agent Waters called soon after with news on the possible kidnapper.

"We tracked one of the burner phones from the text messages. It was still on and we traced it to a garbage can in the alley behind Dion's on Wyoming. From there, we traced where it was purchased and they had surveillance footage. We got him. His name is Colton Ellix. There's only one problem," she said, her voice tinged with panic.

"What?"

"He died two days ago in a car accident. He was trying to outrun a squad car that, at first, wasn't even after him. He thought they were, took off. The officers pursued, but he exited at Rio Grande during rush hour traffic doing at least a hundred. He killed a pedestrian as well as himself."

My heart sank. "She's still alive, Kit. You need to look into all his holdings, anywhere he frequented, his past. Where did he grow up? Does any of his family have land?"

"You're preaching to the choir, hon. We're looking into everything, but he didn't have any property. He was renting a small house in Algodones, but we searched it and the surrounding properties. The neighbors said they hadn't seen him in a few days."

"Where did he know her from?"

"He worked for my brother," Agent Waters said. "Did a few side jobs around the house for them and watched the dogs when they were out of town."

"He had access to everything."

"Exactly."

"Okay, then, what about your brother? Did he have any property that Ellix would have known about?"

"He had some land in Rio Rancho. They were going to build a new house, but there's nothing out there." When I didn't say anything, he added, "I'll get a patrol car out there immediately."

"In the meantime," I said, speaking mostly to Kit on this one, "I'll do what I do and see what I can come up with."

"And what is it you do?" Agent Waters asked.

"What I'm hired to do," I said, being as vague as humanly possible. "We need everything you have on him."

"Already en route," she said.

"Oh, and Beep's here."

A long silence ensued and I let it all sink in. Women had been having babies for years, though. It was all the rage. Not sure why it was such a difficult thing for her to digest.

"Well, say hi for us," Kit said.

"Okay."

"Oh!" she shouted. "Beep. *The* Beep. Oh my gosh, Charley, congratulations. Are you here in Albuquerque?"

"Nope, still out here at the convent."

"You had her there?" she asked, appalled.

"Yeah. In a well. It's a long story."

"Okay. Well, congratulations to you both."

"Thanks. Get us those files."

"They'll be there in an hour."

As soon as Cookie got up and got her hair under control, I set her to find out everything she could on our potential kidnapper. They found no evidence that he really took Faris, but I knew one way to find out for sure.

I had Denise take Beep to change her and lay her down for a nap. I was going fishing and she didn't need to be around when I caught anything.

I walked into the office while Cook was making coffee. I took a deep breath, closed my eyes, and summoned Colton Ellix.

Nothing. Either I was losing my touch, or he'd already crossed. And if he was kidnapping girls, then I was pretty certain I knew which direction he went. But that was the problem. He'd crossed and I needed to know where Faris was. According to Rocket, she was still alive. I checked. But again, the good news was given with a dire warning. She wouldn't be for long. That told me she was imprisoned where she was either going to suffocate or die of dehydration. Those were the most logical reasons for why she wouldn't have long to live. He could have hurt her, however, and she could be lying somewhere with an infected wound.

There was simply no telling, but I wasn't about to give up yet.

I took off in search of Osh. Only two beings on this earth knew my celestial name, and he was one of them.

I found him in the kitchen raiding the fridge. We still had a lot of food left over from the caterers and the cookout.

"No," he said before I could even get a word out.

"But you haven't heard—"

"No," he said again, standing up with his arms full of leftovers. "And that's final."

"How do you even know I want something?"

"It's how you walk. You have a determined walk, your footsteps harder, when you want something you know you can't have. So, no." He dumped his haul onto the countertop, since we no longer had a table, and went in search of a plate and utensils.

"It's a really simple request."

His shoulder-length black hair had been slicked back, still wet from a shower. It glistened almost as much as his dark bronze eyes. I'd never seen eyes quite that color before.

"Nothing is simple with you, love."

Glancing around, afraid Reyes might be near, I stepped closer and pleaded. "It's important."

He took a plate out of the simple cabinets and turned to me. "It always is."

"I need to know my name."

He stilled, looked me up and down, then asked, "Why?"

"The man who most likely kidnapped my client's niece," I said, trying to get him to connect with Faris, let him know she had family who was worried about her, "died two days ago, and she is being held somewhere. We need to find her. She's going to die soon if we don't."

Without breaking his mesmerizing gaze, he pulled a knife out of a drawer behind him. "No." He took out two pieces of bread, preparing to make a BBQ sandwich while I struggled to come up with some leverage or a trade or something, anything, to get him to comply.

"You said when I learn my name I will understand so much more. I will have all my powers. Everything I am capable of in a few, tiny syllables."

"And what would you do with that power?"

"I need to summon the guy from hell. I can't do that right now. I need more . . . mojo."

He shook his head as he took out some lettuce and tomatoes. On BBQ? Oh well, to each his own. At least he was eating a tad healthier than I did seven days out of the week.

"The kind of mojo you would get . . . it's not like you think. And besides. It's not my gift to give. It is something you will learn with your passing. Rey'aziel would never forgive me."

"Why would you need his forgiveness for anything?"

He paused, put both hands on the counter. "We all need forgiving at some point."

"Is that why you're doing this? Is that why you're helping? You need forgiveness?"

He turned to me then, as though I'd offended him. "What do you think?"

"I think you're not really afraid of Reyes."

"No, I'm not, but if we fought and I killed him, you'd never forgive me."

"I'm not worried about you killing my husband, Osh."

"Look, we don't know what will happen when you learn it. That's what he's really afraid of. He thinks that you might ascend. That you might quit your human body and become the grim reaper for real. That you might leave him. Or worse."

"What can be worse?"

"That you will go back to your dimension. That you'll leave him forever."

"But I wouldn't do that."

"There is no way you can know what you will and won't do once you have all your powers. Or what you can and can't do. Hell, love, *we* don't even know. Not really. You're not just the grim reaper. You're also a god. The first pure ghost god. Do you have any idea what that means? It makes Lucifer and all his power look like child's play."

"Then why not give me that power and end all this? Beep is in danger because of him. Because of the hellhounds. Why not just let me fix it so we can get on with our lives?"

"It doesn't work that way, love."

I was growing more frustrated by the minute. "Why? Why doesn't it work that way?"

"Because if you will notice, you have power over souls, right? You have the very rare ability to mark them."

"Yes, and?"

"That's it. We believe that when you agreed to come here to this dimension, you had to agree to abide by the rules of this universe."

"Man, you people love rules. And what rules are those?"

He slapped his bread together, turned to me, and took a huge bite of his sandwich. Mumbling, he said, "God gave humans the power over their own lives. They have the power to make their own decisions. To make their own mistakes. To follow the dark one or not. God kicked Lucifer out of heaven but not out of the game entirely. There's still a war raging, and you have no power to stop it. Only humans can really stop the war. Can really put an end to Lucifer. But, as you are well aware, there is a lot of evil in this world. Some people will always choose to follow him. And with every human he wins, his powers grow."

"So, you are telling me I have no dominion over Lucifer? Over his demons?"

"I'm saying you cannot destroy him. Only a human born of flesh and blood can."

"I'm human. Have been since the day I was born."

He grinned, took a huge gulp of water, then leaned into me. "You're no more human than I am."

"Wait. Are you telling me that is why all the prophecies say that Beep will destroy Lucifer?"

"She's human."

"With supernatural parents. Surely, if she is going to take on Satan, she has to have some of our powers."

"She does. She will. Just like you, her powers will grow as she gets older. But she was still created from the human sides of you and Rey'aziel. She was still born a human. She will ultimately have power over things you don't and never will. You can't break the agreement the God of this universe made. It's—" He stopped to think about his next words. "It's bad form."

"So that was it. That's why our Beep is going to face off against Lucifer?"

"That surprises you? After everything you've read? After everything we've uncovered?"

"I was just hoping—"

"To find a loophole."

I lowered my head. "Yes."

Osh bit down in frustration. "Yeah, me, too. Of course, there's something else you have to consider."

"There's more?" I asked, growing disheartened.

"You have to think about what you are, how powerful you are. If you learn your name before it's time, you might not be able to control that power. You could kill everyone around you in the blink of an eye."

"So, that's a definite no to my celestial name?"

His mouth formed a thin line. "Sorry, love. I don't want to have to kill Rey'aziel. Not yet, anyway."

This time I leaned in. "I think Rey'aziel can take you."

"Every other creature in hell thought they could take me, too. They were wrong."

I stole his sandwich and took a bite. "Then I guess it's a good thing you're on our side."

A sweet lopsided grin softened his face, and I had to remember once again that he only *looked* nineteen.

I walked upstairs to check on Beep. The trip was much easier now that I wasn't harboring the little fugitive. I wasn't about to give up on talking to Colton Ellix. I had a backup plan. It scared the hell out of me, and I didn't dare tell Reyes, but it was a plan nonetheless. Reyes wouldn't see it that way, though. He'd have me drugged and locked away so I couldn't carry out my plan until it was too late to do anything about it. But at that point, Faris would be dead. I was not going to let that happen if there was even the slightest chance I could stop it.

I tiptoed up to the door to our bedroom. Quentin and Amber were in there with Beep. Quentin held her much the same way Reyes had, like a crystal football in danger of cracking should he hold her too tight, while Amber taught him how to give her a bottle, an expert after only a day.

I longed to breast-feed Beep, but I was out for so long after the whole well incident that they'd had no choice but to bottle-feed her. I didn't know if she'd take me now, but I wanted to try. Not, like, right at that moment. Quentin might get embarrassed. But soon.

I watched Amber as she interacted with my beautiful daughter. She had a particular sheen about her. Her hair shimmered in the morning sun filtering in through the curtains. Her skin sparkled. Then I realized she still had some glitter on her face from the wedding. But she was so pretty. A wingless fairy, tall and strong with delicate features and an all-knowing sense of the world. Then again, she *was* a teen. They did know everything. The thing about Amber, however, was that she approached her worldly knowledge with respect.

Spiritualist, I thought as I looked at her. It seemed appropriate. Important, even. Her deep connection to all things around her, all things in nature, gave her a sense of the bigger picture.

She giggled when Quentin let the bottle drop too low. "Up," she said, pointing skyward. He obeyed immediately, his blue eyes sparkling as bright as the smile he flashed her.

"What?" Amber asked Beep as though the little rascal had spoken to her. She giggled again. "I think so, too," she told her. "His is bright and clear as a summer day."

Wondering what she was talking about, Quentin shrugged at her.

She signed to him. "She said your aura is nice."

He raised his brows and nodded, not believing her for a minute. I, on the other hand, was beginning to wonder. Maybe Amber really was a fairy.

She looked down at Beep again and nodded. "Okay. Okay, I promise. It would only upset her anyway."

"Upset?" Quentin said with his voice, deep and soft as it was. "Who?"

Amber pressed her lips together seeming to regret something that was about to happen. "Charley," she said.

Quentin knew I was standing there. He could see my light. He gave me a sideways glance, then went back to his duties. He also knew Mo was standing by them, waving to Beep, touching her face. Mo glanced up at me, her hands clasped at her chest in adoration.

I gave her a wink, then left them alone, my curiosity burning. Amber had a powerful connection with every living thing around her, but to have a conversation with a newborn? That was novel.

I felt a coolness waft over me and turned to see that Sister Maureen, or just Mo, as she insisted on being called, had followed me out.

"Thank you," she said, using a gesture of tipping a hat. She pointed to the bedroom. "She is beautiful."

"I agree," I whispered. "My contact at the Vatican sent a report to the higher-ups there. They will be looking into your and your sister's deaths as well as the priest's, naturally."

She thanked me again. "You told them? My sister tried to save me?"

"I told them everything, Mo." I walked to her, a deep sorrow for what she went through tightening my chest. "You can cross through me."

She lowered her head. "I— I don't think he wants me."

"Mo, of course he does. If he didn't, trust me, you'd be elsewhere."

"You don't understand. I sinned beyond redemption."

"Who hasn't? You should have been at my house Halloween night my senior year of college. You ain't got nothing on a French maid with a Jason Voorhees mask. That's what forgiveness is all about, and I have a feeling God will understand. We all get lost, sweetheart. He knows. I promise."

She gave in at last and took a hesitant step forward, then another, and another until her face brightened. I could tell she saw someone, most likely a family member. She looked at me one last time, her expression full of gratitude, then stepped through.

She'd seen her father gunned down in Chicago. The memory had the weight and force of a freight train behind it. It knocked the air from my lungs as I watched a gunman roar up the street in a classic Ford. He stuck his head out the window, his arms full of the automatic weapon he carried, a tommy gun, and showered bullets down on the pedestrians.

Sadly, he was after one man, a mob boss from a rival family. But Mo's father, a baker carrying a fifty-pound sack of flour, had been gunned down in the process. He didn't even know what hit him. He had the sack on a shoulder, holding it steady with one hand, and Mo's hand in the other. They were looking at the Christmas-themed pastries he'd made in the window. Santa. Christmas trees. Stars. All brightly colored and begging to be eaten. By her and her sister, of course, who was home with a fever.

One of her father's best customers was a man named Crichton, a crime boss, though she didn't know it at the time. The shooter wanted him, but the rival family had also wanted to make a statement, to kill anyone they could on the boss's turf.

Mo jumped when the gun went off, and she watched as the man, seeing her shocked expression, aimed the gun right at her. But the sack had fallen off her father's shoulder. He'd been shot in the head, and the sack took the two shots that were meant for her head.

The car sped off, leaving the agonizing screams of the survivors in its wake. Mo stood there in a cloud of flour with a death grip on her father's hand. But the angle of his grip was wrong. She turned and saw that he was lying facedown in a pool of his own blood.

The sounds died away. The cloud settled, looking like snow all around her. And her father lay motionless. Then everything went away for a very long time. She ended up spending several months in a psychiatric hospital. Her mother, thank goodness, refused to let them perform insulin therapy on her. She saw it no less barbaric than electroshock. When the doctors told her to just sign her daughter away to them, claiming she would never come out of her stupor, she took her daughter out that very day, brought her home, and made her chicken soup.

Mo felt to the day she died it was the chicken soup that had healed her, and though she never spoke again, she did find her way back to reality, slowly at first, and over time her mother and sister helped her recover.

She and her sister grew even closer. They made up signs, their own secret language, so Mo could talk to her, and while her mother insisted she learn real sign language, she never forgot the language she and her sister made up.

Her good memories hit me, too. Her cousin's birthday party where she ended up bringing a puppy home because her cousin was angry that it wasn't a pony. So her aunt gave it to her to teach her son a lesson. The boy had a pony a month later, thus her cousin learned nothing from the experience, but that was okay, because Mo and Bea had a puppy named BB, short for Big Boy, that they served tea to and taught to sneeze on demand. And I now had irrefutable proof that dogs did indeed go to heaven, because that was who Mo saw first when she stepped through me, followed by her sister and then her parents.

———

It took me a moment to recover after she passed. I was so happy for her, to be in the place she belonged, with her family again. I was also sad that it took over seventy years for her to be reunited with them, but from what I understood, time didn't matter much on the other side.

Cookie texted me asking me where I was at.

Right here. Where are you?

Right here. Why can't I see you? she asked, playing along.

I descended the stairs, still walking a little slower than I'd like, and strolled through the house toward our office.

Garrett was busy in the dining room, scouring a small portion of the text that he felt might be relevant to our situation, namely being held hostage by a group of angry hellhounds. I didn't dare disturb him, but Osh did. He was in there, too, and he tossed a Cheez-It at him. Garrett didn't acknowledge the Daeva or his antics.

Osh turned toward me as I walked past, his eyes narrowed. Had he figured out my plan? How could he have? It was a freaking awesome plan. No way would anyone figure it out. Not in a million years.

"So," Cookie said when I walked in, "I have a plan."

"Me, too." I sat in my chair and snatched the file papers out of her hand.

"This is everything I could find out about Colton Ellix. He has the usual. Poor social skills. Very arrogant despite it. He was accused of stalking a girl when he was in high school, but that was long before they took that sort of thing seriously. He told the principal they'd been secretly dating, and when people found out, she accused him of stalking. The principal laughed it off, chalking it up to teenage hormones."

"What happened with the girl?"

"That's just it. She disappeared about a month later. She was never found."

"So, he's been doing this awhile."

"I don't know," she said, pointing out another report. "He has never, not once, had another report filed on him. No complaints. Just always kept to himself."

"That doesn't mean he hasn't abducted more girls."

"True, but look at this." She lifted out a spreadsheet. I was allergic to spreadsheets, so I opted not to touch it. "I have a detailed account of everywhere he's lived. The high school incident happened in Kentucky. But his family moved around a lot, mostly in close range to other relatives. I get the feeling they were mooches. Once that relative got sick of them, they moved on to the next, claiming one hardship after another until someone new took them in."

"So, not a stable home life."

"Not at all, but I've searched and searched. There were absolutely no missing persons cases in any town they lived in. At least, not while he lived there. I even widened the search to a hundred miles. Nada. And that's taking into account when he left his family. He was only sixteen when he moved in with a friend."

"Still no missing persons?"

"Not one that wasn't solved. But here's the most interesting part," Cookie said, getting excited. "Look at the girl who went missing when he was in high school."

She showed me a picture of a girl who could have been Faris's twin. "Wow."

"Right? I mean, that can't be a coincidence."

I sat back and compared their pictures. Every feature was strikingly similar.

"You know what this means?"

"Yes," she said, nodding. Then she shook her head. "Well, no, not really."

"It means he was relatively new to it. He wasn't seasoned."

Her eyes crinkled at the corners as she tried to grasp what I was getting at.

"It means that he made mistakes. Probably a lot of them. Sure, he planned this. Thought it through. Went over every detail with a fine-toothed comb, but I promise you, he screwed up."

"Of course. He had to have. Repeat killers learn how to avoid mistakes as they go, how to cover their tracks better."

"They eventually screw up. They all do, but this guy had only done this once. And since he didn't do it again, I would say he probably didn't mean to kill the girl the first time. Maybe he genuinely thought that if he could just get her alone, he would win her over. When she either cried and scared him or tried to fight him, he killed her."

"Maybe she threatened him and he panicked."

"Could be. Either way, I think the first one was an accident."

"But when the guy he starts doing odd jobs for turns out to have a daughter that looks just like his former crush?"

"Those old feelings come bubbling up and he can't resist trying to win her again. I'm just wondering which feelings came to the surface."

"What do you mean?"

"Was it the old feelings of love or was it the feelings of betrayal? I think Faris's life depends on which emotion held more sway. So what's your plan?"

"I think you should go get him and drag his ass back here."

I sat speechless. "Cook," I said at last, my voice a harsh whisper, "how did you know what I was going to do?"

"No way," she said, just as shocked as I was. "I have to admit, I was mostly kidding. I mean, go where? He's already crossed, right? Then—"

This time she sat speechless. "You are not thinking what I'm thinking."

"Bet I am," I said with a wink.

"Charley, no." She stood, scanned the halls to make sure no one was looking, then closed the door with a soft click. She sat in front of me and whispered, "Charley, you can't be serious. I mean, he's . . . there. Look at what we are dealing with here. Hellhounds at our gates. Spies in the closet. Departed trying to push you down mountains. If that's what's up here, what do you think will be down there?"

I shifted in my chair. "I didn't think of that. I haven't really worked out the particulars, but, you know, it'll be a surprise. They won't expect me."

"That's for sure. I know you said Reyes went to hell to get that rock on your finger—"

I couldn't help a glance at the orange diamond on my ring finger, the cut stunning, the color surreal.

"—but he was born and raised there. He knew the layout. How on earth are you going to waltz in, find Mr. Ellix, interrogate him, then pop back out again without you-know-who finding out?"

"Reyes?

"Satan!" she screeched.

"Sorry," I said, testy thing. "Like I said, I haven't worked out the particulars."

"So, we're in agreement. That's a crazy idea and we will never have one like that again."

"Cook, all our ideas are crazy. That's setting the bar a little high, don't you think?"

She squared her shoulders. "Yes, but they aren't all *that* crazy. You know, batshit."

"Don't worry," I said, patting her knee. "I have insider information."

"From who?"

"Garrett."

"You're going to make him go to hell again, aren't you? That poor guy."

"What? No. I'm going to tell him . . . Well, I haven't gotten that far yet. It's a work in progress, but I'll figure it out. He can tell me what I need to know."

"This is the worst idea we've had yet."

"No way. Remember the time we tried to train that ferret to steal a file from that corporate guy's office and this guy died?"

"Oh, yeah. Okay, the second worst. Who would've guessed he was that allergic to ferrets?"

"I felt bad about that. And if he hadn't swindled the life savings from half the residents at Sunny Days Retirement Center, I would've felt *really* bad."

13

So, Mr. Ellix was pretty new to kidnapping. I could only hope he hadn't tried his hands at other parts of the gig. I prayed he hadn't violated her. If so, it would be even harder for Faris to recover. But it seemed like he'd wanted that girl's approval in high school. Her love. Maybe he was seeking the same from Faris. And raping her would not get her approval or her love.

That was a bridge I'd have to cross when I came to it. Right now, I needed a baby. And a beer.

I strolled into the dining room, carrying my beautiful daughter in my arms. I'd practically had to rip her out of Gemma's but I'd called dibs in the well, so she had to give in. I couldn't get enough of her. Of holding her. Of counting her fingers and toes, marveling at how long they were. She'd been swaddled in soft pink and gray and wore a crocheted beanie on her tiny head. Her fists were curled tight and resting on either side of her nose. It was the cutest thing ever. I'd been trying to figure out who she looked more like, but alas, I'd been in denial. Of course she looked like Reyes. Thick black hair. Impossibly long eyelashes. Straight, strong nose with a curve at the tip. Full, perfectly formed mouth. She was going to knock 'em dead. Like, literally. We'd have to teach her to use her powers for good.

Garrett looked up and didn't know which item to take from me first: Beep or the beer. He decided on Beep, then the beer. Probably a wise decision. As he bounced around with her, cooing about how she was going to save the world, I scanned the piles of copied documents. Many had Garrett's handwriting on them. Since going to hell, compliments of Mr. Reyes Farrow, he'd been obsessed with the prophecies. With the past, as well, and the future, and how Beep would one day destroy the underworld.

"So," I said to him, thankful that Osh had left the building. Or at least the room. "I have a question for you."

"No."

Damn it. Osh had gotten to him.

"Then give me back my kid."

He gasped at me melodramatically for Beep's benefit, though she slept through his whole performance. "Already using your child to get what you want out of people. That's shameful." He looked down at Beep. "Your mother is like everyone at the nuthouse rolled into one. She's a nut roll. Can you say 'nut roll'?"

Oh yeah. Garrett Swopes, the tough-as-nails bounty hunter who took bullets to the chest like others took splinters, had gone bye-bye.

I sat there for-like-ever while Garrett told Beep all kinds of stories about me that were mostly untrue. He tended to exaggerate. Honestly, like I would've gone out with Greg Nusser for backstage passes to Blue Öyster Cult. Not even. I went out with Brad Stark for the backstage passes to

Blue Öyster Cult. I went out with Greg Nusser for tickets to 3 Doors Down.

Denise came to get Beep then, saying it was time for her bath and I needed to learn how to bathe her. Like I didn't know already. Sadly, it was much more complicated than I'd thought, mostly because a wet Beep was a slippery Beep. And she did not enjoy that one iota. Denise said she would grow to love bath time. Until then, I was totally investing in those noise-reduction headphones.

Next Cookie came to hold her, because God forbid she feel the touch of a mattress on her back. Then she and Gemma took turns feeding then burping her all while I sat waiting for Reyes to go do something. He was spending all his time with Beep and me. What the hell? Did men do that?

It was a nice feeling, though. All of us together like a real family, as opposed to one being held together with duct tape and hellhounds. Reyes made the most adorable dad, especially when he let her sleep on his chest as we sat in the theater and exposed her to the world of hobbits. His heat, I was sure, kept her toasty warm on the chilly autumn day.

Then, when I least expected it, Uncle Bob came in for his turn at the little doughnut. That's what he called her. She looked more like a cherry éclair to me. Reyes checked his watch and made some lame excuse about going for a run. He didn't run unless being chased. And even then, running from danger had never been his strong suit.

"Okay," I said, a little too happy about it.

He was totally meeting Angel again. I could tell. I could see it in his eyes.

Oh well. His timing was perfect. I had a girl to save, and while I'd been hoping Kit would call with good news, we had yet to receive any news at all.

I called her just to make sure they hadn't found anything. They were still checking the area where Ellix had lived and worked.

With no other choice, I went into the laundry room. People went in there only if they had actual laundry to do. They rarely just showed up for no reason. This was the most likely place I could try this thing without being interrupted. With Reyes secretly meeting my traitorous investigator, now was the perfect opportunity for me to take my plan for a test run. But I needed a little assistance first.

I summoned Angel, just to make sure I wasn't missing something before risking life and limb to break into hell.

He popped in, his expression almost bored. At least he wasn't annoyed.

"Having a secret meeting with my husband?" I asked, my voice sharp with accusation and innuendo. Mostly accusation.

"Man, *pendeja,* you think that all I do is your husband's legwork?"

"So, you're not meeting with him right now?"

"No. What the hell?"

"Then who are you meeting with?"

"I was checking out the chicks at the mall."

"Coronado or Cottonwood?"

"Coronado, why?"

"I miss the mall," I said, suddenly nostalgic for the good old days when I could shop without being ripped apart. "Do they still have that store that sells those little ice cream dots? That is some crazy shit."

"I don't know. I don't eat."

"Right, so, can I visit someone in hell?"

"Dude, I'm not saying it again. You can do anything—"

I waved an impatient hand. "I know. I know. I can do anything. You keep telling me. But really, can I? And if you're not having a secret meeting with Reyes, who is?"

"Probably that old couple he keeps talking to."

I stilled. Like, for a really long time. Long enough for Angel to look worried.

"What old couple?" I asked at last.

"The one he keeps meeting with. I don't know their names. They're old."

I stilled again as my brain struggled for an explanation. Surely . . . No, he couldn't know about the Loehrs. It was impossible. I'd met them for the first time just two days ago. "And how long has he been meeting with them?"

"Couple of months. Why? Are you two getting a divorce?"

"What?" Alarm ran rampant over my nerve endings, much like five-year-olds on a sugar rush. "Why would you say that? Did he say that?"

"No," Angel said, stepping closer. "I was just hoping you'd ditch him for someone more your age."

"I'm millions of years old."

He stepped so close, I had to look up at him, though not terribly. He was only a couple inches taller than me. "Age isn't everything."

He had a gorgeous full mouth and clear brown eyes and if he didn't stop hitting on me, I was going to—

"Wait!" he said, sobering. "Did you say 'hell'?"

"Yes," I said, biting my lower lip.

"You can't just go to hell. There's a void between here and there."

"But the map is imprinted on my husband's body," I explained.

"Yes, on his. Not yours."

It was now or never. I closed my eyes. "Lucky for me, I have an excellent memory. If I don't make it back, explain to Reyes I went to find Ellix." I opened my eyes again. "But I'll make it back. Give me two minutes."

I closed my eyes again, envisioned the map on Reyes's torso, the one that would lead me through the void, and I fell into darkness.

Admittedly, I didn't understand how the map worked. Not until I actually used it. There were paths, almost imperceptible paths, and I wound through them, meeting obstacle after obstacle, but knowing which way to turn, which opening to take. As long as I envisioned the map, as long as I let myself fall into it with complete and total faith that it would get me where I needed to go, I flew threw the void. It felt a lot like a head rush but it was all over my body. Tingling and cold. I hadn't expected the cold. I felt a frost form over my skin, and yet I didn't have skin here.

I looked down and it cracked when I moved my hand, only to reform, creating tiny crystals that spread over me, up my neck and over my face. But I kept envisioning the map, suddenly scared to death I'd get lost in the void. Reyes would find me, though. I knew he would find me if I did go astray. But another thing I didn't count on was the audience I'd gained.

I couldn't see them, but I felt their glassy eyes watching me, their hot breath on the nape of my neck, the prickling of their teeth. Were these beings the demons that had become lost in the void? Were they still trying to make it to the earthly plane, I wondered, and if so, how long had they been there?

In a heartbeat, I was standing on solid ground, a hot wind raked over my skin. It burned like acid, and my skin started to darken. As though I had a disease, I began to turn black, the top layers of my epidermis drying and floating off in thousands of tiny flakes. Wherever the skin peeled off and flew away, my flesh glowed a bright orange, as though I were made of molten lava on the inside. And I burned. Every breath I took scorched my throat, set fire to my lungs. My eyes calcified, leaving spiderweb cracks for me to see through. It was like looking at the desolate landscape through a shattered windowpane.

I stepped forward, the sound of a thousand screams swirling around me, carried on the blistering wind like whispers of agony. The ground broke beneath me, the top layer black with the same molten orange underneath. I tried to take another step, but I was melted to the spot. I couldn't move. Then I looked harder. In between the cracks of inklike crust were people. I could see faces screaming in pain, hands reaching out to me. I gasped and paid the price as the scalding air entered me again, turning my lungs to boiling acid, eating me away from the inside out.

I looked across the landscape again and realized what I thought were boulders on the horizon were people, melting into the maelstrom. They couldn't move either. All that was visible of them was their eyes. Wide. Terrified.

Sorry.

They were all sorry for whatever it was they had done. The screams started to make sense to me. They were a chorus of pleas, apologizing for what they'd done, begging for forgiveness.

I watched as my skin peeled away, just like what was happening to those around me who had yet to melt completely. The skin drifting off them was like fireflies at night. Horrific yet magical.

I had never imagined in my wildest dreams it would be like this. I knew it would be hot. Like my husband was. I realized I was on a surface that descended for thousands of floors beneath me. That was where Reyes was born. That was where Lucifer ruled.

I wouldn't be able to get back. I was stuck in hell, and by the time Reyes found me, I would be a melted glob just like all the others.

But I wasn't like all the others. I was a bit different. This place held no sway over me. At least, that's what I chose to tell myself. I lifted my foot and forced it out of the glassy quicksand. I lifted the other and then forced the fires off me with a thought. My skin began to heal. The darkness drifted off me one last time as I stood my ground. Finding anyone in this sea of condemned souls would seem an impossible feat, but I knew exactly how to get him to me. He was now a bound spirit in the under-world. I could summon it, just like any other soul.

I bowed my head and ordered him to appear in front of me.

The melting, fiery thing that materialized looked nothing like a man, though I could see its eyes, like saucers, afraid. Sorry. Begging for for-giveness.

I decided he'd need his mouth to talk to me. I reached out and touched what I'd hoped was a shoulder. He slowly re-formed and, now that he had a voice again, screamed in agony as a pain like none other consumed him. Continuing to heal him, I waited until he was able to stop scream-ing long enough to talk.

Once he was partially human again, his skin blackened but remained intact. I began my interrogation.

"Where is the girl?" I yelled at him. I had to yell to be heard above the wind and the screams.

He looked confused at first, then surprised. "You're here for her?"

"Where is Faris? Where did you take her?"

"You aren't here to get me out of this?"

"No," I said. I should have lied, but I didn't want him to feel any hope when Faris damned sure didn't. I didn't want him to have that luxury.

His shoulders collapsed the moment he realized he was going back.

"Where is she?" I asked, keeping my fingertips on him.

He glowered at me, his blistering features contorting under the heat. "Why should I tell you? What more can you do to me?"

I took my hand away and he cried out in agony as the lava took him again. What most people didn't know was that hell is only a temporary punishment. You simply ceased to exist after, but you burned for a lim-ited amount of time, the amount depending on what you did to warrant a trip to the basement. After replacing my hand, giving him a small mea-sure of relief, I leaned in. "Because I can make this last forever."

He knew he had no recourse. No bargaining chip. It was agony for a little while or agony forever. He decided to try to get in my good graces.

He lowered his head. "At my house. She's at my house."

"Liar," I said, my voice a husky version of the original, mostly because my throat had been burned to a crisp. "We've looked."

"There is a room. The fireplace pulls out. It's an old panic room. Solid concrete. She's in there." When he looked back at me, his face was full of remorse. "I didn't mean to kill her. Olivia Dern. It was an accident."

The girl from high school. "And what about Faris?"

"She was my second chance. A sign that I could make amends. I didn't hurt her. I swear. She's Olivia born again. Check her birthday. You'll understand."

I had no idea what he was talking about, nor did I care. I only wanted out of the literally godforsaken place.

When I let go, he lunged for me, but it was too late. He'd solidified to the spot and began melting back into the ground whence he came.

"Please take me with you!" he yelled, but his voice was distant and intermingled with the thousands of others.

I stepped back away from him and turned full circle. It was like an entire planet of just melting bodies. But underneath the melted faces at my feet, through the glowing glass, I saw the huge black eyes of demons. The razor-sharp teeth. The thick shiny scales.

They were coming for me. I had trespassed and they were swimming up through the bodies to get to me. I stumbled back and fell, the heat of the molten floor beneath me scorching the skin off my palms. Scrambling back onto my feet, I saw one of them. He walked straight for me, his skin blackening just like mine, his flesh molten just like mine. But this was no demon. He walked purposefully, his gait primal, as smooth as a panther's.

I stood transfixed, unable to believe my eyes until Reyes was upon me, his hand around my throat.

He didn't talk. He didn't say a word. He simply held me by my throat as fury surged through him. Even here I could feel it. His emotions. His palpable anger.

Then we were in the void. He'd never taken his eyes off me, and still didn't, even as creatures tried to follow us through the void. Reyes was too fast. His knowledge of the void now vast.

The blackened parts of his face faded and the frost was back. A thin layer of ice covered his mouth, spiked his dark lashes.

Then his heat blasted across my skin again and he thrust me against the nearest wall.

I didn't move. Instead, I allowed him to catch his breath. To remember who I was and what I meant to him. If he couldn't, if the beast he was in hell had come back in full force, I would have no choice but to disable him. But this was Reyes who held me. In all his glory. In all his rage. It was still Reyes.

He glared at me, his dark brown irises shimmering dangerously. He was trying to get his emotions under control. I let him. I gave him all the leeway he needed. His wide chest heaved and he moved at last, leaned into me, tightened his grip on my neck, but not enough to cause me discomfort. Quite the opposite. But he was too frustrated, too enraged to take advantage of the raw power rushing through his veins. He growled, a low and guttural sound, then hit the wall by my head with such force, he dented the drywall and broke a stud. It cracked loudly.

That was when I realized we had an audience. Osh stood near me as though to stop Reyes should he take it too far. Garrett wasn't far behind him. Angel stood off to the side by the washer, his face averted. Had he ratted me out? No matter. I'd gotten what I went in for.

Last but not least was Cookie. She stood, fear radiating out of her in waves. Fear for me and for Reyes. He could easily do something he would regret later. She didn't want that. Not for either of us.

The soft sounds of a baby breathing drifted to us and we both turned. Cookie was holding Beep, her sweet face like a salve on the stinging wounds we'd rubbed raw. Reyes's biting emotions shuddered through him. He turned from me, from us all, as wetness slipped past his lashes.

"We're okay," I said, placing a hand on Osh's arm to reassure him. "We're okay." I stepped to Reyes, and in a lightning-quick move, he grabbed hold of my arm. Not to hurt or scare me, but to slow time with me. In here, we could talk with no one the wiser.

"Why?" he asked, his voice hoarse.

"I needed information from that man."

"For a case?" he scoffed, and turned from me in disbelief. "You risked everything for a case?"

"I knew I wasn't in any danger."

He was in front of me at once. He dug a hand into my hair, his actions almost cruel. "You are a fool if you actually believe that."

I raised my chin. His opinion of me, of what I did, was a little more than I wanted to bear sometimes. "You keep telling me I'm a god. Why, if that's true, would I be in any danger?"

He let go and stepped back, and I understood.

"I wasn't in danger, but my body was. Is that it? If I accidentally brought one of those demons back with me and it killed my corporeal body, you think I will leave."

"I don't think, Dutch. I know. You'll have no choice. But it wasn't just that."

"Then what? I truly want to understand."

He bit down, welding his teeth together as he tried to explain. "I didn't want you to see . . . my world. I never wanted you to see where I came from. And I damned sure didn't want you to see me in that place. To see the monster."

How ridiculous and vulnerable he could be over the craziest things. I wanted to kick him. But mostly I wanted to rip off his clothes because that was the sexiest thing I'd ever seen. Reyes walking through smoke and ash, literally made of fire, his body startlingly powerful, his allure breathtaking.

His lids narrowed as he tried to read my emotions. Or maybe he'd already read them and thought he misunderstood. Stepping closer, braced both hands on the wall beside my head. Then he bent until his mouth was inches from mine. "You really are a god," he said, in awe of me when he had no idea the depths of my astonishment, of my awe of him.

"And you really were created in the fires of sin."

"You're repulsed?"

"Oh yes," I said, curling my fingers into the hem of his shirt and coaxing him closer. "Completely."

His reaction spoke volumes. He'd actually expected me to be disgusted. As if. Did he truly not understand the measure of his magnetism?

He warred with what to do next. He wanted to be furious. He wanted to rant and rave. But I could think of much better things to do.

Almost reluctantly, he looked to the side. "It's coming."

Time. He meant time was about to bounce back. Even a seasoned expert like Reyes could hold it for only so long.

My reaction to his world had thrown him. He glanced at each of the faces around us, then dropped his hands and strode out of the small room. I wanted to call him back. Mostly because I was in love with him beyond my wildest imaginings and I hated, *hated,* to see him in pain. But partly because in all the upheaval, I forgot to tell him something I'd learned while in his world: Lucifer was no longer in hell. He was here. He was on earth.

Cookie and I called Kit the moment I came to my senses. We sat in my office, then stood, then paced, each of us taking turns holding Beep. Agent Waters had argued with me at first. Furious Kit was wasting her time with me, he informed me every chance he got that they'd already gone through the house with a fine-toothed comb. I told him to quit being an ass and go save his niece.

The house was in Bernalillo and they were in Albuquerque, so Kit sent a squad car over there while they rushed that way. Cookie and I waited with bated breath. Gemma came in and waited with us. Then Denise took Beep to change her and brought her back. Still no call.

When the pediatrician arrived for the checkup, I was grateful for the distraction. We went upstairs and he asked over a thousand questions. Thankfully, Denise stuck around to help.

Reyes walked in, his expression sheepish yet stubborn after his brusque exodus earlier, and we watched as the doctor stripped her down—Beep, not Denise—for the checkup, and while she didn't like being naked one bit, it gave me a chance to look her over, too. I counted her toes and kissed the bottoms of her feet while Reyes tested the fine layer of hair that covered her body. We both marveled once again at how perfect she was.

"How strange," the doctor said in a thick Middle Eastern accent, and we both snapped to attention at his observation.

"What?" Reyes asked, his tone sharp.

"Oh, there's nothing to be concerned about yet, but this little sweetheart has dextrocardia."

I gasped. "Is it serious?"

"No," he said with a soft chuckle. "It simply means her heart is on the right side of her chest."

Right. I knew that; he just took me by surprise.

"I've never actually seen it." He poked around a little more aggressively, thoroughly perturbing his patient. "And it looks like all of her organs could be a mirror image. I'll have to order some tests to be sure."

"But she's okay?"

"Sure seems to be. We'll know for certain when you bring her in. How does tomorrow morning look?"

We both stood there, unsure of what to say.

"Tomorrow morning is great," Denise said for us.

"And she has a very unusual birthmark."

"Birthmark?" I asked, peering closer.

He used the light from his otoscope to examine a mark on Beep's left shoulder. "It's very light. I've never seen anything like it."

I had nothing. Both Reyes and I stood staring down at our daughter. So light, they were almost invisible to the naked eye were the tiny curves and lines that made up Reyes's tattoo. The map to the gates of hell. The key to Hades.

"Gosh, that is strange," I said, stunned.

"But everything checks out A-OK. You had a good midwife," he said. "I'll just need a sample of her blood, and I'll get out of your hair."

"You need my midwife's blood?"

"A sense of humor. That's good. You're getting around well, I see."

"Oh yeah, I'm a fast healer."

"Good. Good to know. My office will contact you with the results of the blood test, but I'm sure she's fine. Healthy, strong lungs, good heartbeat even if it is on the other side of her chest. I'll have my staff dig up some literature for you. It will be there when you arrive tomorrow." He took out a blood-collecting kit with a lancet and a small glass vial. "Just call my office around nine. Peggy will let you know when to bring her in."

"Thank you," I said, still taken aback by the markings.

The doctor took some blood from Beep's heel. And I thought she'd been pissed before. The minute he was finished, I wrapped her up and offered her a bottle. She'd had to be given one since I was out so long, and I didn't feel now was the time to try to switch her to a diet of Danger and Will Robinson. Maybe when she was a little less agitated.

After we bade the doctor adieu, I turned and gaped at Reyes. "How—? Why—?"

"I don't know," he said, indicating Denise with a nod.

"Right," I said under my breath. That would have to wait. For the moment, I satisfied myself with grilling Denise on dextrocardia.

"It only means there's a higher chance that she will have a congenital defect," she said. "Dextrocardia is, by definition, a congenital defect, but it doesn't mean there is anything wrong with her. Everything so far checks out perfectly normal. She just needs to be tested to be sure."

"Denise," I said as we headed back downstairs, "we can't. I told you." I looked at Reyes. Watched as concern hardened the lines of his face. "What do we do?"

"I don't know yet," he said.

"I'll take her in," Denise said.

I stopped on the stairs and looked up at her, as she was a couple of steps behind me. "Denise, Beep is in as much danger from the beasts I told you about as we are." After all, the prophecies that foretold of Lucifer's downfall were about Beep. She was his main threat. Not me. Not Reyes.

"Why—?" she began, then stopped herself. "Charley, she has to be tested. Dextrocardia raises her chances of other complications dramatically. We can't just—"

"We'll figure it out," Reyes said, ushering me down the stairs. But I could tell he was as worried as I.

When we got to the bottom, I took him aside as quickly as I could and

said, "I meant to tell you, I found out something while I was . . . you
know."

He bristled at the reminder of my trip to his hometown.

"Your dad isn't home."

After waiting for Denise to pass, he asked, "Then where is he?"

"From what I gathered, he's here."

It took a few seconds for him to respond. "If he's on this plane, we need
to move quickly."

"We can't leave yet. Beep needs to be tested first. She could have a
serious medical condition, and that's something we'll need to know no
matter where we go."

He lowered his voice even further. "If they find her, it won't matter
how healthy she is. She'll be dead before they can run a single test."

"Then they can't find her," I said, imploring him.

Before the hour was up, I was back to pacing. I couldn't sit still. Couldn't
stop worrying about the tests Beep needed. Couldn't stop marveling at
the map imprinted beneath her skin. Couldn't stop hoping they'd find
Faris. Reyes paced, too, only he did it outside, his mind racing for a solu-
tion. Unless he planned on buying all the equipment the doctor would
need, we would have to take Beep in for tests. We had no choice. Our
escape-to-an-island-paradise plan would have to wait.

The phone rang at last and I lunged for it.

"She's alive!" Kit said before I even said hello.

I gave Cookie a thumbs-up and she rose out of her chair in elation—
carefully, as she was holding Beep.

"Just barely, but we'll take it. Charley," she said, her voice cracking.
"I just— I don't know where to begin. Jonny is very . . . appreciative of
your help. We both are."

"Tell him it was my pleasure. And by the way, you realize he's still in love with you, right?"

The phone went silent for a moment before she spoke again. "He—He was never in love with me."

"You keep telling yourself that."

"Charley, I—"

"Celebrate. Take him to dinner tomorrow to celebrate finding his niece. If ever there was a reason . . . See where it goes from there."

"He'll be celebrating with his family, I'm sure."

"And you are a part of it."

"I have to know. How?"

Though I knew what she was talking about, I said, "That's a mighty broad question."

"How did you know where she would be?"

"I promise to tell you someday. But today, it's kind of a tender subject around these parts."

"I'm sorry, hold on. What?" she said, speaking to someone else. "Okay, I have to go, Charley. Thank you again."

"My pleasure. Give her a hug for me. And just so you know, he didn't—She wasn't violated. Not in that way."

A relieved sigh, then, "Thank you."

"Oh, one more thing. There's something about Faris's birthday and the girl he killed while he was in high school. Some kind of connection." After a moment of silence, I said, "Kit?"

"Charley, how did you know?" she asked.

"Know what?" I asked, suddenly intrigued.

"Faris was born the same day Olivia Dern went missing. The exact same day."

"That's what he meant. He took that as a sign that—"

"Who?" she asked.

Since Colton Ellix died two days ago, I couldn't exactly tell her the truth. Not yet, anyway. "My . . . gardener."

After another moment of silence, she said, "One of these days, you are going to tell me everything."

"Okeydokey. Go. Celebrate."

I hung up, then almost collapsed onto the couch we'd stuffed into the corner for just such occasions.

"Charley," Cookie said, "you realize you have to tell me everything. And I do mean everything."

"You sound like Kit."

"Charley Davidson—"

"I will. I promise. Once I absorb it all myself, I'll tell you. I don't know if you'll believe it or not, though."

"I've seen too much not to." She turned her attention to Beep. "Yes, I have," she said in an animated voice. "I've seen enough to make a grown man wet himself. And they don't wear diapers like you do."

I couldn't wait to tell her about the *birthmark*. That'd keep her up at night.

14

Garrett, Osh, and I sat around the reassembled kitchen table and gazed down at little Miss Beep. She was trying to decide if she wanted to fuss or catch some Z's. It was a hard decision for most of us. She made baby sounds. Nothing on earth made sounds like that. They were a ruse. A ploy. A way to get adults to fall in love.

They worked really well.

But the reason our little moppet was lying on the table—on a blanket, of course—was so that we could see the birthmark. Or, more accurately, so that I could show them the birthmark. Barely visible, she had the lines, the map to the gates of hell, marked on her body just like her father.

"How?" I asked no one in particular. "I mean, those were put on Reyes when he was forged in hell. How did they transfer to Beep?"

Nobody answered. It was a fairly rhetorical question anyway.

And Reyes wasn't there to give his opinion. He'd been pacing outside, but I lost sight of him a while earlier. He was probably off dragging hellhounds around. I bet they hated that. And he was probably still mad at me. So, I went to hell. I'd needed information. That was the quickest way to get it. The *only* way to get it. And because of it, we saved a girl's life. Sure, it was dangerous, but that was my middle names. I'd assumed he was used to that by now. Figured he even liked that about me. Apparently not.

Of course, the thought of a family reunion right here on earth was the most likely culprit of his agitation. Coming face-to-face with one's evil father after centuries apart was enough to put anyone in a bad mood.

Speaking of bad moods, with all the unwanted attention Beep was getting, even she'd started leaning toward the fussy end of the spectrum, so I wrapped her up like a burrito, warmed up a bottle of breast milk I'd collected earlier, and walked around the house crooning and crowing about this and that. It was like dinner theater.

Uncle Bob had taken Quentin back to school in Santa Fe, and Cookie and Amber left, too. Amber had school in the morning, much to her chagrin, and Cookie wanted to get some shopping done. She'd been cooking quite a bit and bringing it out to us.

I thought about cooking once.

Beep and I walked around the house as she ate, partly to look out the windows in the hopes of seeing her daddy. And partly to work off some nervous tension. I'd hurt him by going to hell, and that was only the half of it. We wandered into the laundry room and I explained the washer and dryer as best I could. I turned on the dryer and put her on it. The vibrations lulled her to sleep again.

"Oh, no you don't," I said, picking her back up again. "You have to be burped. If I don't burp you, I'll get arrested by the burp police, and then—"

I stopped midsentence. The wall Reyes broke was adjacent to the locked closet door. He must've triggered a latching mechanism when he broke the stud, because it stood slightly ajar.

"At last," I said as we walked to it. "Are we ready for this?" I asked her.

She didn't reply.

I slid open the heavy door. It creaked along rusted tracks. It was a pocket door, which explained why it hadn't opened when we pushed on it, but as tall and narrow as it was, it had to be at least three inches thick. I peeked inside and, wow, was I not impressed.

"This is it?" I asked Beep. After fumbling in my pocket for my phone, I turned the flashlight on and took a closer look. It was a tiny round room, dusty and cobwebbed. Nothing special about it. The ceiling formed an arch overhead, so that was almost interesting. But there were no shelves. No nooks for storage. No dead bodies. Nada.

"What on earth is this for?" Finding no light switch, I stepped inside and, only a little fearful we wouldn't get the door open again as I'd seen how it latched, slid it closed. Then we stood there. Waited. Turned in a circle. Then I opened the door, utterly disappointed.

"Okay, then," I said, stepping out and giving it another once-over. "This is rather useless in the grand scheme of things."

I turned to leave and came face-to-face with everyone left in the house. They all stared at us with mouths slightly agape.

"What?" I asked, wiping at my face, then smoothing my hair down. "What?"

"Your light," Angel said at last. "It completely disappeared when you were in there."

"Really?" I turned back to give it another once-over. "That's odd, right?"

Osh stepped to the closet. "You have no idea. Your light is eternal. It's constant and boundless. Nothing can stop it from being seen from a thousand different planes."

"I can't see it," I said, my hand raised.

"Try it again, but be careful," he said, suddenly untrusting of the tiny compartment. It did seem a tad ominous. Maybe it was a portal to hell. Or a broom closet. I always felt broom closets were a little shady. Why would a broom need its own closet?

I stepped inside and closed the door again. Then I waited for the signal. Not that we'd decided on one, but surely they'd let me know when they were ready for us to come out. I was beginning to think we'd been punked when I heard a male voice from behind me.

"Hey, pumpkin."

Goose bumps erupted across my skin as I turned. "Dad!" I yelled, and threw my free arm around his neck.

He laughed and hugged me back, being careful not to squish my package. Then he looked down at said package, his eyes glistening. "My God," he said, his expression full of pride.

"Dad, how are you here?" I asked.

He sobered and smiled at me. "This is kind of like a safe room. No one from outside can see us in here. They would literally have to come inside this room to hear anything we say, even the departed, and you would see them."

"Really? This is the coolest room ever. But what happened?"

He smoothed my hair back. "No time for that, pumpkin. If you don't come out soon, that group out there is likely to rip the door off its hinges."

"Oh, you're right. Hold on."

I cracked open the door. Everyone was still standing in awe.

"I'll just be a minute."

Osh grew suspicious. It was like he didn't trust me.

"Why? What are you doing?"

"Reflecting."

I closed the door then turned back to my father. I touched his face and his cool skin reminded me exactly what state he was in.

"Now, what happened? Who killed you?"

"First, you have to know, there are spies."

"I know. I totally busted one. She was living in my closet."

"There are more."

I knew that. I'd known for a while. "Duff."

"Yes."

"More?"

"A couple on the lawn, I think. It's like the Cold War here."

"Wait, are you a spy for the good guys?"

He grinned. "I'm a spy for you, honey. I just had no idea." He glanced down at Beep again. "I had absolutely no idea."

"Okay, but really, who killed you?"

He shook his head. "I don't want you involved in any of that. You're too important. She's too important."

"Dad."

"Charley."

"Dad."

"Charley."

"Dad. And, yes, I can do this all day." I had taken hold of his arm. "And just so you know, you can't disappear as long as I'm holding on to you."

"Really?" he asked, surprised.

I raised my brows.

He turned away, as though unable to look me in the eye. "You know, you always amazed me. From the day you were born, you were different. I knew it, too."

"Dad," I repeated. We didn't have the time for a stroll down memory lane. I wanted to know who had killed my father, and said father was darned sure going to tell me.

"Just give me a sec, hon. You have to understand what happened before."

"Okay." I leaned back against the wall and bounced Beep, but didn't let go of his wrist. I didn't think I ever could again. I laced my fingers through his and waited for him to say what he had to.

It took him a moment. Tears swelled between his lashes. "Once you started helping me solve crimes, people noticed. They didn't know about you, of course, but somehow a few of the cops figured out I was getting . . . outside help. One was dirty. As dirty as they come. He told a businessman whose payroll he was on. As a result, that man became very interested in me."

"All this from my help solving crimes?"

"Yes. And no." He lowered his head, completely embarrassed. "You helped in other ways. Ways you were unaware of."

"Like what?"

"Charley, I wasn't always— I mean, I made mistakes. I— I got in over my head with a situation."

This time I lowered my head. "Did it involve the racetrack at Ruidoso Downs?"

"How did you know?"

I shrugged. "You changed after that. When you got home from your camping trip, you were devastated."

"Ah, yes, you can feel people's emotions, can't you?"

I nodded.

"Why didn't you tell me?"

"Like I wasn't enough of a freak."

"Charley, if there is one thing you are not, it's a freak. But that doesn't explain how you figured out what happened that weekend."

"It took me a few years to piece together, but I realized you'd gone to Ruidoso. There's only three things in Ruidoso: shopping, camping, and gambling. So, what happened?"

He lowered his head once more, embarrassed. "I had what we call in the gambling business a sure thing."

"But you weren't a gambler."

"Normally, no, but I got this tip. The guy said it was all set up."

"The sure thing."

"Yes. And I'd seen him win a fortune once based on a similar tip. So, I bet everything."

"And you lost it all."

"In the blink of an eye."

"Then how did you open the bar? I thought you did that with your savings?"

"That's where you come in. This businessman offered to pay me double what I lost for one name."

I gasped teasingly. "You used me."

"Charley, it's not funny."

"Right. Sorry. But, Dad, really, it's not that bad."

"It is, actually, and it gets worse."

"Oh," I said, understanding. "You gave him the name, and now you were indebted to him, only he knew you had a secret weapon."

"Yes. I led him to believe I had a confidential informant."

"What happened to the first guy? The first name you gave him?"

He bit down, embarrassed to say. "He was never found," he said at last.

"I'm sorry, Dad."

"As you can imagine, I retired soon after. I told him I no longer had access to my CI."

The gravity hit me. "Dad, he could have killed you."

A sad smile thinned his lips. "He did, actually."

That time, I gasped for real. "What happened?"

"He got himself in a bind, needed my informant."

"And you refused. So, your death was my fault, too. Just like mom's."

"Charley, you can't honestly say that about your mother. Not after what you've just been through."

He was right. Beep was worth the risk that went hand in hand with pregnancy.

"And my death was entirely my fault. I was never perfect."

"You were in my eyes." I leaned forward. "And you still are."

"Charley, I used you for years to advance my career. That doesn't exactly qualify me for Father of the Year."

"We work with what we got. Do you think I resent you in any way? I would do the same today. You never placed me in any danger. You caught bad guys that I led you to. We were doing a good thing."

"Yes, bad guys that I asked you to lead me to. That alone placed you in danger."

"Do you blame Uncle Bob for what he's doing? Special Agent Carson? Or her FedEx?"

"No, but you're older now, hon. It's different. You know what you're getting yourself in for most of the time. I just let you advance my career while leaving you completely in the dark as to what was at stake. And then there's the whole Denise issue."

"What about her?"

"I should have been harder on her. I shouldn't have let her treat you that way. But I could sense her fear. She believed, Charley. She always believed in you. For her, that *was* the problem."

"Denise and I are finding our way."

"And I want to thank you for that. You have a bigger heart than people give you credit for."

"Right?" I said in complete agreement. "Now, who actually pulled the trigger? And who is this businessman?"

"No. And I mean it. Your uncle is closing in, thanks to you and that anonymous tip. You've done enough." He smiled down at the little princess, and a soft squeak sounded.

"Uh-oh," I said to her, unlacing my hand to pat her mouth with the blanket. "Someone burped."

"Don't worry, Beep," Dad said. "What happens in the closet stays in the closet."

The door slid open then, and Spanky and the Gang stood in the exact same positions as when I'd closed it.

"We were getting worried," Angel said.

I turned, but Dad was gone. I could smell him on my clothes and on Beep's blanket.

Osh stepped inside and turned full circle. "Seriously, what the hell?"

"I don't know, but we need to have a powwow."

This time I hunted Denise down and gave her Beep for a while. She was more than happy to take her while Osh and I went hunting.

We went into the office, where it was quieter. No need to alarm Denise.

It didn't take us long to find him, since I could summon him right to me. I did so and immediately grabbed his wrist so he couldn't vanish.

"Wh-what's going on?" Duff asked, his eyes wide behind the glasses.

"How does this work?" I asked him.

"Wh-what?"

"And you can stop stuttering now," I added. "How does this work? Who do you report to?"

He looked down at his wrist, then back at me. "You don't know what it's like down there," he said, vying for the sympathy angle. "You are burned alive."

"I know. I visited recently."

He had the decency to look shocked.

"Don't pretend you didn't know that."

"I haven't been able to hang around much," he said, scowling at Angel. "Rey'aziel caught on. Sent the kid to babysit. Can't turn around without him watching me."

I turned to Angel. "Is that what all that was about?"

Angel shrugged. "We're also watching a few more."

"We?"

"Rey'aziel has a whole army of spies watching other spies."

"Why didn't he just tell me?" I asked, appalled. "I thought this was something horrible like you two were trying to figure out which asylum to have me locked in once Beep was born."

He snickered. "We decided that months ago."

Garrett walked in then. "Got him," he said, carrying a tablet. "Duff Newman, executed for killing a woman and her daughter in 1987."

Osh tsked. "Duff. That's not very nice."

Focusing on Duff again, I said, "Once more with feeling. Who do you report to?"

"If I tell you, he'll send me back."

"To hell?" I asked. "You're going back there anyway, sport. It's hot. You might want to plan for that. Take an ointment."

Osh spoke up again. "Why let him live at all? I could use dessert."

"You sure?"

"Positive." That wolfish grin was back, and Duff tried to jerk out of my grip, suddenly terrified.

"Wait," I said; then I turned to Angel. "No really, why not just tell me?"

He lowered his head. "You're too reckless."

"What?" I asked, completely offended.

"You're too careless," he said, unable to meet my gaze. "You risk too much for people you barely know. We couldn't—"

When he didn't continue, I finished for him. "Trust me. You couldn't trust me."

He didn't answer. He didn't have to.

"Well, that little decision almost cost me my life, thank you very much."

"Sorry."

Fury overrode every other emotion as I marked Duff. One thought was all it took, and the symbol appeared instantly. "He's all yours," I said to Osh.

The Daeva walked up to Duff, who decided right then to fight. He managed to slip from my grasp, but Osh had him around the throat in the blink of an eye. He pushed Duff against the wall, the exact same way he had with Sheila.

Osh squeezed Duff's jaw, doing some Vulcan mind meld thing to get him to be still. He froze as though he could no longer move.

"It's better than being burned alive," he told Duff.

Apparently, Duff didn't agree. He shook his head, fear consuming him. "Not this," he pleaded, and I couldn't help but wonder why. I'd been to hell. Why was this worse?

"I wonder if those people you killed said that."

Before Duff could answer, Osh braced a hand above the wall over Duff's head, pressed against him like a lover, then covered Duff's mouth with his own. And while the soul-sucking thing with Sheila had been hot, this was even more so. I felt a warm rush wash over me. It pooled in my abdomen as Osh kept a hand locked around Duff's throat, his mouth on his. Then he pulled back, just a little, just like before, and the light, a light blue glow, shone between them. Duff splayed his fingers and stared at the ceiling as Osh took everything he had to offer. Slowly, Duff dissipated, cracking and drifting away until there was nothing left.

Osh pressed his forehead against the wall, his chest heaving, his muscles weak, while I stood in a convent, in a house of God, with the most impure thoughts I'd had in a while. Boy-on-boy action.

"I need a shower," I said, suddenly warm.

Osh glanced over his shoulder at me. "You know what goes well with shish-kebabed Duff?"

"I don't want to know," I said as I started for the door.

"Cherry pie," he called out after me, laughing softly. "Tart cherry pie."

"Asshole." He knew how sexy that was. He was freaking doing it on purpose.

After about five seconds in the shower, I started groaning. Out loud.

I really did need one, if for no other reason than to work the kinks out of my muscles. I couldn't help but wonder where Reyes had gone off to. Maybe he was talking to that older couple again. Angel couldn't have meant the Loehrs. They weren't that old. Angel made the couple Reyes was talking to sound ancient. And he couldn't possibly know about the Loehrs. I'd only just found out about them myself, and he'd told me months ago he didn't want to contact them.

I turned off the water and wrapped a towel around me. Then I did the all-important phone check. No calls. No texts. Probably a good thing.

Hoping Reyes was okay and wondering if he would suck a guy's soul like Osh so I could watch—because, day-um—I wiped steam off the mirror and was just about to blow-dry my "in bad need of a trim" locks when my phone chimed.

The fact that it could have been Reyes made me a little too enthusiastic. I knocked the phone off the counter and watched as it headed right toward the toilet.

Without blinking, I slowed time, fetched it, then let time bounce back into place.

Being a god definitely had its perks.

Swiping a finger across the screen, I brought up the text and my world fell apart at the seams.

Do not move.

The first line of the text read like it'd been sent by some harmless creep playing a joke. That wasn't the part that slid the world out from under me.

Do not say anything.

The sender was unknown, a blocked number.

Do not alert your friends to this message.

Dread crept up my spine to settle at the nape of my neck.

Control your emotions or Ms. Kowalski and her daughter die.

Whoever was sending the texts knew enough about me and my friends to know that any spike in emotion could summon the cavalry. Not many people knew that.

But the next text contained an image, and the dread scratching at my neck exploded, awakening every nerve ending in my body as a sharp tingling sensation washed over me. My knees gave beneath me, and I sank onto the side of the bathtub.

They—whoever they were—had Cook and Amber. The picture showed them sitting beside each other in a dark room, a harsh light brightening only their features, their hands tied behind their backs, their mouths gagged, their faces dirty. There was a newspaper in their laps. I didn't bother trying to make out the date. No one would go to that much trouble without actually having the day's newspaper.

I couldn't take my eyes off them. They sat leaning in to each other. While Amber stared blankly into the camera, clearly in shock, Cookie looked up at her abductor, her brows scrunched in fear for her daughter's life. Her shoulder was in front of Amber as though she were trying to protect her. And then I saw why. The assailant, at least one of them, had a gun. I could barely see it in the upper right corner of the image. And it was pointed straight at Amber's head.

I covered my mouth with a hand to suppress an astonished sob as another text slipped underneath the picture.

I'm sure we have your attention. Calmly walk out the door, get in your car, and
go to the abandoned gas station at the bottom of the mountain, just before the turn

off in San Ysidro. If anyone follows you, if you alert anyone to the situation, they are
dead. You have ten minutes.

I dragged on my dirty clothes and burst through the door. Speed-
walking as normally as possible, I pressed my mouth together hard and
forced a smile when I saw Garrett come out of the kitchen.

He slowly made his way to the stairs, pausing to ask, "You okay?"

My keys to Misery, my cherry red Jeep Wrangler, were hanging on a
hook by the front door. I hadn't driven her in eight months, but Garrett
made a point to take her to work about twice a month to keep things
running smooth. Swallowing hard, I nodded and walked back to the
kitchen, waiting for him to ascend the stairs. The minute he was out of
sight, I rushed forward, grabbed the keys off the hook, and flew out the
front door.

The sun hung low on the horizon as I ran for Misery. I hopped in and
started her on one try. Backing out of the drive while trying to seem non-
chalant was excruciating, but I didn't want to alarm anyone, so I took
my time. Hopefully, if anyone looked out, they'd think I was just moving my car to a different location. Dying inside. The fear coursing through
me was so powerful, I thought I would be sick. Clearly, I was not sup-
pressing my emotions, and yet Reyes was nowhere to be found. He must
have been angrier with me than I thought, but even at his angriest, he
would never leave me hanging. I couldn't imagine why he wasn't mate-
rializing beside me, but I was both relieved and concerned.

I raced down the mountain, taking the 25 mph curves at 75.

A motorcycle appeared out of nowhere, the driver waving me to
pull over. I ignored him and pressed the gas pedal until it would go no
farther.

He pulled ahead of me, missing an oncoming car by inches, and waved
again. I stared straight ahead. Was he one of the abductors? Two more
motorcycles appeared in my rearview, speeding up behind me. I consid-

ered slamming on my brakes to take them out, but I didn't want to lose the time. It took more than ten minutes to get down the mountain from where we were. I didn't have a second to spare.

Just as the last curve came into view, the gas station only minutes from there, the motorcycle swerved in front of me. My reflexes took over. I jerked Misery to the right and didn't have enough space to fix the over-correction. I went headfirst into a shallow ravine, bouncing over the bumpy drop until crashing to a stop at the bottom. I flew forward, my seat belt biting into my shoulder as my head hit the steering wheel.

Then someone was knocking on the window, jerking on the door handle. I tried to restart Misery, to no avail.

"Charley, damn it!"

I finally turned and saw Donovan. Biker Donovan. *My* Donovan. It didn't make sense. Why would he be here? I looked back at the other two, and sure enough, his sidekicks, Eric and Michael, were also with him. They had lived beside the abandoned asylum Rocket grew up in. Arte-mis, my guardian Rottweiler, had originally been Donovan's. He'd led a rough life—most bikers did—but he had a heart of gold. If not for that whole bank-robbing gig, he would still have been in my life in one form or another.

"Move!" he shouted through my window a split second before he drove a leather-clad elbow through it. He reached in, unlocked the door, and dragged me out of Misery kicking and screaming. Eric, the one I'd al-ways referred to as the Greek prince, was right there, helping him.

"What are you doing?" I yelled, pushing them off me once I'd gained my footing. "I have to go! They have Cookie and Amber!"

Donovan held his palms toward me, gesturing for me to calm down. "Who has them?"

My phone rang before I could come back with a biting reply. I pulled it out of my pocket, my hands shaking uncontrollably. It was from Cook-ie's number.

"Cookie!" I screamed, pressing a palm against Misery for support. "What happened? What do they want?"

"Charley, what are you talking about? What's wrong? Is Beep okay? Oh my God, did something happen to Beep?"

"No, what? Where are you? You've been abducted. You and Amber."

"What?" Cookie screeched. She dropped the phone, and I heard footsteps, a frantic voice, then more footsteps. "Charley, damn it," she said when she picked up the phone again, panting. "If this is a joke—"

"Cook, you haven't been abducted? You're— You're okay?"

"Of course we're okay."

"Amber's okay?"

"She's right here. We were just about to head out there. I was calling to see if you needed anything before we left Albuquerque."

I fell to my knees in relief. "Why did you pose for that picture?" I screamed at her. "What kind of sadist are you?"

"Charley, you're scaring me."

"Join the club. That was a horrible picture. And you had red eye in it."

"Honey, what picture are you talking about?"

Donovan was right beside me. He lowered himself onto one knee and kept a hand on my back.

"What's going on?" she asked, but I looked up at Donovan.

Donovan!

Donovan?

I blinked, knowing in the back of my mind that my mouth sat agape. Which couldn't be flattering. "What are you doing here?" I brought the trio surrounding me into focus.

Eric stood beside us, his lean frame at the ready.

Michael stood back as usual, coolness wafting off him as he rested against his Harley, arms crossed over his chest, an amused smirk on his face. "Still causing hell, I see."

I scrambled to my feet, then threw my arms around Donovan's neck. He lifted me off the ground and hugged me tight.

"What are all of you doing here?" I asked when he set me back down. "You're wanted men. You can't be here."

Eric nodded. "That's what we tried to tell that guy. Nobody listens to us."

I shook my head, trying to absorb a thousand layers of information at once. "What guy?"

Donovan grinned. "That man of yours, sugar. We've been holed up across the road from you, keeping watch."

"Reyes? Reyes asked you to come? Why? And keeping watch for what?"

"This," Michael said, smirk firmly in place. "Said you have a habit of running off when you shouldn't. Seems he was right."

I was so flabbergasted, I didn't even know how to respond. Why would Reyes bring these guys here? He knew I had a weak spot in my heart for them. A really weak spot. As in, Donovan-was-an-incredible-kisser weak spot.

Then something a tad more important hit me. Cookie and Amber hadn't been taken. Someone wanted me off the grounds, the sacred grounds. They wanted me dead. I whirled around, watching the road from where I'd just come, waiting for the sounds of paws tearing through the forest. For the sound of snarls and teeth gnashing as they drove closer and closer to the kill. Because I finally remembered why I was not to leave the convent. But the only sound I heard was the breeze whispering through the trees. A bird calling out overhead.

Slowly, realization dawned. There was a reason the Twelve didn't follow me. They were going after Beep. My hand flew over my mouth, and a paralyzing fear gripped me.

"Sweetheart," Donovan said, trying to coax me back to him.

"I have to go back. Now!" I started for Misery, but Donovan tucked an arm around my waist and hauled me toward his bike. "I'll take you. We'll come back for your Jeep later."

"Yes. Yes, good idea." I hopped on the back of Donovan's Harley and wrapped my arms around him. "Please, drive fast," I said before he brought Odin, his Harley, to life with a roar.

"My favorite way to drive!" he yelled back to me. Only after we started back did I realize I'd left Cookie hanging on the phone, probably frantic. And my phone lay somewhere between here and there.

15

LIKE THE SUICIDAL RACCOON,
I, TOO, WILL FUCK UP YOUR ALIGNMENT IF YOU RUN ME OVER.
——T-SHIRT

The second we pulled to a stop, I tore off the bike and ran for the front door despite Donovan's insisting otherwise. When I got inside, I was met with exactly the scene I'd been expecting. The first things I noticed were the bloodied bodies of Osh, Garrett, and Reyes. Denise sat in a corner, her fear so great, she was probably crippled by it. And the hounds, the ones who couldn't come onto sacred ground, stood encircling Beep's bassinet.

My lungs seized when I saw their silvery black hides shimmer, then disappear, their massive heads more shadow than substance, and their razor-sharp teeth glinting off the low light. A terror of nightmarish proportions ripped through me so fast, I could hardly focus. With legs shaking, I lowered myself onto one knee.

I had so few options. With Osh, Reyes, and Garrett down, what could I do?

I could slow time, but they would only match it before I could reach Beep. I could let the energy inside me explode, the light like acid on their hides, but they'd recover too quickly for me to get to her. I could offer my life, but could hellhounds be bargained with? And Lucifer wanted Beep, all because of a few verses some guy wrote centuries ago. He wouldn't settle for me when he had the very being prophesied to destroy him at his fingertips. Or his hellhounds' claws.

Artemis took up position beside me, her hackles raised, a low growl reverberating from her chest.

Garrett was out cold, but Osh got slowly to his feet, a smile on his face as he dusted himself off. "I live for this shit," he said, but he wasn't looking at the hellhounds. In fact, the hellhounds seemed quite at ease. He was looking at Reyes as he followed suit and stood. He cracked his neck and rolled his shoulders before testing his jaw.

I blinked in confusion. Was Osh betraying us after all? Reyes hadn't wanted to trust him, but I thought we could. I really thought he was on our side.

I rose to my feet to try to reason with him. Osh, I could reason with. The Twelve, not so much.

"Charley, no!" Denise said. She started to get up, but I held up a hand to stop her.

Still, her cry was enough to get the attention of the others in the room.

" 'Bout time," Osh said, doubling over and panting as the bikers came in behind me.

Reyes watched Osh for a moment, turned his attention to the bikers, then focused on me. And I suddenly understood. The man before me, while in Reyes's body, was not my husband.

He stared at me a long moment, and what I saw was like something from a dream. Black fog drifted off his shoulders and down around him like a great cape. It pooled at his feet. His lips parted and he ran his tongue over his bottom lip. Or, Reyes's bottom lip.

Enough with the gawking. "Lucifer, I presume."

"You are more beautiful in your true form, but this isn't bad either. You'll taste good, I'm sure."

"What did you do with my husband?"

"You mean my son? The son I created to carry out a mission, and he couldn't even do that."

"And yet you don't seem disappointed."

Osh was easing closer to me. Lucifer offered him a disinterested glance, then asked me, "Why would I be disappointed when my son did exactly as I knew he would? He always defied my orders. Why should my order to kill you be any different?"

"So, you knew he would disobey you?"

"It's in his nature. He was never one to follow the rules. And I knew he would want to be with you, the Val-Eeth, the last of her kind, the most beautiful and the only pure ghost god ever to exist. He always was attracted to power."

"You know nothing about me."

"I know that you are the first god of pure light, the first pure ghost god born of two ghost gods ever to exist. I know you are the thirteenth. I know you have inherited all the power from all the gods ever to exist in your realm, and yet here you are, playing games with me. I am honored and appalled that you would think so much of these humans to risk your life for them. You must realize you have left your realm vulnerable. No telling what you'll go back to."

"What do you want?"

"So many things. Where to start?"

The conversation left me fighting for air. It was Reyes. It was his voice. It was his beautiful face. But absent his mannerisms and his convictions and his compassion. This being was nothing like my husband. And yet I couldn't help but wonder why anyone in this room, including my precious daughter, was still alive. Clearly, he could sic the hounds on us anytime he wanted. What was he waiting for?

"Actually, I have all I want right here. I've taken over my son's body, a feat that took some doing, as I first had to weaken him by making him worry about you and your creation so much he couldn't sleep. I had no idea it would take months to get him to the point where I could overtake him, but it was certainly worth the wait. I mean, look at this." He flexed and stretched, trying out his new body. "I do believe he is as beautiful as I was."

"More so, I'm sure."

"Well, there you have it. I made a good choice, because the other choice was to track down the champion, the escaped Daeva, and take him instead. I'm just not sure I would look good in teenager."

Lucifer's admission surprised Osh, who'd clearly had no idea that he had been an option.

"But don't worry, traitor. I have plans for you."

"Why do you need a body at all?"

"Have you seen the looks my kind gets in this world? Also, I didn't want to live like a vampire. We can live in the light only if we have a human host. But you know that. Do you also know that no human can contain me? So I created a son." He checked his nails and smiled in approval. "You should understand before we go much further, I've been preparing for this very day for centuries. But one doesn't just escape from hell. One needs a map, so the mapmakers slaved for thousands of years to create a key to the gates that held me in. We lost millions to the void in the process. I couldn't risk it falling into the wrong hands, so I imprinted it on my son. In him, actually, thereby creating not just a map, but also a key, a portal. Then I destroyed the original and all those who helped create it, save one."

He focused on Osh again, accused him with a glare. "One was never found. Naughty boy. Did you eat my mapmaker?"

Osh said nothing.

"I wondered where he'd gone off to, but since you are the only Daeva ever to escape hell and make it to the other side, I'll assume you had something to do with his disappearance. And so," he said, refocusing on me, "I was stuck once again. I was hardly going to risk the void without the key, but then one day, I was minding my own business, melting the faces off a few thousand humans, when my son decides to risk a trip back home for that trinket on your finger."

The orange diamond. I pressed my mouth together to keep from gasping.

"Following him out of the void undetected proved far easier than I imagined. It's such a vast thing and he was traveling at the speed of light, him being a portal and all. And then I was free. Well, free-ish."

He hooked his hands behind his back as he explained, and I couldn't figure out what he was waiting for. Why was he telling me all this? Why he was stalling?

"I was quite tired of living in the shadows. The remedy for that was also easy. Weakening my son was not. But when one is plagued with nightmares of his wife and child being ripped apart by hellhounds every time he closes his eyes, he's bound to miss a few nights' sleep."

I leveled my best scowl on him. "You tortured him."

"Naturally."

Osh was about five feet from me, and I wondered what he was up to. Then I happened to look at Garrett and realized he wasn't out. He was faking. Great. They probably had a plan. I was so bad at plans, I wished they would have clued me in to theirs.

"You realize this is not going to end well for you," I said.

"And how can it not?"

"There's an ancient text that says our daughter will be your downfall."

"You humans," he said, the laugh that escaped him not even remotely similar to Reyes's, "stumbling upon words that mean nothing, trying to decipher the undecipherable. The man who wrote them was an imbecile."

"Yet here you are in all your glory to destroy her. Is that not a confirmation of the documents' legitimacy? You are going to fail here today." At least I hoped so. The more he stalled, the more I worried.

"My dear, I have contingency plan upon contingency plan. Even as we speak, there are twelve dormant parasites from twelve different dimensions waiting inside human hosts. They've been here for decades, in this realm, on this planet, and they are just now awakening. Trust me when I say they are very cranky when they first wake up."

"Twelve parasites? You sent the twelve? The *bad* twelve? Then who summoned the hellhounds?"

That was when I took a really good look at the hounds. They were not snarling at my daughter or snapping at her. They . . . they were protecting her. A new hope sprang to life inside me. The only person in the room they seemed focused on was Reyes. Their heads down. Their ears back. Their teeth glistening. But every single one of them was turned toward Reyes. No, not Reyes. Lucifer.

Then I noticed a man. Like the hounds, he was hard to see. His visibility shifted with the light. A shimmer of gold here. A glint of silver there. In fact, he seemed made of light. Pure and powerful.

One of the hounds nudged him, and he rested a hand on its head before disappearing into the shadows again. He was clad in armor like a prince from an ancient Asian dynasty.

"Mr. Wong," I said as I stood stunned by the mere thought of it.

Though not tall, he stood with the beasts, his shoulders wide, his stance sure and strong as his other hand rested on the hilt of a sword.

He bowed when I finally saw him, as though he'd been waiting. *"Tsu lah, Val-Eeth."*

He spoke in an ancient language that I recognized but didn't quite understand.

I thought back, tried to reconcile what I was seeing with what I knew to be true. The Twelve never actually attacked me. They attacked others, anyone whom they saw as a threat. Me, they simply tried to drag to safety. To keep me out of harm's way.

"Who sent you?" I asked Mr. Wong.

"You did. Before you became human, you sent me to be your protector, your sentry until you finished your duties here and went home."

"You are like an archangel, only from our realm?"

He nodded, accepting that analogy.

I wanted to run to him. To hug him. To beg his forgiveness for that time I tried repeatedly to put a lampshade on his head. But with the outcast up from the basement, salutations would have to wait.

Lucifer was actually quite interested in our conversation. I got the feeling he hadn't expected backup.

"What happens to the human hosts of these parasites?" I asked Lucifer. We were in a standoff, but he was taking it all in stride, letting us ramble and ask questions. I had a feeling he wouldn't normally do such a thing. He was biding his time, perhaps expecting backup of his own.

"They are all already dead."

I closed my eyes, horrified.

"Easier to control when they have no mind to fight back."

"I understand. But this is between you and me. Let my family go."

"We're bargaining now?"

"We have twelve hellhounds that I'm pretty sure would just as soon rip your face off as look at you. We have a testy Daeva with a score to settle. We have the equivalent of an archangel who loves to use that sword of his. And we have me, the Val-Eeth. Surely you'd be willing to make a trade."

"I'll give you the woman," he said, bargaining, again, to bide his time.

But so was I. I wanted Donovan and the guys out. And Garrett as well.

I glanced at Denise as she crouched in the corner. She gazed at me, seemingly grateful she was part of the deal.

With the barest wave of my hand, Artemis sank into the floor beside me then rose from the staircase right above Denise's head.

"Was the story real?" I asked her. "The one about the blue towels? About the angel you saw in the hospital? About your mother's car accident and your father telling you that sometimes a blue towel was more than just a towel?"

She frowned, confused, but couldn't help a quick glance at her boss. He didn't move. With a resigned sigh, she stood. "Yes, it was all real. But she was too much of a coward to tell you herself. Still, it was the perfect way to get inside." She looked at Lucifer. "May I have her now?" she asked.

"Manners," he said, scolding. "We have more guests coming."

My chest tightened the second realization sank in. He meant Cookie and Amber. And knowing Cookie, she'd called Uncle Bob. He was surely on his way back here, and possibly with Quentin. That's what he'd been waiting for. Because the more people I tried to save, the more chances he would have of getting to Beep. And if not him, then Denise. Or whatever was inside Denise.

Apparently the hellhounds had thought of that as well. Before I could say anything, one lunged forward, catching Denise by the throat. Artemis launched herself off the staircase and clamped on to Denise's arm.

I gasped and watched in horror as she changed. Her face stretched as a row of long, needlelike teeth grew out of her mouth. She shook Artemis off then latched on to the hound. It cried out, but another was on her back. It sank its teeth into her rib cage, until her fingernails grew into sharp, steely points. She fended him off her with one, clean swipe.

They turned on her, growling and snapping with Artemis right beside them as she did the same. The fact that Denise was a snarling, garish parasite wasn't that surprising. It was more the fact that she didn't kill Beep when she had the chance. She'd had ample opportunity, and I had no idea when she'd ceased to be Denise. Days ago, apparently. Possibly weeks. Then why wait? And how could a demon, a being of pure evil, pass so effortlessly as a human? It had delivered a human baby, for heaven's sake. It had quite possibly saved Beep's life. And yet we'd had no idea what she really was. Even Artemis didn't know.

The bikers had joined in the fight. Donovan, unaware of the hounds in the room, broke a chair over Denise's head, and Eric was using a fireplace poker as a sword. Michael just kind of stood back and soaked it all in. He was never one to rush into anything.

A third beast surrounded her, and I could tell she expected Lucifer to help her. How foolish to expect quarter from a man who would create his own son just so he could inhabit his body. Ethics were not his strong suit.

She hissed at the beasts, swiped as Eric got a little too close with the poker, and fell when the hounds converged, each ripping a piece of her apart.

I turned away. Even knowing the real Denise had probably been dead for days now, it wasn't easy to watch.

Once the beasts were finished with her, they slowly circled Lucifer. Only, that happened to be my husband's body they were about to rip apart.

I summoned Artemis back to me before glancing at Mr. Wong, now able to see the incredible power that encased him, and silently pleaded with him not to let the Twelve kill my husband.

"You sent me to protect you at all costs," Mr. Wong whispered to me, though I could hear him clearly. "He is a threat. There is no help for it."

Fine. I was back to fighting hellhounds.

"Hey!" I yelled at them, crouching down as though I would attack them.

"You would give up your life for his?" Lucifer asked.

"Of course, you idiot."

He smiled. "Rey'aziel is very, very unhappy about that."

"Yeah, well, he would be."

A hound snapped at him, and in that instant when his focus swept to the hound, Osh was at my side. He no longer had a choice. Reyes was about to die, and I was the only one who could send Satan back to hell and save my husband in the process. He wrapped his arms around me, leaned in, put his mouth at my ear, and whispered my celestial name.

What hit me next was like an epiphany times infinity. It all made sense.

In an instant, a power like I'd never felt before flowed through me like lightning in my veins. Just like Reyes told me, with the knowledge of my name came billions of memories. I remembered my realm, my people, the gods that came before me. The memories were like flashes of camera light, only a million at a time. Then another million. Then the next. I remembered the creation of my universe and every universe thereafter. I remembered the wars. So many wars. So many lives lost, both celestial and mortal, each species of intelligence a little different from the others, yet each capable of a love greater than life.

And I remembered my decision to shift onto this plane. Though Reyes had seen me centuries ago, I saw him first. Knew he was capable of greatness. Called dibs.

God promised to leave earth to humans, to leave them to their own devices. He could only intervene if asked, if prayed to. In His infinite wisdom, however, He found a loophole. Another god could keep Satan at bay. And that god's human child could destroy him.

I understood. I knew why my daughter—our daughter—was such a threat to Lucifer. She truly was born a human. She was conceived from both of our human sides. There was nothing supernatural about her conception. About her birth. She was human through and through. True, she would be a human with extraordinary gifts, but she was human nonetheless, and she would be his downfall. This was why I'd agreed to come. I knew my purpose, and I knew hers. I knew what she would be capable of.

But for now . . .

I smiled at Lucifer, at the monster inside my husband, and while he looked like the man I'd fallen in love with centuries ago, the man who would do anything for our daughter, for me, he was not. He didn't have a key to the void like Reyes did. Locking him back in the basement would give our daughter time to grow, to become stronger, to learn how to defeat her grandfather and destroy him forever.

Lucifer had raised his hand, blocking the light flowing out of me. Then he realized what had happened. He panicked.

"You have no jurisdiction over me!" he yelled, backing away. "Your ordination precludes authority over anything other than mortals. Only one born of humans can command me, can embrace or deny what I offer. Put simply, that was the deal."

"I *am* human."

"You are a god hiding behind the rotting layers of human flesh. You are no more human than I."

He had a point.

I walked over to him, grazed my fingertips along the hides of the hounds as I wound through them, and stood nose to nose with my husband's father. I placed a hand on his chest, moved it seductively to his heart. Interest leapt within him. Then I reached inside him, searching for the immortal being cowering there.

He grinned and wrapped one hand around the back of my neck and one on my jaw, preparing to snap my neck.

His voice grew hoarse. "Honey, in this universe, I'm the big, bad wolf," he said, enjoying the thought of my death. "That shit doesn't work on me."

I grinned back and every muscle in his body flexed as he twisted my head around. Or tried to. Even with all his strength, with all his incredible power, he was no match for the seven original gods residing within me.

I reached in farther and he grabbed my arm, fighting the agony I was putting him through, stunned.

He was even more stunned when I ripped him out of my husband's body. Reyes crumpled to the floor, unconscious as I held his father.

Lucifer was massive, his body taking up half the room, part demon, part grotesque, but a part of him was still an angel, too. The beautiful being he once was had become a shell filled to the brim with hatred, judgment, and indifference. Evil.

He was struggling to breathe under the pressure of my hold. "How?" he asked, his voice straining.

"Honey," I said, mocking him, "I'm a god. That shit works on everyone."

I looked to the side. The hounds had moved back, given me room to work. I leaned over Reyes, placed one hand on him, used his power, his key, to open the gates of hell.

Lucifer fought me, but it was like a gnat fighting an eighteen-wheeler. The gate opened, and with one last gesture—my sauciest wink—I tossed his ass off our plane.

The gate closed and I collapsed across Reyes, petting his hair, begging him to be okay. Just then, Beep started crying, and I rushed to her, relief flooding every nook and cranny of my body because she was okay. I took her to Reyes as he stirred. Osh had knelt beside him, too. Then Garrett and Artemis joined us.

Reyes opened his eyes and turned onto his back. I touched his face. Smiled. Told him we were okay. But the turbulence in my husband's eyes left little doubt that I was wrong.

16

EARTH: THE INSANE ASYLUM OF THE UNIVERSE.
—T-SHIRT

"But I don't understand," I said as Osh and Garrett helped Reyes to his feet. He swayed a little, then repeated the words he'd ripped straight from my worst nightmare.

"We have to send her away. Now."

"You mean, we're going away with her like we'd planned. We're taking a helicopter to that island."

"The island doesn't matter anymore." He strode to the kitchen as we followed.

"I saw his plans," he said. "My father's. We— We have no choice."

He started throwing things in a bag, Beep's things, her bottles and formula.

"I saw his plans. He will not give up until she is dead."

"But I'm a god," I said, arguing with him. "I know my celestial name. Surely between the two of us, we can protect her."

"You don't understand. You *are* his plan. You are the beacon of light that is going to lead his soldiers right to her."

"Yes, demons. We've handled them before. We can do it again."

He stopped just long enough to tell me, "Not his demons. Not this time. Demons from other dimensions. Stronger. More powerful."

He made a call while ordering everyone around us to do this or that. They helped him pack Beep up. But I just wanted answers. I seemed to know everything I'd ever wanted to know, but suddenly it all meant nothing.

"So we fight them. Like always," I said when he got off the phone.

"He sent a group to lead them."

"Okay," I said, needing more.

"Gods from another dimension, three of them, and their dimension makes hell look like a water park. They are ruthless and powerful beyond belief, and they are more potent than even you."

"There is no such thing," I said, my temper flaring. The earth quaked beneath our feet.

He took hold of my arm to calm me. "More potent. Not more power-ful. Not even close, but you have distinct disadvantages. You care about those around you. They care only about the destruction of anything and everything standing in their way."

"The gods of Uzan?" Osh asked, paling before my eyes.

Reyes offered a curt nod.

"Here? In this dimension? They'll destroy it."

"Exactly. They'll destroy everything on earth to get to her. My father is not going to give up until our daughter is dead. And your light, the same light that is a beacon of hope for the departed, is now a death sen-tence for our daughter. That is how they will find her." He forced another blanket into an already bulging backpack. "He planned for this, Dutch. All of it. He set this in motion centuries ago, from the time the prophe-cies were first written."

"If he wanted her dead so bad, why didn't Denise kill her when she had the chance? She could have done it at any time."

His mouth thinned. "He wanted to do it himself. At first. Now he doesn't care."

"This is insane," I said, scrubbing my face with my fingertips, unable to believe what was happening, but he kept working, ignoring my ideas, promising me we'd come up with our own plan once Beep was safely away. "Is this because you can't trust me? Because of my impulsive nature?"

"No, though it would serve you right."

I couldn't argue that, and I knew he wouldn't even consider such a move if there were any other option. "Surely, we don't have to send her away this minute."

"What do you think he was waiting for?" Reyes asked, facing me head on. "Lucifer, as he spoke to you, drawing out your conversation, stalling."

"The gods? They're already here?"

"They've been here, waiting for word from my father."

"But how? How can Lucifer command such beings?"

He went back to work. I wasn't even paying attention to what he was packing. "He doesn't command them, but you don't get to be the king of hell and not make a few nasty friends. We fought alongside them more than once."

"You fought with them?"

"Dutch, you saw what I am. That surprises you?"

"Everything about this surprises me."

A knock on the front door caught my attention. Uncle Bob answered it, his expression grave. The Loehrs walked in with Mr. Alaniz, the PI, trailing them. I sank into the nearest chair. Not this. Not now. Why were they here? What would this do to our already splintering relationship?

"Anything you want to tell me?" Reyes asked, his movements sharp and quick. "I asked you not to contact them."

"I know," I said, shame engulfing me.

"So I did it instead."

I blinked up at him. "What?"

"After a while, after the thought of Beep and having a family, I understood what you meant. They deserved to know what happened to me. So I contacted them months ago."

"But, how did you know I contacted them as well?"

He indicated Mr. Alaniz with a gesture.

I gaped at him. "You were in on it the whole time? From the beginning?"

Mr. Alaniz nodded, shame lining his face.

"Even the letter and the ultimatum that I tell Reyes the truth?" I said to the man I thought was *my* PI.

"I was trying to force your hand," Reyes answered for him. "You'd contacted them against my wishes. I wanted you to tell me. To be honest with me."

I wanted to apologize, but all I could think about was my daughter being sent away from me because I was the one thing in the universe that would lead to her death.

"I saw something else," he said, his voice thick with sorrow. "It was my father who had me kidnapped in the first place, taken from the Loehrs."

"Reyes," I said, aghast. "I'm so sorry."

"Don't be. They were my only contingency plan."

"What do you mean?" When he didn't answer, I put two and two together. "They're going to take Beep?"

"For now, until we can figure out our next step."

"But that would mean you knew this was going to happen. You prepared for us having to give up our child."

"I suspected. It was always a possibility."

"I didn't!"

He bowed his head. His sorrow was just as great as mine, his pain just as agonizing. "They're good people, Dutch. They'll take good care of her until all this is over."

"But they're going into this blind. They don't know who she is. What she's up against. They'll be taking her under false pretenses, and they'll be in danger."

"You're wrong," Mrs. Loehr said. I turned to her, studied her kind face, her olive skin, her hair, just as thick and black as it had been when she'd first lost Reyes. "We knew Reyes was a gift from God. We knew he was special. He told me his name the moment he was born. Rey'aziel."

" 'The beautiful one,' " I said, translating his name.

"Yes. That is one interpretation," Mr. Loehr said. "But it actually means 'God's secret.' "

I blinked in surprise. They were right. In the ancient angelic language, it meant "God's secret."

Reyes scoffed gently. "I appreciate the euphemism, but God did not send me."

"Actually, he did," Mrs. Loehr said. "And nothing you say will ever convince me otherwise." When her voice cracked, Mr. Loehr placed a gentle arm on her shoulder.

"You were an answer to our prayers." She focused on me then. "We will keep her safe until you come back for her. And then we pray we can be a part of her life."

My throat tightened at the thought. My heart ached, struggling to beat under the weight of my sorrow.

I looked at Mr. Wong as he walked up to me. He had allowed everyone to see him. A good thing since he'd taken a turn with Beep and, to everyone's chagrin, refused to give her up. Until now. He handed her to Mrs. Loehr, her eyes bright with emotion as she cradled my daughter in her arms. All I felt was the good in her. The love. The desire to help her son, her granddaughter, in any way she could.

It hurt too much to look at Beep, so I looked at Mr. Wong instead, suddenly very aware of who he was.

"You're like . . . like my second-in-command."

He bowed his head in acknowledgment.

"And your name is most decidedly not Mr. Wong."

"Just as your title is most decidedly not Your Majesty, Your Majesty. But, if I may be so bold, they will both do for now."

I smiled at him. "You knew Osh would tell me."

"I'd hoped, as I was forbidden to."

"By whom?"

"You."

"That's right," I said, remembering. "And the hellhounds?"

"They are yours to command," he said. "As am I."

I stood and walked to the hellhound I'd stabbed all those months ago, recognizing him. He'd hovered over me for quite some time after I'd stabbed him. I thought at the time it'd been preparing for an all-you-can-eat Charley buffet, but he'd actually been protecting me. All along, everything they had done was for my—and Beep's—protection. Even patrolling the border of the sacred ground was to keep me on it. Not the other way around.

I touched the wound I gave him. "I'm sorry for that."

His response was something akin to a purr but more like the low hum of an idling Bugatti engine. He nuzzled my hand, pushed his head into my side.

I heard a crash and turned to Reyes. He stood on unsteady legs, his expression blank, void of emotion. He'd knocked over a small table. The shattered glass of a vase shimmered on the floor. I doubted it registered.

"We're ready," he said to me, to the Loehrs.

We led them to the door, the room deathly quiet.

"They'll need protection," I said, glancing around at everyone who had gathered to say their good-byes.

I could now see imprints of light on people, like fingerprints. Their character, their pasts, their probable futures, all written in their auras. The lights shifted and danced on and around them and were as easy for me to read now as the morning paper.

Just like in the prophecies, there were twelve summoned and twelve sent. Mr. Wong summoned the hounds from hell for Beep's protection. Satan sent his twelve parasites, hid them among us. But he also sent the gods of Uzan. Reyes and I would have to become hunters. We'd have to find them before they found Beep. It would take time, but we had to succeed.

Still, the prophecies spoke of an army, Beep's army beyond the twelve. Her confidants who help her wage war on Reyes's father in the future. And they were there with us now. Every member of her army had somehow found us. Become a part of our lives.

I marked them all as we led the Loehrs to their car. The sentry, the scholar, the spiritualist, the healer. I even marked the three guardians, and it just goes to show that the bravest hearts often lie in the least likely candidates. No matter where Beep's path led, these people were destined to be in her life.

The departed who had gathered on the lawn watched. They'd just wanted to see her. They shuffled closer for a glimpse, their faces full of hope. Hope. It was an emotion I hadn't expected from them. Then one by one, they disappeared.

Sensing my distress, Mrs. Loehr granted me temporary custody. Holding her to me, fighting the sobs that threatened to wrench free, I looked at the Thirteenth Warrior, the one who, according to prophecy, would tip the scales either for or against her. The one who would be the doom of every being on earth if he failed: Osh'ekiel.

Beneath the powerful exterior lay the heart of a king. And he would love her. The question was, would she accept him? Would she see the good buried beneath the bad? Would she recognize that he was created that way? It wasn't a choice. It was an imposition. I marked him last as he ran a fingertip over the folds of her tiny ear.

The sob finally wrenched free as I handed my daughter back to Mrs. Loehr. I couldn't believe I was losing her after having just met her, but the thing that broke my heart even more was the fact that neither Reyes nor I would be there on that fateful day. The day she would challenge the devil to a duel. While I could see that as clear as the stars in the sky, what I couldn't see was why we weren't there for her at the appointed time. Would we die before it happened? Nothing other than death could keep us from her in her time of need, so then why would we not be a part of her army? Why would we not fight side by side with her?

Only time would tell—and fate could be altered. This could all be altered. I knew how the universe worked now. Time was anything but linear. Prophecies were anything but concrete. We could change it all.

They buckled Beep into her car seat and turned to say . . . what? What did one say in such a situation?

"Wait!" I ran into the house and grabbed Beep's registration form for her birth certificate and a pen. Then I stepped onto the porch and gestured for my husband to join me.

"What do we name her?"

He shook his head sadly.

"We need to name her after you."

"No," he said, a line appearing between his brows at the thought. "We can't name her anything that will lead my father's emissaries to her. Her name has to be completely untraceable."

"How about common? Or, at least, not completely uncommon."

I bent to write, and he nodded, giving me the go ahead.

"This is ink. No erasing."

"I trust you completely."

I tried to smile, failed, then wrote a name on the registry. My celestial father, for all intents and purposes, was named Ran-Eeth-Bijou. My mother, Ayn-Eethial. And my name, the name they gave me when I was created, was Elle-Ryn-Ahleethia.

My hands shook as I wrote Beep's real name: *Elwyn Alexandra*—a version of Reyes's middle name—*Loehr*. My vision blurred as I looked up at my husband for approval.

"It's perfect."

I folded the paper, put it in the envelope with a note I'd written Beep weeks ago, and took it to the Loehrs. As we stood below the starry sky, I couldn't watch them take Beep away. I closed my eyes, the act only encouraging more tears to fall. Then I just listened. I listened to the sound of the engine as the Loehrs backed out of the drive, tires crunching on pebbles and dried grass. I listened as they wound through the mountain pass, until their car was only an echo bouncing off the canyon walls. I listened until the only sounds I heard were the soft sobs coming from Cookie and Amber. The stalking-off of Osh. The beat of the hounds' paws as they followed the car. They would never leave her, and that was no small consolation. Then I heard the thud of Reyes's knees hitting the ground, his breath catching in his lungs.

I felt arms around me. Pats on my shoulder. Promises that it would get better. But my sorrow only grew. It built and spread and swelled until it swallowed me whole. I glanced up at the stars, at Beep's planet, and I could no longer suppress the force inside me. A primal scream surged out of me with the release, the energy bursting forth in a blinding flash, and I exploded into a million shards of light.

I pressed my fingers to my head, marveling at the agony therein, wondering why it felt like my brain had just exploded. I was on my back. I wondered about that, too. I didn't remember being on my back. I didn't remember being much of anything, my head hurt so bad. Pain rocketed through it in nauseating waves as I tried to figure out where I kept pain medication.

Then another sensation hit me. A biting cold like I'd never felt before, and I realized I couldn't remember where I was. Wondering if I'd sleep-walked, I tried to open my eyes. They wouldn't budge at first, but they were being pelted with ice-cold water, and I needed to find out why.

It took a minute, but I finally managed to pry them open enough to constitute two slits. Rain fell in huge, sleet-filled drops, stinging my face when they landed. I raised my arms to shield my eyes and saw a huge Rott-weiler standing over me. The moment my gaze landed on him, he whim-pered and licked my face. But his affection was just as cold as the rain.

A yellow light floated above me. A security light. Pebbles bored into my back and scraped my elbows as I struggled to a sitting position. I pet-ted the Rottweiler, assured him—her—I was okay. She finally let up and stepped back to give me some space. Still groggy, I looked to my left, then to my right. A dark alley stretched out in either direction. I focused on a faded sign that hung on a door directly in front of me. It read THE FIRE-LIGHT GRILL. To the left of that, a historical marker on the building itself read THE FIRE HOUSE, EST. 1755, SLEEPY HOLLOW, NY.

Okay. That answered that.

With legs made of lead, I took a crack at standing. Once I gained my footing, I stumbled toward the door. Even though it was a back door, I turned the knob and went inside, holding it open for the dog. That would garner a code violation and probably a swift kick out of there if they didn't call the cops on me first.

Thick brown hair hung in clumps over my shoulders and down my back. I had to push it out of my face repeatedly with blue, glacial hands. I could only imagine what the rest of me looked like. I glanced down at my waterlogged boots and shook my head. No need to worry about looks at the moment. There were more important things to consider.

I stepped inside a dark hallway and walked forward. A small room filled with supplies sat on the right, and a door with an OFFICE sign on my left. Ahead of me was a kitchen. I forced my frozen feet forward, taking it one step at a time. The café itself was dark, but one man was busy in the brightly lit kitchen, cleaning up for the night. A large man with a head of thick black hair slicked back, he wore a cook's apron as he emptied smaller garbage containers into one large one. He stilled when he spotted me. Reached for a weapon. Raised a spatula.

"What are you doing in here?" he barked, using a naturally baritone voice to his advantage.

I raised my hands. The blue ones that shook uncontrollably.

Another voice came from behind me. A female one. She must have come out of the office. "What's going on?" she asked, her tone sharp.

I turned to her. In her early forties, she was large, but she had bright red hair straight out of a box and a pretty round face that had probably seen a tad too much partying in its day. Her heavily lined brows slid together.

"I just need help," I said, showing my palms to her as well.

The dog whimpered, but they didn't seem to give a lick about her.

"You can't be back here."

"I know. I'm sorry, I was just— I mean, I was wondering—"

"Spit it out, girl, before you turn into a chunk of ice. I don't think I've ever seen that shade of blue on anyone before."

"Right," I said through chattering teeth. "I was just wondering . . . if . . . if you know who I am."

"Why?" she asked, jamming her hands on her hips. "You somebody special?"

"No. I mean, I was wondering if you know my name."

The man chuckled. "Don't you?"

I turned to him, hugging myself. "No," I said, my whole body quaking. "I— I don't have a clue."

Excerpt:
Reye's POV

"I found her."

I turned to the kid, Angel, and tried to keep control of my emotions. I knew it wouldn't take him long to find her if she was still on earth. My fear was that she'd ascended. That she was no longer on earth and had taken her rightful place as grim reaper. Or even god of her realm. She'd come into her powers. There wasn't a damned thing I could do about it if that was her choice.

"Where is she?" the Daeva asked.

The Daeva's inquiry gained the attention of everyone else in the room, since they couldn't hear the mutt. Didn't know he'd gotten back.

Cookie, her eyes red and swollen, stood and glanced from the Daeva to me, then back again. Dutch's uncle Bob did the same while Amber and Quentin watched with wide eyes.

Gemma, who'd been sobbing almost uncontrollably, paced the kitchen floor, but she stopped and questioned me, her expression hopeful. "What? Did your guy come back?"

"Angel. Your sister's investigator. He's back and he says he's found her."

She covered her mouth with a hand, then rushed to Cookie and hugged her.

I turned to the kid. "And?"

"She's so bright now, it's hard to find her center. To find her in all that light. But she's in some town in New York."

"New York?" I asked.

"Like from the story. That town with the headless horseman. Sleepy Hollow."

"What the fuck is in New York?"

The kid shrugged as everyone once again turned toward me askance.

"I don't understand," Gemma said.

"Neither do I." Swopes was getting angry. The unknown did that to humans.

"She's only been gone an hour," Gemma said. "How could she possibly have gotten to New York in an hour?"

But the Daeva knew. He'd stilled the minute the kid said it.

I stepped to him, anger coursing through my veins like liquid fire. "Why are you surprised, slave? This is your fault."

He stood and stepped toe-to-toe with me. In all honesty, the fact that he looked like a kid meant nothing. He was centuries older than I and had been the deadliest Daeva in hell. On any other day, if he got really lucky, if the planets aligned and the tides shifted the gravity of the earth a centimeter to the left, he might have a snowball's chance of kicking my ass. Today was not that day.

He seemed to have something to say, so I fought the urge to break his neck outright.

He leaned in until I could see the minute details of his irises. "You'd been evicted, fuckhead. Daddy had taken over your digs and was about to kill your daughter. What would you have had me do?"

"Not that," I said, trying to suppress my natural inclination to rip apart first and ask questions later. He'd done the unthinkable. He'd told Dutch her name. Her celestial name. And now all that power coursing through her veins would be almost uncontrollable, as she'd proved with her trip northeast.

Swopes had moved closer to the Daeva and me, knowing what we were capable of.

A slow grin spread across the Daeva's face. "Afraid she'll figure out exactly what you are, what you've done, and leave your insignificant ass?"

The thought of a fight caused a spike of adrenaline. A welcome spike. "The only thing I'm afraid of is how much I'm going to enjoy burying your body tonight."

"You're nothing more than primordial ooze that slithered up from the basement, and she's a fucking god."

"A god?" Gemma asked, her voice thick with emotion. "Is that meta-phorical?"

But the Daeva wasn't finished digging his own grave. I gave him all the time he needed. Handed him a shovel.

"Why would you ever believe yourself worthy of her?"

"There are innocent people in this room," Swopes said.

"Reyes," Cookie said. She'd stepped closer. Placed a hand on my arm. Looked up at me with those gorgeous blue eyes of hers. "Please, find her."

After a long and tense moment, I swallowed back my anger—and my sudden thirst for Daeva blood. She was right. We needed to find out what was happening with Dutch, not start a war.

"There's something else," the kid said.

I glared in impatience.

"I think she's lost her memory."

The Daeva, anger still surging through him, grabbed his dirty T-shirt. "What do you mean, you think?"

The kid pushed him. "Get off me, *pendejo*." He brushed his shirt, as though that would help, before continuing. "I mean she doesn't remember who she is. But, I don't know, maybe she remembers other things."

Quentin, who could see the kid as well as I could, was telling Amber what he could understand. Going by his signs, he'd pretty much nailed it.

Amber stood and walked to me. "Is that right?" she asked. "Charley has lost her memory?"

"What?" Now it was Gemma's turn to place a hand on my arm. "Reyes?"

I shook her off and grabbed my jacket from the back of a chair. "I'll find her."

"Wait," Gemma said. She sank into a seat at the table and spoke between sobs. "We need a plan. You can't just go up to her and force her to come home. If she doesn't know who you are, you could do more damage than good."

"I won't force her to do anything." I started for the door when the Daeva decided to press his luck again.

"Listen to her first," he said. He'd grabbed hold of my forearm, and the seething anger I'd felt before came back ten times stronger.

But Robert was beside me, too. "Please, Reyes," he said. "Gemma is very good at what she does."

After another long and tense moment, I'd calmed down long enough to sit at the table and listen to Dutch's sister go on and on about Dutch's psyche. About how fragile it had to be at that moment with everything she'd gone through. And now she vanished before our eyes only to end up somewhere in New York with no memory.

"She must have suffered a psychotic break, Reyes. We need to give her time to recover."

"I'm not leaving her up there alone," I said, making sure my tone spoke volumes on the subject.

"I'm not saying that." She blew her nose and then continued. "I'm just saying, we need to reveal her past to her slowly, to let her try to find her way back on her own."

"So, what's your plan?" Robert asked her.

She thought a moment, then glanced at him. "How much vacation time do you have saved up?"

"As much as I need."

She smiled. "Okay, here's what we do."

We got as much information from the kid as we could about where Dutch was and who she was with; then Gemma laid out a viable plan for us. One that involved most of us going to New York. Amber and Quentin had school, so they would stay back, but the rest of us were headed to the Northeast. I chartered a plane. We would leave in seven hours. Not soon enough, in my opinion, but the others had to make arrangements.

The longer we waited, however, the more danger Dutch would be in. With no memory of who she was—of what she was—she was more vulnerable than ever before, and my father had emissaries out there just itching to separate her head from her body. Not to mention the three gods of Uzan. Throwing them into the mix was like bringing nuclear weapons to a knife fight.

Everyone left to clear their schedules, leaving me alone in the house with the Daeva. He stood without saying a word and started for the stairs.

"You're wrong," I said.

He stopped but didn't turn around.

"I've never believed myself worthy of her."

"At least we have that in common." He took the stairs three at a time, and I couldn't suppress my doubts about him. Why was he here? What did he have to gain? I'd been suspicious of him from day one, and my suspicions grew stronger by the minute.

Finally, after a long wait, I said, "You can come out now."

Dutch's father appeared in front of me. He was almost as tall as I was. Thinner, though. Lighter. "I'll keep an eye on her until you get there," he said.

"I have the kid for that."

He hesitated. "I'll help."

"How did you know about the spies?" I asked him. I'd been very curious since he told Dutch about them. How had he known about them in the first place?

He shrugged a bony shoulder. "You understand how it is. You hear things on this side."

Before he knew what I was up to, I grabbed him by the throat, making it impossible for him to disappear, and shoved him back against the fireplace. I couldn't actually choke him, since he was already six feet under. I just felt better with my hand around his throat. "I won't ask again."

He scoffed. Fought my hold. Failed. "What can you do to me that hasn't already been done?"

With a smile as sincere as a used car salesman's, I leaned in to him. "I can send you to hell."

He stilled, but only for a minute. "Bullshit. You can't send someone to hell."

"I'm the portal. I can send anyone anytime."

"Look," he said, giving up the struggle. "It's not what you think."

"Enlighten me."

"I had no idea what Charley was. I swear. Not until I died. Only then did I discover that my wildest imaginings didn't even come close. I mean, seriously? A god? But you know what your father is planning for her. And for my granddaughter."

"Better than anyone."

"Well, I did what I do best. In my early years on the force, I went undercover, sometimes for months at a time. I collared more dealers than anyone in APD history."

"Ah, so you're undercover. Doing what, exactly?"

"I'm a spy. What else?"

His treachery stunned me. "You're spying for the very people who want your daughter dead?"

His mouth formed a crooked smile, mostly because I still had him by the throat. "I am. I told you, I'm undercover. And I know who Duff was reporting to. The man in the black Rolls. I've seen him. He's one of your father's emissaries."

"You're not impressing me, Mr. Davidson." I prepared to send him back to hell. He was better off in hell than spying on his daughter for my father.

"Think about it," he said. "You knew me before I died. Do you really think I went to hell?"

He had me there. He was a good man for the most part.

"It took me months to get in with them. To convince them I'd been sent by the big man downstairs. And the more we talk about it, the more likely you'll blow my cover. So if you wouldn't mind getting the fuck off me."

He shoved my arm and I lost my grip, but he didn't disappear. Least he had balls.

"Still don't believe me?"

"Your word is not evidence," I said, giving him a long leash. If he disappeared now, I'd know he was lying, and next time there'd be no exchange. I'd throw him into hell before he knew what hit him.

"In your room, underneath the slats on the bed."

Fine. I'd bite. I strode to our room, the one Dutch and I had shared for over eight months, and lifted the bed off its frame. A picture floated to the ground. I stepped into the square bed frame and picked it up, though I didn't need to look. It was the picture Dutch had of me when I was around fourteen, the one she'd managed to get from a crazy old lady who lived in a building I'd once inhabited growing up. The man who raised me, Earl Walker, used to take pictures of his handiwork. This one was of me tied up, bruised and bloodied. But I'd endured worse. Still, I felt the emotion that charged through my wife when she looked at it. I wondered why she kept it. She'd even brought it here. Why?

"To remind her," Leland said. He'd appeared beside me. "She thinks she is going to prevent anything like that from happening to you ever again. She thinks she is your savior, and it's going to get her killed. Just look at what she tried to do tonight. She tried to trade her life for yours."

As gratingly right as he was, he hadn't convinced me of a damn thing. I put the picture in my back pocket and started to pack. "This isn't evidence."

"I was just making a point."

"And that point is?"

"That the man who did that to you—the man you made a quadriplegic and who you think is in a care facility drinking his meals through a straw—is the man in the Rolls."

He'd caught me off guard. I shot around to face him.

He nodded. "The emissary has been inside him for weeks. Who better, after all? He knows more about you than anyone. Knows how you think. Your weaknesses. Your habits."

"No one knows how I think."

"But Earl Walker knows better than most. The beast inside him, the emissary, finally killed him yesterday and now has complete control of his body."

"Thank God for small favors."

"Those things are bloody hard to kill once they've burrowed inside a human host. These aren't your average demons."

"I know that. I was there, remember? I saw what one did to your bitch wife."

"Then why didn't you know about Earl Walker?" he asked me.

I stopped.

He nodded. "I think your father let you see exactly as much as he wanted you to see. There's still a lot you don't know and a lot I can help with. I'm in, Reyes. Let me do what I do best, but first let me help with Charley. She's my daughter. I have a right."

There was no denying that Leland had been a good man when he was alive, but death did things to people. Their good nature didn't always survive the trip into the supernatural world. I was beginning to think, however, that Leland's did.

"I want reports every two hours," I said, stuffing a handful of shirts into a duffel bag.

"You got it. But, Reyes, there's a reason I told you all this."

I gave him my full attention. "More good news, I assume?"

"Not really. I just find it odd that Charley ended up in Sleepy Hollow, New York, of all places."

I shook off the dread clawing its way up my spine, and asked, "Why?"

"Because that's where Earl Walker is now."